TIME AFTER TIME

Volume 6: The DeLaine Reynolds Journey

First Edition 2020

Dedicated to:

My cher, Darrell
I can only imagine....

AUTHOR'S NOTE

As always, I want to thank you, my favorite fans, for continuing this incredible ride with DeLaine and me. I like to include her as a part of this author note, because while she is completely fictional, I feel as her creator that she is telling this story just as much as I am writing it. Through DeLaine, I'm able to share an inspiring tale to countless readers who become just as invested in reading about her life as I did in creating it.

DeLaine's tale is not a smooth one, and it isn't about to get any easier either. Like with the last book, she is maturing and doing so in a rapid way. Not everyone gets to grow up in a stable environment. As I've shared this story, I've had many of you share your own stories of hardship in your growing up years. You are the people I want to reach the most.

As kids of dysfunctional families, we learned early about pain, suffering, trust issues and many other subjects so many never have to learn. I've found there are more of us out there than I could ever imagine. Some of those *'normal'* kids didn't have such *'normal'* lives as I always thought. Most of the time dysfunction hides from others. I hope that DeLaine's story shows that we can overcome and become stronger for it.

The last volume dealt with some very mature subject matter and I feel as if I must write a disclaimer for this novel as well. Many mature themes are presented. I discuss more about alcoholism, drug addiction, domestic violence, teen pregnancy, teenage sexuality as well as date rape. Because the subject matter continues to mature with the characters, I feel it is important that my readers are aware that there are violent episodes involved in DeLaine's story. I would never want to write something that will be a trigger for anyone who may have issues with any of the above matters. I've taken from my own experiences for many of these subjects. Only I will ever know all of the true tales from the made-up ones.

While certain events are inspired by real people and happenings, the story itself is *fictional*. Characters' names have been changed from the people who inspired them and some characters were inspired by no one or by several people and are what I called mashed up characters. If you recognize a character as someone we may have known, I appreciate your eye to the detail in my description.

I thank you for taking this incredible trip with me and I look forward to continuing DeLaine's story. She still has an amazing journey ahead of her just as we all do in the real world! Peace to you all and remember to support indie authors, artists and musicians by writing reviews for their works in appropriate sites. These reviews help continue our abilities to producing books, artwork, and music for everyone who enjoy our masterpieces.

Prologue

Sighing, I sat down at my desk where I put on my makeup. I looked in my lighted mirror and wondered when I'd finally feel some sort of happiness again. I'd made the decision, before I came home from my annual summer trip to Wichita Falls, to stop living in two worlds.

I became two different people for each home town that I entered. In Wichita Falls, I was the old DeLaine. The DeLaine that felt like my most authentic self, but once I went back to Corpus Christi, I became another DeLaine entirely. Gone was the girl who believed in love and forever with Kevin and out came the jaded and cynical teenager I'd turned into. I partied, I drank, and I smoked cigarettes and pot. I made out with other boys and even had sex with Chance Cahill. I didn't like myself at all. I lived for my time when I could be with my best friend, Bailey and the boy I loved with my whole heart, Kevin Strong. That had to wait for the hottest part of the year and only for a few brief days out of each summer. I wanted to graduate high school so badly, so I could leave the DeLaine I hated and find that girl I felt slipping away more with each month I lived in Corpus Christi.

I'd promised Kevin I would give myself a chance in Corpus this school year. I wouldn't call or mail any letters to him. I would be open to having a real boyfriend and not just screw around with Chance Cahill because he was there. I hated that Kevin even knew about Chance. I also promised to be more involved with school and to party less. The stupid thing is I was the one who came up with the unfathomable idea in the first place.

I glanced at myself in the mirror once more as I opened the black, liquid eyeliner I would stroke across my upper eyelid with the practiced ease I now used. My eyes were red from crying myself to sleep the night before. I held my instant photo of me standing by Kevin the first summer after I'd fallen in love with him, as I cried. It was before I'd left for my annual summer trip to Corpus Christi. My life was completely opposite then what it was now. I'd lived in Wichita and had a demon spawned step brother named Geoffrey that haunted my every move. Now I lived in Corpus and the demon spawn was replaced with Satan's bride, my mother, when she was drunk. I snorted when I thought that.

I hated thinking of my mom that way, but when she was drunk, she was a maniac. She was sometimes violent and always angry it seemed. I'd had to learn evasive moves when it came to dealing with her and sometimes, I wasn't quick in evading her wrath.

I felt even worse thinking that because she was actually taking me shopping for school clothes. I was excited to go because I was still an all-American teenager of the 80's and loved shopping. I hoped we didn't end up in a beer joint on Leonard with my mom three sheets to the wind and me having to be the adult and drive her home.

I was looking at a huge year of change and hadn't really liked the idea, but knew it was something I had to do before I completely lost who I was from all the dual living I was doing. I wasn't so certain I could make it for an entire ten months with absolutely no contact with Kevin. We'd already survived so much. I had promised to try, so I came home from my summer trip, literally a shell of how I normally was. This time, gone was my normal exuberance from spending so many beautiful moments with Kevin and in its place was my dogged determination to be as brave as he always thought me to be. I was grateful I still had Bailey, but even our relationship had taken some dings over this last summer.

Chapter 1

I'd lost so much weight during the summer that none of my clothes fit very well. I was excited because I didn't often get to go shopping, but my step-dad, Ray had given Mama a big chunk of money and told her to take me shopping. I didn't care if she was going with me. One thing about my mom was she had great taste in clothes and knew how to dress and accessorize. She also knew my style and when she bought me clothes out of the blue it was always something I ended up loving.

I thought we would shop mainly at K-Mart or Wal-Mart, but Mama surprised me when she took me to the mall too. I'd found a few things at the less expensive retail stores, but nothing that really jumped out. When we got to the mall, we found one shop that had so many cute clothes I felt like I was in heaven. I grabbed size 12's to try on and was flabbergasted when they were literally falling off of me. I knew my 14's were too big, but I didn't think I'd lost *that* much weight. I asked Mom to get me a size nine and she brought me a nine and a seven. I laughed when I saw the seven and told her I hadn't worn a size seven since I was in 7th grade. She smiled at me and remarked, "Well, you have really lost *a lot* of weight, DeLaine! You might be surprised. Try the nine, but then try the seven too." I shrugged my shoulders and walked back into the dressing room.

Curious, I put the size nine on the small bench in the dressing room. I decided to try the seven first, to prove my point that I was still a big cow. When I pulled the black jeans up and pulled the button together, I managed to zip it, with no trouble or holding of my breath. I stood up straight and looked at the large mirror in amazement! *I was wearing a size seven again.* That meant I must weigh somewhere under 130 pounds which was phenomenal in my opinion. I looked at the tight black jeans and liked the soft curves I saw of my hips. I pulled the t-shirt off that I'd worn that was really large on me too and grabbed one of the blouses I had liked. I put it on and stood back looking into the mirror. I actually looked *good,* I thought. I turned around and looked at my butt and was amazed at how flattering the jeans were, but more than that I was amazed at how thin I had become. I wanted to jump up and down. It had been hard to lose the weight. I'd been regimented in what I ate, except while I'd been away, but even then, I'd tried hard to be careful. I only drank a couple of cokes, and the rest of the time I drank water or lemonade.

I twirled back around and put my hand on my hip. I'd never realized that I wasn't a *pig.* I wasn't *ugly.* I had a nice little body now. It was a tight one, but it had womanly curves that I could finally appreciate and not feel ashamed of also. I looked at the swell of my breast and realized I'd lost some weight there too, but they were still plenty full. They were heavier than most girls and one of the things guys seemed to notice on me the most and had been for far too long. They looked good with the thinner body I had. Smiling broadly, I wondered what others would think when I got to school. Finally, my mom began to call for me to come out. I strolled out to model the lovely size seven pants that she'd brought up. I was so excited to show someone that I was actually pretty now.

When my mama saw me, her face lit up, "Oh DeLaine, you look stunning! Those are the sevens, aren't they?" I nodded my head and she crowed, "I told you that you would fit into them! You don't realize how much you've lost! C'mon, there are a few other things I want you to see. I found a couple of dresses if you want to look." I smiled and nodded my head. I knew I'd need some dresses because I'd signed up for Vocational Office Education. I knew there would be days I'd have to dress professionally. My mom wanted me to take every business class I could, so I could work in an office and not be a bartender, like her. The next year I knew if I stayed with it,

I would be able to go to school for half a day and go to work half a day. I thought that would give me an opportunity to save money to *escape* at least. I felt a little shiver through my back and was excited now for school to start.

By the time we finished, I'd gotten an entire new wardrobe and was shocked at how much we actually bought. I was good about buying things that could be mixed and matched, as well as three new dresses. As we walked through the mall, Mama told me that we needed to get my eyes checked before the school year too. I nodded. I'd worn glasses since I was 6 years old and was blind as could be without them. I hated having glasses, but couldn't see anything without them. We walked into the eye doctor's office in the mall. I had my eyes examined just as I had every year. While we were sitting in the darkened room, the optometrist brought up the subject of contacts. I'd always wanted them, but Clarice had told me they were too expensive, and Daddy had said no. They thought I was too young for them, and wasn't responsible enough.

Mama looked over at me in the dim light of the exam room and shocked me when she asked, "Do you think you'd like contacts?" I sat there in the dark stupefied. Was she just dangling it in front of me or was she serious? "Seriously, DeLaine? Do you think you'd like them? Do you think you can take care of them properly?" I nodded my head and my mom looked at the eye doctor and had him explain everything to us about contacts. He told us that my eyes were definitely very bad and he would like to put me in soft contacts, but he was worried as bad as my eyes were, I might have to switch to hard lenses. He explained everything that would need to be done to care for them as far as disinfecting daily and cleaning them with some other kind of cleaner every week.

I was thrilled thinking of wearing contacts and no longer having the big, heavy glasses on my face. After the exam, the doctor left the room. I smiled like a ninny at my mama while we waited for him to come back in the room with a trial pair of contacts. We had to see if I could get them in and out without any problems. I could feel my body basically humming in anticipation. I thought about what Kevin would think if he saw me without glasses. I quickly felt a bit of a damper come over me and my mood, but quickly hid it from my mom.

The optometrist's assistant came in to show me how to insert the contacts. Once I had them in, it felt strange to be looking out of my eyes and being able to see without having glasses. I had been blind without my glasses, for so many years, that the ability to see without feeling the presence of something I thought of as just another appendage was amazing. I grinned as I looked around the room and told my mom and the assistant how bright everything looked. It was like I'd been sightless and now I could see. Everything had a crisper and more vivid quality. I hoped that my mama would let me get them.

By the time we walked out, I had the contacts and was walking on air. I had gotten basically a whole new wardrobe, and could once again fit into a size seven. I also got rid of the ugly glasses I'd been strapped with for almost 11 years. I had to wash off my eye makeup, in the optometrist's office, in order to put the contacts in. I was walking around looking washed out, without makeup, but I didn't care. I felt *gorgeous*. Everything that had happened that day was almost more than I could stand. I had a strong, heady feeling and every time I looked at my mom I smiled. She returned the smile and I hoped that this year truly would be different. I didn't know what it was that made Ray give Mama the money so freely. I also didn't know what had Mama acting almost like a *normal* mother, but I was thrilled to be basking in whatever was the cause of it. The result was almost miraculous to me and I never wanted it to end.

When we got home, I showed off all the new outfits to Ray and he smiled with each one. I knew he honestly didn't care. He even smiled when he heard about the contacts. I was so thrilled, and even though my eyes burned a little, they said it was normal because my eyes had to get accustomed to them. I honestly thought that maybe my life here might be looking better. I didn't know if Kevin or Mrs. Strong called my mom ahead of time, to tell her I would be going through a hard time this next year.

My happiness was short lived. By the end of the first week of school, my mama was back to her old antics of drinking to the point of belligerence. Ray would try to hide and I would follow suit. I felt so betrayed the first time she got drunk after I got home. I thought that this time though was much different. She was even more violent. She and Ray got into a physical fight. I mercifully was able to sneak into my room. I felt a tug at not helping her, but I couldn't say I blamed Ray for hitting her back after she picked up one of my baby pictures and smashed it over his head.

As if Mom's drinking again wasn't already a crappy thing, I found out the first weekend after school started would be the last weekend the Game Room was going to be open. After that it would be closed. Kelly, Robin and I were all deeply saddened by this news. It was the place that was ours and where we could safely hang out on the weekends and be away from our parents. During football season we could go to the home games, but other than that there wasn't a whole lot we could do.

We moped every time we walked into the Game Room before the final weekend to find even fewer electronic, video games. The guys who had all worked at the snack bar, through the years, had become our friends. Even when they quit working there, they still hung out up there also. We all speculated about what would happen. Someone said we would have to cruise Sonic more. I couldn't imagine cruising Sonic would be all that fun. It wasn't like it was a building and we could sit inside of it.

The only good thing was that I had gotten my driver's license before I left that summer, so Mama was more liberal with me driving around Annaville. She still wouldn't let me go to the South side of town where the malls were. The 'in town' kids cruised Everly Drive like we did on Kemplar in Wichita Falls. There wasn't a lot to drag on Leonard Street, in Annaville, and Sonic was not that big. We heard that the dance hall was going to start having dances every Saturday night and that was a little better, but we couldn't always afford to go out there. I had hoped that my junior year was going to be a lot different, but it was shaping up after the first week to look a little bleak.

That first weekend after school started was a long weekend. We started school a week before Labor Day, so when we got out on Friday, we had a three-day weekend. By then life at home had gotten back to its extremes. I was once again riding the tides of my mother's moods. I was excited to go to the Game Room that weekend, even if it would be the last one. I was going to get to debut my contacts and new clothes for the people I ran around with from Woodway High. If they were anything like the kids at Calvin High, I thought it might shape up to be a little exciting to see the responses.

My first week had been so strange. Every day I left school smiling because so many people didn't seem to even recognize me. On Wednesday of the first week, I was walking down the hall when the cutest boy in my class, who happened to be a surfer I'd gotten to know a little the year before, stopped dead in his tracks when he passed me in the halls. I didn't realize it until I heard him say, "DeLaine???" I turned my head and saw him checking me out. I had worn the little, black dress I'd gotten during my shopping excursion and some black heels. I felt good in that dress and liked how I looked in it. I smiled at Surfer Boy and he mouthed the word, "*WOW*"! I shook my head with a smile and turned back around. I didn't want him to see the beet red blush I felt creeping up my neck. That was pretty much the response I was getting around Calvin all week. There were some kids who actually thought I was a new student. When I told them that I'd had a class with them the previous year and described the class and myself, it was always amusing to see the look of disbelief cross their faces.

When I walked into the Game Room with Robin and Kelly that last Friday night it would be open, there weren't a lot of people in there. I was surprised, but figured it was because we'd gotten there a little early and it was mostly daylight still. I had purposely taken great pains to dress up and do my hair and makeup just right. Kelly and Robin both almost fell over when they came to the door when I picked them up. They pulled me into their house and we all talked at once. It was good to see them. I sometimes took for granted their friendship when I had so few in the place I now called home. I was happy to see them though and they both seemed ecstatic to see me as well. We went immediately into their room so they could finish getting ready.

Amid all the hair spray that was choking us out of their bathroom and all the talking, it was a wonder we made it to the Game Room before dark, but we did. I told them all about my summer trip to Wichita Falls and Oklahoma City. They told me all about what had happened while I'd been gone; like who hooked up, who broke up and one other extremely interesting fact. Chance Cahill had gotten an apartment with a guy who had graduated from Calvin in 1982 also. I didn't know him since I hadn't gone to Calvin until the senior class of 1983. His name was Lonnie Littlejohn. I was shocked to learn that Chance had moved out of his house. When I thought about it, I realized that he would be 20 in another month, so it made sense, I supposed. Kelly told me about a few parties she'd gone to at their apartment. She thought Chance was going to be so freaked when he saw me. I just laughed. I wondered what he would think if I was getting the responses at Calvin that I was.

I thought about Kevin any time I thought about Chance. I felt almost guilty every single time too. I stood there as Kelly and Robin chirped out more gossip. I felt my thoughts turn inward briefly as I thought about Kevin telling me to get a *real boyfriend* this year and quit messing around with the *Cahill asshole*! I chuckled softly and the girls turned to look at me. Robin was the one to ask, "What? What's so funny?"

Shaking my head, I murmured, "Nothing, just thinking about Kevin telling me I needed to find a *real* boyfriend this year and get rid of that *Cahill asshole*!" This made my two best friends from Corpus Christi break into fits of giggles.

Kelly cackled, "Oh yeah, right, like that's ever gonna happen! You know you got it bad for ol' Chance!" I smiled at her and felt a weird stab of some emotion. I couldn't quite put my finger on it. Was it jealousy? Anger? Finally, I just smiled at her and nodded my head. I didn't know what else to do. I knew that Kelly had messed around with Chance too. It hurt when I found out and when I had caught them together it hurt even more. I didn't have any claim on Chance, so there was no way for me to tell her off. I realized I was feeling the exact same way I had when I heard Bailey and Jax had dated for a while. I didn't have a claim on Jax either, but I couldn't understand liking or messing around with someone who had once meant a lot to one of your best friends.

While we were sitting around the Game Room chatting with the few that came in before dark, Kelly came up to me and stated, "You know that Chance and Lonnie are probably having a party. That's what they've been doing since they got their apartment. They just party there that way they aren't out drinking and getting in trouble."

"Really? How do you know, Kelly? You been to a lot of them?" I asked her feeling the uncomfortable feeling creep back into me. I didn't like it, but I also felt hurt when I felt it too. It was an odd feeling and one I wanted to go away.

Around 9 o'clock, just when I was about to give up on seeing him, Chance Cahill walked into the glass door of the Game Room. I felt my breath hitch just a tiny bit as I remembered our last night together, before I left for Wichita Falls. I wondered if he'd even notice the changes in me. I wouldn't have to wait long to find out. Chance's face broke out into a huge grin and he walked over to me. "*Hey Beautiful!*" Chance cooed sweetly. I realized it sounded almost like the weird *'come-on'* voice Kevin had used the last night he came to Bailey's with Freddie Black. I started giggling and

Chance looked truly affronted. "What? I thought that was sweet!" Chance declared.

"You've just never said anything like that to *me* before," I tittered, trying to stifle my giggles.

Chance looked at me strangely, and then I saw his entire demeanor change. He looked like he had just figured out a great mystery. I realized he hadn't even known who I was. "DeLaine?" Chance asked softly. I looked at him and nodded my head. "Holy Shit Girl! What the hell did you do while you were gone? Jesus, you look *completely different*! Holy Shit! That's fucking wild! I mean, I'm sorry but I didn't have a clue it was you!" he stammered.

I kept the smile plastered on my face, but I felt deeply hurt even though I'm sure his remarks weren't meant to hurt me. He'd seen me with my glasses off plenty of times since we took them off when we made out. I didn't think I'd continued to lose that much weight while I'd been gone. I could understand the goofy boys at Calvin freaking out over the change, but Chance was someone I'd been *intimate* with. I thought he'd be complimentary, but not completely taken by surprise enough not to recognize me!

"It's me." My smile became a tight one on my face. I was trying desperately to keep my composure. I wanted to jump up and knock the hell out of him and burst into tears all at the same time. I chose to sit there and stuff both of those feelings down deep and give him my tight smile. I hoped he realized what a total jackass he'd been. When he kept going on about how great I looked and how shocked he was it was me, I knew he'd never get how much it hurt to have him not even recognize me. No matter what he said positive about me, the only thing I heard was how unbearably *ugly* I'd been before. Now that I was skinny again, and didn't wear glasses, I was now a *babe* or something.

Chance leaned over and bragged, "Hey, I got an apartment with Lonnie from Calvin's class of '82!" I nodded my head and told him I'd heard. He looked over in Kelly's direction where she was flirting outrageously with Lee Bass, who was the new love of her life. She'd messed around enough with him, but now she was putting it on full throttle for them to get together as a couple. Finally, Chance asked, "We're having a few people over in a little while. You wanna come over?"

I looked over at Kelly and then Robin. I told him I had to take them home. He seemed to weigh the information and finally he shrugged, "It's cool. Bring 'em over with you." I told him I needed to ask if they wanted to go. I knew that was stupid because they'd both be in it just for the beer. When they said yes, I returned where Chance was sitting and told him we'd come over for a little bit, before I had to get them home. He smiled really big and said he had to get more beer. It was almost 9:30 and I told him we'd probably be there within an hour. He grinned and leaned over and whispered in my ear, "You know, when I saw you I thought, 'DAMN! That girl is gorgeous and looks so familiar!' I'm sorry I was a dumbass and didn't realize it was you at first."

Looking at my feet, I felt my stupid heart leap up in joy. I tried to make it get back in its rightful spot. I wasn't supposed to be hung up on Chance Cahill anymore. I was supposed to get a *real* boyfriend this year. I'd *promised* Kevin I'd try. Chance Cahill wasn't going to be that guy. He didn't want to be tied to anybody, no matter how much a part of me would love to say he was my boyfriend for real. Finally, I looked into his sweet, round face and smiled a more genuine smile. "Thanks, Chance," I whispered unsure what else to say. He smiled with his beautifully, straight, white, toothy smile and winked one of his blue eyes. Then he was striding purposely out the door.

We went to the apartment that Chance Cahill shared with Lonnie Littlejohn. When I met Lonnie I was surprised, because I didn't remember ever seeing him anywhere before. Even more surprising was learning who all he ran around with, because they were all more or less others that I knew as well.

Lonnie was cute in a unique way. He had some of the blondest hair I'd ever seen. It was almost white it was so light. He had a very ruddy, red complexion and light blue eyes that looked like washed out watercolors. He was funny though and after you talked to him, he began to seem cuter. I knew it wasn't the beer talking for me because I was walking around with a Sonic cup full of lemonade. I was the only person in the entire apartment who wasn't drinking, I thought.

I sat at the small dinette set most of the evening with Lonnie, Chance's little brother, Scotty, and a rotating mix of people in the other three chairs. I was shocked when I came in and found Carla Feldman. She was already drunk when I got there and she was really loud. I'd hung out with her a little the year before, so I considered us friends, even though it seemed like a strange friendship. We basically shared Chance, which was a little weird too. She was squealing loudly when she saw me and kept gushing about how good I looked with my contacts and new clothes. There were several people who were surprised by my transformation and in many ways I felt like the *Ugly Duckling* must have when he transformed into the gorgeous swan. I always knew I wasn't anything that special, but was surprised so many others were impressed with my new appearance.

Around 11 o'clock, Chance had rotated into one of the two extra chairs at the table. "Hey, you wanna come see my room?" Chance whispered in my ear. I was surprised he could make a whisper be heard over the din of people and music. I looked over at him and arched my infamous eyebrow. I saw the smile growing on his face and a part of me wanted to, in hopes that maybe Chance WAS the one I was supposed to have as my boyfriend. It would save me a lot of pain in trying to find one. I thought it defeated the purpose of me having a real life, like Kevin, and even his mom wanted for me.

Smiling back at him I nodded my head just slightly. I wasn't sure what I was going to do once I went to his room, but I hoped it would be right whatever happened. I wondered briefly when we were walking through the small living room full of people if Chance could make me have the same exquisite feeling that Kevin had done only a few weeks ago. I was still in awe of how mind blowing an orgasm was. I knew it felt good when a boy touched you, but when everything finally worked *right,* and an orgasm occurred, I realized what the big deal was. I thought about it and realized that boys always knew that heady release, because they always had an orgasm. For them it was over once it happened. Girls I didn't think *always* had one.

When Chance turned to look at me, I felt myself blush immediately. I'd been thinking about such personal stuff while I was following him. I chastised myself inside my own head. He didn't have a clue what was running through the now fertile fields of my almost 17 year old brain. Then I thought about that word...*fertile.* I realized Kevin and I still hadn't used any birth control. I felt my insides completely convulse all at once. It caused me to have a huge cold chill run down my spine. Chance asked if I was okay. Nodding my head I turned and looked at the small bedroom. I was shocked to see he had a twin bed. I had a queen sized bed in my bedroom. I couldn't imagine having to sleep on a twin bed again. Chance was a 'grown-up' and he was still sleeping on a kid's bed.

I was frantic inside, worrying about when my last period was and when I was supposed to start again. I couldn't believe we'd been so stupid again. It was insane of me not to think about it after what Carla had gone through at the end of our freshman year, with Chance no less!

Chance came up behind me and reached around, pushing the door closed to his room. I stood there stock still, wondering what I should do. I felt so weird. I was worrying about whether I was pregnant with Kevin's baby, and about to do something with Chance Cahill. I didn't know if I was just gonna mess around with him or actually have sex. He put his hands on my shoulders gently and I felt as he gently rubbed them. It felt good, but it felt wrong at the same time. I was feeling too weird about the whole thing.

"Uh, Chance, it's getting late, I need to get Kelly and Robin home," I stated, stepping forward to where I was now away from his warm and wonderful feeling hands.

Turning me around, Chance drawled, "Nah, it's just a little after 11! You'll have them home by midnight! We won't be in here long."

Looking up at him with our mouths only inches away I couldn't help but begin to giggle. "Gee, don't worry about the romance on my account!" I spouted, flippantly.

Chance looked at me curiously. "What's that supposed to mean?"

"Well, shit, if it's a little after 11, and I have to have them home by midnight, it takes at least 20 minutes to drive all the way to the other end of Leonard, where they live, that leaves roughly 25-30 minutes of *romance* for us." I was trying not to appear mean-spirited.

Chance looked at me and nodded his head. "Okay, so what's wrong with that?"

Shaking my head as I remembered the beautiful night I'd spent with Kevin and then the weird fumbling around on the side of Bailey's house, I realized that Chance would never *get* what it meant to take his time and make me feel special. "Chance, 30 minutes isn't a lot of time," I noted quietly, trying not to sound too bitchy.

He walked up and put his arms around my waist and began to kiss my neck as he murmured, "But it is, DeLaine! Just hang on and I'll show you 30 minutes can feel like an hour."

When his mouth found mine, I kissed him eagerly, glad to feel familiar lips on my own that I liked and knew what to expect from them. When his hand began to slide slowly up my shirt, I could feel the roughness of his hands. They were calloused and permanently stained from the refinery he worked at. I began to think about how Kevin's beautiful, graceful hands were going to end up looking like that soon.

Suddenly, I pulled away from Chance's kissing and pushed his hands down and away from me. I knew from the bulge I'd felt in his blue jeans, against my stomach, that he was not really in a way to take no for an answer, but I was praying he would. "Chance, I'm sorry, I *can't* do this!"

"*What*??" Chance exclaimed, as his blue eyes became round with surprise.

"I'm sorry, I just *can't*. Not tonight, I'm sorry. I just…I don't know…I just don't feel right about it." I groaned miserably.

Chance looked at me and asked, "Wait, you don't feel right about it, *tonight*?" I shook my head and Chance flopped down onto his bed, "Jesus *D*.! You coulda saved me a hard-on if you didn't want to do it, by not agreeing to come back here!"

I looked at him angrily, "First of all, my name is DELAINE…it is NOT "D"…second, I'm sorry you have a hard on, and I'm just not feeling it. You don't seem to be too distressed though, or in danger of it falling off, because I said no. I'm sure once I leave, you can go out and Carla will be more than happy to come back here and take care of that for you. We're interchangeable like that for you, aren't we?"

"Fuck!" Chance complained, as he flung the rest of his body on his bed. "Jesus, DeLaine! What is your hang up about Carla? I thought we already got through this shit at the first of the year!"

I looked at him and felt myself begin to calm down. Finally, when I knew I could talk reasonably, I stated, "Yes, we did. We've talked about a lot of stuff, but you know what Chance, I don't want to just fuck you. I want a *real* boyfriend! I'm sick of just being an *easy fuck* for you."

"Like I'm the *only* one," Chance muttered.

"What did you just say?" I asked him, with the edge coming back to my voice.

"Nothin' DELAINE!" Chance sighed, as he sat up.

"Oh bullshit, Chance Cahill! You are the ONLY guy here that I've had sex with, so you better watch your fucking mouth!" I was feeling the anger come back. If I wasn't mistaken I felt the faintest tickle of winged flames against my gut.

Chance looked at me and barked, "The only one HERE? What the fuck does that mean?"

I looked at him in shock. "That is none of your fucking business!"

"If I'm screwing you, I think in a way it is," Chance fumed quietly.

I began to laugh. "You know you are *un-fucking-believable*!!! How many girls have you fucked in Annaville, and you are worried about who or what I do outside of Corpus?"

"Well, if you've got a boyfriend where you go every summer or you get the Clap or some shit, don't you think I should know *who* it is?" Chance asked me seriously.

"You are fuckin' crazy dude!" I snarled. "I'm the one who needs to worry about *the Clap*! Who knows what some of those whores you fuck are carrying around. For your information, yes, I have a *boyfriend* in Wichita Falls that I see when I'm up there!" I stated. Part of me thrilled at referring to Kevin as my boyfriend because it was the first time I'd ever been able to do it. It still wasn't the real truth, but Chance didn't know that!

Chance looked at me curiously. "You mean, you were with *me* right before you left this summer and then you went up there to see *him*? Man, that's pretty shitty, DeLaine!"

I stood there for a minute trying to figure out how suddenly I was the one doing something wrong for telling Chance I didn't want to mess around. Shaking my head, I said as I opened the door, "You know Chance, I want us to be friends, but I wouldn't hold my breath if I were you when it comes to us *ever* having sex again!" Glaring at me as I walked out of the door, Chance kept his seat on his twin bed. I walked over to Kelly and told her we were leaving. She was sitting on Ryan O'Malley's lap, playing quarters on the square coffee table that took up most of the space in the small living room.

"I'm not ready to leave yet," Kelly pouted.

"Yes you are," I stated forcefully. "Get your shit and get out to my car!"

"Gee *Mom*! Why you gotta be like that?" Ryan asked me. I looked down at him. He was stoned and I knew that I didn't have time or patience to deal with someone who was baked.

"C'mon, Kelly," I pleaded, a little more gently. She poked her lip out and looked at Ryan.

"I'll take her home *Ma*, you don't gotta worry about her," he grinned.

I smiled sweetly at him, "Yeah, I doubt it. I'm gonna take her home so she doesn't get grounded for being late. I have to get home on time too, because my mom *will* kick my ass. I mean that in the very literal sense, if I come in after curfew....say goodnight, Kelly! Bye Ryan!" I turned to find Robin and found her playing quarters in the dining area where Lonnie and Scotty still sat.

Shaking my head as I walked over to Robin, I felt guilty that we drug her around with us when she was younger than us. I wondered why they were playing two different games of quarters, but realized it didn't matter. I needed to get my charges and get the hell out of there! I told Robin we had to go and thankfully she didn't give me any hassle. We both had to go back and finally pry Kelly away from Ryan with a little help from Scotty. He was such a sweet guy. I wondered why I couldn't be attracted to him instead of his stupid brother.

I was relieved when I finally got them home and could drive with the radio turned down. I had gone out and not drank one drop of alcohol. I hadn't even *thought* about it. I pondered about that deeply as I drove. I didn't know if I was going to drink again. It felt odd that I hadn't really *wanted* to, even after getting mad at Chance. I just couldn't believe that things were once again changing in my life.

The Game Room was closing. I wasn't sure what this next year was going to hold for me, but I knew it was going to be different just after the first week of school! I was excited about

Theater Arts. I was even excited about the Office Education class. I sighed as I drove down the winding road home.

Chapter 2

The Game Room closed the next night. It seemed there were a lot of people I usually saw every weekend that I no longer saw. Kelly, Robin and I decided to take each weekend as it came for the time being, until something came to take the place of the Game Room. I could still drive us around and it seemed more people were beginning to have house parties or field parties, so we started going to a lot more of those.

Carla Feldman ended up moving into Calvin school district. She had gone to Woodway since kindergarten. She was so upset, but because I'd been a transplant from Woodway, the Vocational Office Education teacher, Mrs. Davis, thought it would be a good idea for me to be her buddy. We laughed about it. That class encompassed two class periods, so Carla and I spent a lot of time together.

She was shocked that I'd left that Friday night from Chance's apartment the way I did. I found out that he did in fact go out there and they ended up messing around. Part of me wanted to be mad at him, but part of me just didn't care. Soon Carla was a part of our trio which turned my trio with Kelly and Robin into a foursome. Since I was the only one with a driver's license, I was the one delegated to drive us everywhere.

The rest of September life seemed to be a monotonous grind. There was never anything different. Every day was always the same it seemed. I went to school and came home, did homework, ate dinner, and watched TV. On the weekends I went to either a football game, that I honestly had no interest in, or drove through Sonic over and over. Saturday's there was always a dance now. When we tired of driving through Sonic, we usually ended up over at Lonnie and Chance's apartment.

Chance didn't speak to me for about two weeks after I told him off, but one night when I was over there, he finally came over to me. I tried hard not to roll my eyes when I saw him. He leaned against the wall nonchalantly, holding his beer in his hand. We were watching everybody else playing some kind of stupid drinking game. I found that I hardly drank now. If I did, I would usually nurse a beer all night, just so everyone thought I was drinking still.

"Who came up with this dumbass game?" Chance asked me, grinning his toothpaste commercial smile.

I shrugged. I wasn't sure I really wanted to start this all over again with him. I couldn't believe he had enough guts to come up to me, but apparently he did.

"Are you ever gonna talk to me again?" Chance asked sweetly.

I jerked my head to look at him and declared, "I didn't know we were on a no speaking term!"

"Well, you left a couple weeks ago pretty pissed off," he admitted, quietly.

I began to shake my head and chuckle. I got up and walked over by the wall next to him. "Pretty pissed off is putting it *pretty mildly,* dude! I was mad as hell! You better be glad you had a hard on and couldn't get up!"

Scotty Cahill was playing the beer game and heard the word *hard-on,* turning around asking us what we were talking about. Both of us shook our heads and Chance jerked his head back towards his room. I looked at him like he'd lost his ever loving mind. He tilted his head and looked at me as if I were being unreasonable. I couldn't believe it, but I followed him.

"Look, I'm sorry for what I said, okay? I guess I'm just an asshole. It's none of my business if you have a boyfriend in Wichita Falls. It must be awfully hard though only getting to see each other once a year. Does he date while you're here?" Chance asked, congenially.

Not sure how to answer, I finally muttered, "Well, um, he wants me to find a boyfriend this year. A *real* boyfriend." I shrugged my shoulder up, uncertain how to explain this.

Chance patted his bed next to him, and I again looked at him shrewdly. I wasn't sure if I should trust his friendly advances. Finally, I walked over and sat next to him, but far enough away that if he tried anything, he couldn't sneak up on me to do it. "So you broke up with him?" Chance asked.

"No," I shook my head. "He just wants me to be more *involved* here. I dunno. It's like I've only *half* lived here. He doesn't want me to call or send any letters. It's kinda complicated." I explained, throwing my hands in the air.

"So does he know about us?" Chance asked quietly. I nodded my head. "Do I need to be worried?" Chance looked at me, concerned.

Laughing, I exclaimed, "Only if you ever go to Wichita Falls looking for Kevin Strong. Then I'd say yes, you should be EXTREMELY worried!" I continued to giggle.

"So, is he some kind of *bad ass* or what?" Chance asked me, with a small smile playing on his mouth.

I thought back to when I was in 7th grade and Kevin had beaten Duke Reed so badly he broke his nose. I couldn't help but laugh when I said, "Actually yes, he beat one guy up three times over me, in junior high. The third time was on the football field and he broke his nose."

Chance looked impressed, "Shit, okay, I won't be making any trips to Wichita Falls any time soon!" I smiled at him. "Seriously, DeLaine, so what does he mean, he wants to break up? Do you all date other people? I mean what the hell is this thing you have with this guy?"

Smiling I murmured, "It's a *complicated mess*. Just say that I promised him that I would live this whole year in Corpus, and not half here, and half there, like I have been doing. I'm going to *really date*. No more just messing around. I'm sorry about the other night, but well, I just felt weird being with you after spending so much time with him."

"I can understand that," Chance whispered, softly.

I looked over at Chance. I realized he could be really sweet when he wanted to be. "I just don't want to screw around with just you, Chance, and not be open to find someone to really date, for real. Plus, this year there is so much happening. I'm in a bunch of stuff at school, there is a lot opening up for me right now. I just don't want us to be tied up in this…well…this *whatever* it is. If I'm going to go all this time without Kevin, then I want it to be for a reason. Next summer I want him to know that I really did try to live my life *here*, even though I'd rather be *there*.

Scooting back on the bed, Chance grabbed one of the pillows, and put it behind his back as he rested against the wall. "So, tell me about this." Chance sounded sincere.

"Shit, Chance, it will take me *hours* to explain it all to you," I remarked quietly, looking at the warm beer I was holding.

Jumping up, Chance said, "Let me go get us another beer and *let's just talk*."

I looked at him shocked and then asked, "Um okay, but do you have any cokes?" Chance looked at me funny and told me he would look in the fridge. He was back in just a couple of minutes and he kicked his boots off as he leaned against the pillow on the wall. He pointed at the head of the bed and told me that I could use the other pillow to do the same. I smiled gratefully.

Once I was settled, I told Chance most of the story of me and Kevin. I didn't understand why I was telling him everything about me. I realized I was telling him a little more than he'd ever known about my personal life. I explained how I had been living for my time in Wichita Falls and only half living here. I told him about Donna, and how much Kevin and I had both adored her. I was shocked that we sat in his room with the door slightly cracked open, talking until it was time for me to leave. By the time I looked at the small, diamond studded watch I wore, I found I had just enough time to get home. I'd told Chance Cahill most of my pathetic love life. I didn't give him intimate details, but he knew about me and Kevin, as much as I was willing to share with him. He knew about my wanting to live in Wichita Falls still, and how hard it had been for me to leave. He knew about Clarice and Geoffrey and my mom.

When I stood up to leave, I realized that Chance wasn't drunk either. He'd only gotten up the one time to go get a beer and managed to scrounge up a coke for me. He stood too and walked over to me. I felt myself stiffen immediately. He reached around me and hugged me. When I realized he was only going to hug me, I felt my muscles loosen a fraction. I was still leery, but when we came apart from the embrace, he kissed me on the forehead, and then stepped away.

"DeLaine, any time you need to *escape* from your mom, you come here, okay?" Chance told me, quietly.

I hadn't been looking for a place to escape, but I was touched that he had picked up on that part of my story. I nodded my head. "Thanks, Chance," I whispered.

"You're gonna have a life this year! I really believe that! Just remember that no matter what, I'm your *friend*, okay?" Chance looked at me tenderly. I felt an overwhelming urge to cry, which I normally reserved for when I was around Kevin. Chance was being sweet. I realized I wasn't very good at accepting kindness. Thankfully no tears were shed and I only nodded my head.

Chapter 3

Because I was hanging out at Chance and Lonnie's house, I began to get friendlier with Scotty Cahill too. He was such a polar opposite of his brother. While Chance and I were now more friends than anything else, there was still an undercurrent of what we'd been before between us. Scotty on the other hand had always been just my friend. We'd hung out some at the game room. He would call me Rizzo which always caused me to giggle.

I sometimes wished I found him even a little appealing. He was the kind of boy I thought would make a great boyfriend. Sadly he was always getting his heart broken. I'd actually threatened to kick one girl's ass one Friday night at the game room during my sophomore year that had cheated on Scotty. I always felt protective of him, but didn't think he saw me as anything other than "Rizzo" from the movie *Grease*. He once told me when he was a bit inebriated that I was the coolest chick he'd ever known. I was surprised when he said that. I didn't think I was cool in any way, shape or form. That's when he dubbed me "Rizzo" of Woodway High School.

As if Chance's words were a spoken premonition, I began to get so involved in school; it seemed I was home less and less during the week. Even though it caused me to stay up well past midnight, most nights, trying to finish my homework, I felt happier than I ever had before.

The auditions for the school play were held at the end of September. I was really excited for them. I was nervous, because I'd never gotten up like that before. I found I was completely different in my Theater Arts class. It was the Beginners' class and it had mostly underclassmen. I liked the teacher a lot. He reminded me of Ichabod Crane and everyone in school detested him, except me, it seemed.

Mr. Magnus was a tough teacher. He was an actor in the community theaters, and had a booming, commanding voice that always got everyone's attention. He didn't tolerate a lot of silliness. For some reason, I made it my mission to get him to smile once, at least, every class period. At first he was a tough nut to crack as Mr. Strong had called me so many years before. Somehow, I managed to see a little bit of light when we talked. Sometimes I would tell him some lame joke I might have heard that day to see if I could elicit a smile. When he began to curve his mouth at the corners, I would feel victorious. I didn't understand why I liked him so much, but I did. He tolerated a lot more out of me than he did the others in his class, which was surprising.

We had worked on what to expect during rehearsals and we'd done a few little skits. I found that I could become *anyone* I wanted to be, when I was acting in a scene. I felt almost a lightness of being when I took to the stage.

The day of auditions, we had to come after school and audition against all the kids in Mr. Magnus's advanced Theater Arts group. They were all in their second, third or fourth year of theater. One of the kids in there was a guy named Pete Mulligan. He was also involved in the community theater groups and had been acting since he was a little kid. He had been in all the school plays since his freshman year and now was a senior. This was his last year and he usually got the lead in the plays. Everyone thought he would get the male lead no matter what part Mr. Magnus made him read. I watched intently as our teacher walked all the older kids, who had been with him for more than a year, through scenes from the play. I wanted a part in this play more than I'd ever wanted anything. I really wasn't sure what part I wanted. I just wanted to be in front of bright lights and *shine*. I wanted to do something finally that my parents might see and be proud of. I couldn't play music, but maybe just maybe I could be an actress. I wondered if my daddy would ever come to see me in a play. I wondered then if my mom would stay *sober* enough to come to it.

While I was lost in thought, thinking about my parents, the girl sitting next to me nudged me and I looked up. I realized Mr. Magnus wanted me to go up on the stage. I'd watched all the older or more experienced kids read every single scene that Mr. Magnus was having us do, in order to audition. He kept Pete up there forever it seemed. I realized Pete was really cute, but he was really out of my league. If I'd ever thought Kevin was out of my league, I'd been sadly mistaken. Pete Mulligan was even *more* out of my league than anyone else I'd ever known. I walked up the side stairs to the stage on shaky legs and felt stupid for being nervous.

Pete handed me one of the scripts they'd been reading from and Mr. Magnus began our first scene. I read the part, but felt stiff and weird standing there. Gone was all the silliness I usually had when I was in theater. Now I had some stiff body I was encased in, that felt like I had cement blocks surrounding my limbs. As if he understood, Mr. Magnus stopped Pete and me mid-sentence. "Okay, Pete, you and DeLaine do the shakes!"

Pete looked at him and demanded, "*Magnus* are you *crazy*?" I was shocked that he had called our teacher that and that he'd had the guts to even say the rest of his sentence.

Mr. Magnus gave Pete a piercing look and shook his head. Pete blew out a big puff of air and he leaned over half-way and began wiggling his arms, body and legs. I wasn't sure what in the world Pete Mulligan was doing, but I *wasn't* doing whatever it was. Finally, Pete looked at me and commanded, "Bend over! We're doing this so *you* get the jitters out of your system!" I quickly leaned half-way and began to shake myself and looked at him. "Just do what I do!" Pete instructed, quietly. I nodded as much as I could while leaning down. After a couple of minutes Mr. Magnus told us to stand up and shake the rest off and continue with the reading. I was shocked. I felt much better and could even tell in my voice that I seemed to put the right emphasis on every word I read from the script.

Before the auditions were done, I'd been up on the stage as long, if not more so, than Pete Mulligan, which was a little of a shock to me. I read every female character with Pete and then different ones with different people. The very last scene we read was a powerful scene where the male lead and the housekeeper, who had more lines than the female lead, but was considered a supporting character, had a massive argument.

We were using some type of British accent and I'd managed to do things like that all the time growing up. I'd perfected a version of one a bit, and was happy to be able to show it off. During the scene, Pete's character grabs the housekeeper and she yells at him to take his hands off of her. I'll never know where it came from, but for some reason when he grabbed me and turned me around wildly I shouted forcefully and with as much conviction as if he were really jerking me around, "TAKE YOUR BLOODY HANDS OFF OF ME!"

Pete Mulligan was a great young actor. He went with my adlibbed line and we ended up doing even more of the scene than we'd done in the past. By the time Mr. Magnus realized it and stopped us, I was in *full character,* even though I had no clue what that meant exactly. I just knew that at that moment I *was* this evil housekeeper who was conspiring with the character that Pete was reading.

Mr. Magnus yelled, *"CUT"* and Pete immediately shut down and it took me a moment to come back into DeLaine Reynolds' body. I stood on the stage with Pete Mulligan feeling horribly exposed suddenly, wondering what in the world I was doing up there. Finally, our director declared, "That's it folks, I'll post the cast list in the morning on the bulletin board." And with that he turned on his heel and walked out of the small auditorium. I stood there, not really certain what I should do. I didn't have any friends yet in there.

I looked over at Pete Mulligan and he gave me a perfunctory smile and walked off the stage. I watched all the teenagers begin to scatter. I turned and slowly walked off the stage. I hoped I got at least a little part. Mr. Magnus had me read for the housekeeper the most, but he'd read me for *everything*. He'd read Pete and me off of each other a lot, but he'd mixed in enough other people for me to feel uncertain *what* he was doing.

The next morning I went to school a little early and was anxious to see if the cast list was posted yet. As I walked through the halls up to the front where the information bulletin boards were, I noticed a large throng of Theater Arts kids who were all in the advanced class checking the list. One of them came over to me as I was walking up and chided, "Oh just wait, Mary is going to be *so* mad at you!"

I turned to look at her funny because I didn't have a clue *who* she was talking about. I walked up and saw the cast list typed neatly. I scanned it and wasn't surprised to see Pete Mulligan's name at the top in the male lead's role. I was surprised by the second character just because I had only seen her read a couple of times. When my eyes rested on the third character in the lineup I was shocked to see my name in black bold letters. I had gotten the part of the evil housekeeper. I had someone else lean over while I was reading the list tell me how mad Mary was going to be with me. I didn't even know *who* Mary was. I was still in shock that I'd actually gotten a part at all. I hoped in a way I'd get a tiny role, but to have the third lead character in my first play felt pretty heady.

Later that day, Mr. Magnus pulled me out of my accelerated English class. "So, listen, everybody else in the play is in my advanced class. I suspect you've done some acting somewhere else, so I'd like to change your schedule and put you in the advanced class so we can do some rehearsals during class periods as well."

I stood in the hallway looking at Mr. Magnus. I wasn't sure what I was supposed to say. Finally, I remembered I had to answer and asked, "Um, so how can you do that?"

Mr. Magnus told me he wanted to change my World History classes. That would give me a much harder teacher, in order to move me into his advanced class. I told him I was worried I wouldn't do well in the History class. Mr. Magnus began to laugh and I watched fascinated at his bobbing Adam's apple. "Why DeLaine, you'll enjoy Dr. Vandergriff's class *much more* than that *pathetic* excuse for a class you're in now! Trust me my dear. A brain like yours needs to be challenged! You aren't getting that now with open book tests and no teaching! Dr. Vandergriff will enjoy you thoroughly as one of his students. He is one of my dearest friends and a mind like yours is the kind he loves to challenge."

Looking at him uncertain what exactly he meant by that last sentence, I finally nodded my head. "Does my mom have to do anything?" I asked, suddenly terrified she'd have to come to the school. Her drinking had been exceptionally heavy the last month and she and Ray had argued much more as well.

Smiling he shook his head. "No, we aren't *dropping* any class, we are merely *rearranging* so the counselor has assured me that it will be nothing more than you going by his office before you go to World History today. Give Mr. Ussery a paper that you'll receive from the counselor. Once he signs it, you come to my advanced class. I sign it and then Dr. Vandergriff will sign off too. From then on you will come to my advanced class, instead of Ussery's history class. Then you will go to Dr. Vandergriff instead of Theater I. Okay?"

"Okay," I replied, taking a deep breath.

Sensing me feeling a little apprehensive Mr. Magnus asked me if I was okay with it. I nodded my head. "Yeah, but I'm just curious. I'm the only person in *Theater I* who got a part in the play. *Why*?"

Surprised Mr. Magnus responded, "My dear, do you not know how *talented* you are?" Shaking my head, he smiled sympathetically at me, "Dear, you are a diamond in the rough. I look forward to helping you to realize your *true brilliance*." I suddenly felt overwhelmed after he said that. It was one of the nicest things an adult had ever said to me. I smiled at him feeling a little flush of embarrassment too. "And you must remember darling, you are an *actor*; don't blush when you are complimented! You deserve it! Only if you do not deserve it should you ever blush." I nodded and smiled at him. He was so *inspiring* to me.

The weeks that followed were filled full of hard work. I was rehearsing every single day for an hour in class, then we would rehearse for at least four more hours, if not longer every night. We built sets on Saturday afternoons, and still managed to rehearse for at least an hour every Saturday as well. Those crazy intense weeks were some of the most fulfilling of my life to that point.

I learned that Mary was a 4th year Theater student who had wanted the role I landed in the play. She felt it was her last chance to have a lead part since she was a senior. Mr. Magnus reminded her there would be the Spring play that we would do also and that we would be taking that one to competition as well. I didn't know exactly what that meant, but I was excited by all of it. Mary was the stage manager on the fall production and even though she was miffed throughout all of the rehearsals at me for winning the role, she remained civil.

Pete Mulligan and I spent more hours together than any of the others. We had the most scenes together and sometimes I wished I had gotten the female lead because he got to kiss her. The female lead was his wife, even if she really wasn't in the play as much as I was. The first rehearsal Pete ran up to me and jumped into my arms completely startling me, hollering some kind of gibberish. What amazed me more was that I caught him and was able to hold him as he wrapped his long skinny legs around my waist and hugged me tight. Once I set him down on the stage carefully, he hugged me and welcomed me to the stage. I was flabbergasted at how warm, gracious and funny he was. We became exceptionally close. He taught me a lot about the stage, lighting and even makeup. When we began to do full makeup and dress rehearsals I was shocked when he walked in with his own makeup kit. He had the makings of anything needed for stage productions. Pete kept me in stitches through everything. We had to be extremely physical in one scene of the play where we fight. I had worried about it when I first realized I got the part, but after just a short period, Pete Mulligan was someone I trusted explicitly.

The more Pete showed me about the theater, the more I yearned to know. He pushed me out of my comfort zone by having me rehearse scenes with him in different accents. He had me improvise scenes even though it took me *forever* to understand what exactly *'improv'* meant. As much as Mr. Magnus was my theater arts teacher, Pete Mulligan was as well. He kept me on my toes at every rehearsal and saved my butt on more than one occasion when I flubbed lines that I knew. Thankfully Pete had enough experience to get us through the scene. I was mortified afterwards but he just laughed it off and told me not to worry.

As I began to get more involved at school, which kept me out of the house, I also began to notice that I was garnering more male attention wherever I went outside of school too. One night I sat in a Circle K parking lot, after getting gas, and a very large guy opened my passenger door and fell inside of my car. I was shocked when I saw the most beautiful, green eyes looking back at me that I'd ever seen in my life. They were even more beautiful than Jax's green eyes, which I didn't think could ever happen. I was about to yell at him when he looked at me seriously and declared, "Oh my God. You are the most *beautiful* woman I've ever seen in my entire life! *Will you go out with me*?"

"What?" I screeched! "I don't even know *who* the hell you are!"

He looked truly chagrined and he stuck out a huge, meaty hand that was at least three times the size of mine, "Hey, my name is Rick."

Before I could even muster a *Rick Who*? another guy I knew came over to my car and opened the passenger door. He hung out with Chance and Lonnie, but I couldn't remember his name. He knew mine though, "Hey, DeLaine! Sorry about that! C'mon Rick! Let's go big fella!"

"Wait a minute," Rick began to slur as the other guy hooked his arm with Rick's. "I gotta know if she'll go out with me. *I think I'm in love, man*! I want to marry this woman!"

I began to giggle at all the nonsense he was spouting off, but the more I looked at him the more intrigued I became. He wasn't small by any means. He reminded me of Jethro Bodine on the *Beverly Hillbillies* because he was very tall and stout. He didn't appear to be fat just a big ol' boy as they say. He had sandy brown hair that was a little shaggy and a strong Patrician type nose. His eyes though were what burned in my mind. They almost glowed like a cat's, they were so green. They were the most intriguing eyes I'd seen yet, and I was quite the eye person. I thought it was probably because I had just plain old, dull, brown ones, with no excitement until I cried.

Finally, the large guy named Rick was safely hauled out of my car by two guys, and the heavy Thunderbird door closed. As I was putting the key in the ignition, I felt the whole car shake. I turned to see Rick hanging through my passenger window that was rolled down. "I'm serious! You are *gorgeous* and I wanna go out with you! You're gonna be my *girlfriend!* I'll find you my beautiful *mystery woman*! I will find you again!" By the time his buddy came and got him again I was laughing so hard my stomach hurt. The other guy had actually said my name and this *Rick* guy didn't even hear him. I felt flattered, but I also thought he was funny as all get out. I was glad my Saturday night ended on a high note as I drove home.

The next week it began to get cold. It wasn't the normal November cold. It was much colder because so many cold fronts were blowing through on a continuous basis. The refineries smelled bad every single day, since the North winds were blowing. I hated any time I had to drive on the highway. I felt bad for Kelly and

Robin because they lived closer to the refineries, but they said they just got used to the odor.

We were getting closer to the actual performance of our play. I was beginning to get nervous. We were now doing full dress rehearsals without makeup. We wouldn't do makeup again until the last week Mr. Magnus had told us.

The rehearsal for Thursday was cut short due to Mr. Magnus having a migraine. I knew that my mom wasn't expecting me until at least 9:30, so I decided to cruise through Annaville a little bit to see who all was out in the windy cold. I could at least drive through Sonic and get a coke. If Mom asked, I'd just tell her that Pete brought it to me on his way to rehearsal. I smiled at my believable lie and drove on into Sonic, which for some odd reason appeared packed. I finally found an open pocket beside a big pickup truck on a lift, and some kind of Blazer on one too. I felt small and low in my Thunderbird beside the two behemoth trucks.

I ordered my coke and lit a cigarette while I was turning up the radio. I had slowly begun to drink cokes again, but I was still not really drinking beer or any alcohol. I hadn't smoked pot since the night in front of Bailey's house with Kevin and Freddie Black. I was trying not to drink too many cokes because I didn't want to gain weight back, but I loved them so much. I usually tried to only drink them on the weekends, but every once in a while, like now, I'd splurge.

I had rolled up the electric window after placing my order because the cold was so awful. I couldn't believe how frigid it was and it was only November. In Corpus it didn't get this cold usually until late December or January. I heard someone outside my driver's side. Thinking the car hop had brought my drink, I reached down to grab the dollar lying in the seat, next to me. I pushed the silver button to roll the window down and when I turned to give the dollar to the car hop I was surprised to see no one there. I could still hear a faint noise like someone was hollering though. I looked around wondering who it was. Suddenly it became clearer and louder. I looked up on the left of me and saw the mysterious *Rick* who thought I was *so* beautiful. He was sitting in the big, black vehicle that looked like some old Blazer.

"Oh my God! *I found you!* I've been looking all over for you! I couldn't get Dalton to tell me your name for the longest time. He kept telling me he didn't know it and then he finally told me he just knew your first name. *Diane?*"

I looked up into the glowing, green eyes and snorted. "*Nope*! If you don't know my name, then you must not have wanted to find me too badly!"

"Aww, c'mon darlin', I'm bad at names! I forgot my own the other night, but I didn't forget *you!*"
Rick grinned sweetly, looking down at me.

I grinned and shook my head. "Nope, Sorry! You don't know my name. Can't let you in!"

"I didn't even ask to be let in, now did I, little girl?"
Rick was still smiling.

Shaking my head, I admitted, "Nope, I guess you didn't! But you still don't know my name. I don't think you're *that* in love with me!"

I saw Rick turn his head and talk to the driver. The huge, black vehicle began to back out. I looked at him astonished that he had taken me so seriously. I thought we'd just been having a good round of playful banter. The truck came to a stop, and I saw the passenger door open up. Rick *stepped* out. He didn't jump out; he *stepped* out of the tall, lifted truck. Just as I realized that Rick had to be at least 6'3" the car hop came with my medium coke. I gave her the dollar and turned back around only to see that Rick was gone and so was the tall Blazer. It had finished pulling out while I was talking to the car hop, but I thought Rick was getting out to come talk to me. I felt disappointed when I realized it was gone and Rick along with it.

I sat back and pushed the silver button to close the window against the cold. It was actually starting to drizzle which was a bummer. I knew that I should just go on home early. As I was about to put the car into reverse there was a tap on the passenger window. I turned around and jumped when I saw Rick's green, cat eyes glowing at me.

"Shit you scared me! I thought you left!" I giggled, as I rolled the window down.

"What's wrong, *little girl*, you afraid the big bad wolf is going to come and get you? Unlock the door!" Rick teased me. I popped the electric lock and he slipped into the passenger seat where we had originally met. When I began grinning he looked at me and asked, "What? Why are you laughing?"

"Well, first of all, I was remembering how I met you the other night at Circle K, when you dove into my car. Second, I just realized how tall you are. You look a little *cramped* in here and this is a big ol' car!" I was trying hard to hide the smirk.

Rick looked at me appraisingly, "Okay, so your name isn't *Diane*. Is it Dian-*a*?" I shook my head smiling. I knew he'd never guess my name. I knew that the guy he had been with knew good and well what it was, because he'd said it as he got a very drunk Rick out of my car. Rick scratched his head, "Okay, not *Diane* or *Diana*. But it's kinda like that, right?!" I smiled indulgently at him. Finally he suggested, "Okay, let's make a bet. I bet you that I'll figure it out on this next try."

"So, if you do what happens?" I asked him.

"Well, I bet you that if I can get it right on the next guess, I get to kiss you. If I don't, I'll get out of your car and *never* bother you again." Rick flashed his pearly whites. I liked his smile. He wasn't beautiful like Kevin, or cute like Jax. His eyes were mesmerizing, but he was rugged looking and handsome.

I tilted my head looking at the massive mountain of a guy sitting inside of my car. His head literally touched the headliner. Finally, I nodded my head, "Okay, I'll take that bet because there is *no way* you can guess my name." I felt certain he'd come up with some other girl "D" name, but it certainly wouldn't be DeLaine.

Rick looked at me and leaned towards the middle of the car, "You better get ready to pucker up *little girl*." I laughed and told him he was awful sure of himself. "DELAINE." My mouth fell open, but Rick's caught it as he moved in and kissed me firmly on my mouth. It wasn't a long passionate kiss, but he definitely let me know he was in the car with me.

When he pulled away from me, I asked, "*How did you…?*" Then I realized he'd known it all along. It was a ruse to get a kiss and he'd played it well. I couldn't believe I'd been that gullible.

Rick smiled, "By the way, has anyone ever told you that you are the most beautiful girl in the world?" I just shook my head and he stated, "Of course they have! *I did*! And you really are the most beautiful girl in the world, DeLaine! That's a beautiful name by the way. It's a name you can really get your mouth around. I grinned and felt myself begin to blush a little. I was beginning to feel a little hot in the car with the heater blasting and all of Rick taking up so much room in my car.

"You have to stop that. It's a little embarrassing." I replied, quietly, looking down.

Rick looked at me seriously, "But you shouldn't be embarrassed. I just think if a woman is beautiful, someone should tell her. You obviously haven't had anyone do that in a long time."

"I'm not sure if anyone has ever put it *quite* the way you did," I giggled.

"Well, I am a big dude, and tend to be pretty loud, and well…I believe in just speaking my mind. So, when are you going out with me?" Rick asked with his face set so seriously.

"I don't know *you*," I replied.

He rolled his eyes, "C'mon! Not this again! You know me! This is the second time you've met me now. I think that you should agree to at least one date now, since we've officially met twice."

"I'm not sure I'd count Circle K," I was arching my eyebrow.

"Yep, it counts!" Rick laughed, as his big voice boomed inside the walls of my car. "If it didn't count I wouldn't know your name, would I?"

"Okay, you got me there!" I shook my head. Suddenly, Rick hushed me and held his finger up. He reached over to the radio and turned it up. Kenny Rogers and Dolly Parton were singing "Islands in the Stream".

"That's *our* song!" Rick boomed.

"Good grief! That's not our song," I replied.

"Of course it is!" he was smiling, then he began to sing parts of it. I was pleasantly surprised to find he had a rich baritone singing voice and wasn't that bad. He saw the spark of surprise in my face and said, "Yeah, I know I sing good! I was in the All State Choir at Calvin for four straight years!"

"Wait! You went to *Calvin*?" I asked surprised.

"Yep, class of 1981," Rick told me. I looked at him stunned. It seemed since the Game Room closed I was meeting more people who were from Calvin. Most were like a lot of my friends from Woodway, and had already graduated from high school.

"Wow! How come I've never seen you before?" I asked him surprised.

"I guess you've been running around with the *wrong* crowd. From what I hear you've been a hostage at Woodway for a while! You finally got out of their hold and into the best school in this whole God forsaken town!" Rick exclaimed.

I looked at him and decided that I liked him, but I was also a little head strong. I picked up my cigarettes and lit one. Rick didn't say anything so I was happy to know that he wasn't going to give me constant grief about smoking. "Do you smoke?" I asked him calmly.

"Nah, unless I'm really drunk! So, can I bum a cigarette?" he asked.

"Wait, you said only when you're really drunk are you saying you're drunk NOW?" I asked him feeling a little nervous because he'd been completely plowed when I'd met him at the Circle K.

Rick's laugh was big and booming, but it was warm and comforting too. "No darlin'. It's a work night! No beer except on Fridays and Saturdays and sometimes a Sunday afternoon!" I smiled at him knowing it was better than every chance he got. "I was just messin' with you *little girl*!"

"You really need to quit callin' me *little girl* you know?" I scolded, a little defensively.

"Hmm, well I don't know any woman who wants to be called *Big girl*!" Rick responded in his easy drawl.

"I guess you're right!" I agreed not sure what to say next.

"How 'bout I call you *Lil' Bit*?" Rick suggested softly.

My head shot up as I looked at him in shock. I felt as if I'd just seen a ghost. I'd called Kevin's little sister, Donna *Lil' Bit*. How could Rick have known? I opened my mouth to respond, but couldn't think what I should say to him.

"Bad name too?" I shook my head. "Okay, you gotta help me here darlin' 'cause I'm gonna call you somethin' that only *I* get to call you." Rick smiled.

After a brief hesitation I said, "I used to have someone very special to me that I called *Lil' Bit.* She died a couple years ago."

Rick nodded his head and said, "That sucks! I'm really sorry. I don't want to make you feel bad."

"You know what, I think that you are *supposed* to call me that," I stated faintly, uncertain how I knew it.

Rick looked at me curiously. "What? Why would you say that?"

"Long story," I was smiling again. "But I think you are supposed to call me that."

"Well, *Lil' Bit*, when you goin' out with me?" Rick began his persistent quest to get me to agree to go out with him.

"Are you going to the dance Saturday?" I asked him.

He smiled, "Are you kidding me? Of course I'm gonna be there! Especially if my sweet *Lil' Bit* is goin'!"

"How 'bout we meet there?" I suggested quietly.

Rick began shaking his head. "Nope, no way! I want to pick you up and meet your daddy and do everything right! I don't believe in girls and guys just hookin' up! I want to do it right!"

I groaned inwardly. I didn't want him to come to my house. As unpredictable as my mom was I never knew who she was going to be if someone came over. I thought I might actually like this boy. He was even older than Chance, but he reminded me of a warm, safe, giant, teddy bear. "Um, my parents are divorced," I finally stated quietly.

"Okay, well, then I need to come meet your mama, I guess?" he asked me curiously.

"Yeah, well, the thing is, she's a little…*unpredictable* sometimes, as far as what her mood is. I'd rather just meet you at the dance." I admitted.

Rick sat there for a while as the drizzle outside began to turn into true rain. I saw him raise his head in the infamous chin nod that Kevin used to do. Then he waved. I looked across and saw the big truck he'd been in when I first pulled in. Finally, he agreed, "Okay, look, I'll meet you at the dance, but I'm *not* counting it as a date, so you still owe me one, okay?" Smiling at him I nodded and he slipped his class ring off. I looked at him curiously. "How big is this ring on your finger?" he asked me.

Laughing I slipped it onto my index finger which was my biggest one, "Well, um, gee, I don't know, but I'd say *quite a bit*!"

Rick opened the door and stepped out before I knew what he was doing. "Well, you keep it for me and bring it to the dance on Saturday okay?"

"No wait! Rick, *take it back*! You can't give me your class ring," I cried out.

"You're just babysitting it for a couple days! See you Saturday, *Lil' Bit*!" Rick grinned, then the door was closed and I was sitting there, holding a very heavy, class ring. I watched as he stepped up into the jacked up vehicle trying to figure out what happened.

When I got home later that night, I took the ring out and looked at it closely. He had been in football which wasn't a big surprise. It had his class year and his name. I realized I didn't even know his last name. Looking inside the ring I saw a faint inscription that looked like R. Ge st. I looked closer and finally realized that it actually said R. Geist. It was so large. I'd seen other girls wearing their boyfriend's class rings and had always wondered what it was like to wear a boy's ring. Of course Jax had been in junior high when we were together, but I know it made me feel good to wear his letter jacket. Kevin never had a class ring and now he never would I thought a little bitterly. Then I realized it didn't really matter. I'd never wear it if he had one anyway.

I remembered seeing other girls who put tape and yarn and even ribbon wound around the ring to make it fit because usually boys' fingers were larger than girls'. I remembered that my mom had a long cylinder of ribbon she used on presents when she felt like making them all fancy. I got up and went to the spare bedroom and got the roll with the green, red, gold and snowflake ribbon wound around the large cardboard cylinder. It was the perfect width and was smooth and satiny. Rick's ring was gold so I tried the gold ribbon. It didn't match it exactly but it was still a good color. I hurried into my bedroom and grabbed the Scotch tape out of my desk drawer and began to slowly wrap the ring with gold ribbon. I didn't know how much it was going to take. I was definitely grateful it was a large cylinder of ribbon! By the time I finished, it fit my finger comfortably without falling off.

I giggled as I finished wrapping the ring in ribbon and decided he'd learn a valuable lesson about giving his ring to a girl when he had to unwrap all the gold ribbon off of it. When I finished, I smiled at the completed project and realized it was already midnight. I knew I had to go to sleep or I'd never get up the next day. I kept the ring on my finger as I fell asleep, so I could feel its weight. I wanted to believe that this boy really thought that I was beautiful and wanted to go out with me. I didn't know why in the world he'd think that. Working hard, I pushed the negative comments out of my head, and began to drift out in my field of yellow flowers to the world of my dreams. I wasn't surprised when I heard Donna's tiny giggles just as sleep claimed me for the night. Did she send Rick to me because it was what Kevin wanted, I wondered briefly as I fell asleep. I wouldn't know the answer to that because the night went dark and I was asleep.

Chapter 4

That Saturday I went to the dance with Kelly and Robin. I was anxious for Rick to show up. I'd told them about my two encounters with the mountain of a man, who jumped into my car and told me how beautiful I was. I showed them the ring too and we all giggled when we thought about what he'd do when he saw how much gold ribbon I'd wrapped around it.

As the night wore on, I was becoming more anxious because I never saw Rick come in. I saw Chance, Scotty and Lonnie and went over to them. I was surprised to find out Chance knew him. He looked at me funny when I asked him. "What's goin' on? Do you finally have a *real* boyfriend?" Chance asked. I just shook my head. We all sat at one of the long tables in the dance hall. More of our crowd came in and sat with us. I watched the door like a hawk, but Rick never came through the door.

While I sat there watching everyone dance, I was surprised when Scotty moved next to me to chat. He leaned over and spoke in my ear so he could be heard over the country music that was blaring out of the huge speakers. "You sure are watching everyone dance around." I nodded my head and gave him a half smile. "I really have to learn how to dance."

I turned and looked at him perplexed. I didn't really know how to two-step very well either, but I would try if anyone ever asked me. Scotty smiled really big and leaned over to tell me that he'd finally asked Sara Barker out for the next country dance in Orange Grove. I was a bit surprised. Sara Barker went to Calvin too and was in my class. She was one of the popular kicker girls. I couldn't stand her and thought she looked like a horse. Why would Scotty Cahill be even remotely interested I wondered?

When I didn't say much, Scotty asked what I thought of her. I sat there for a minute and thought about my answer. I could tell he was excited that she'd accepted his invitation for a date, but I thought she was a bitch and he was definitely too sweet for her. "Scotty, I don't want to hurt your feelings, but I'm not real crazy about her."

"Why?" He asked me.

I sat there for a second then said, "Well, number one I think you are too good for her and number too she's just a snotty twit!" I grinned and stated for good measure, "Plus she's got a horsey face!"

Scotty looked a little crest fallen that I hadn't shared in his excitement in a better way. "I think she's pretty," he responded quietly.

I really felt bad for being such an obnoxious friend. "I guess to a guy she is pretty," I began trying to appease his hurt feelings. "It's probably just me." Scotty nodded his head and looked out at the dance floor. I really wanted to make it up to him. He was one of those people you couldn't stand to hurt.

"Hey, Scotty, my mom used to teach dance a long time ago before I was born. Maybe she could show you a few steps," I offered. As soon as the words came out of my mouth I felt awful. I worried he would come over and see what an insane drunk she was. I regretted offering him dance lessons when I knew my mom was so unpredictable. Before I could withdraw the suggestion his face lit up and he began to thank me profusely. I swallowed hard and gave him what I hoped looked like a genuine smile but was afraid it came out rather sickly.

I tried to figure out how to get out of this mess I'd just created. Suddenly I realized if he came over on a Saturday morning she might actually not be drunk yet. When she wasn't drunk she was funny and loving. If he could come before her switch was tripped I might still come off not being such a bad friend. I told him I'd call him later in the week and let him know if she was up to it. He quickly hugged me and I felt even worse for having been so mean about this girl he liked.

The rest of the night we sat beside each other talking. I still kept my gaze constantly towards the door, hoping Rick would come in. He never did.

When I was driving Kelly and Robin home, I felt so disappointed. I had thought maybe this Rick guy was special, but he didn't even keep our date at the dance. I guessed he just wanted to see if he could get me to like him by saying all the stuff he'd said. Driving home from Kelly and Robin's house I had hot tears rolling down my cheeks. I didn't think there was any hope of ever finding someone else other than the one person I truly loved. I couldn't have him, I thought bitterly, as I wiped my hand across my face.

The next week at school I was sitting in VOE when one of the girls named Mandy Manson whispered across the table, "Hey, DeLaine, are you dating Rick Geist now?"

I looked at her curiously, "What? No!"

"Isn't that his ring on your finger?" she persisted.

I looked at the huge class ring that I'd kept on my finger since Saturday just because it felt nice to feel like someone liked me, even if he didn't show up when he was supposed to. "Um, yeah, but we aren't dating." I replied.

"Why do you have his ring then?" Mandy persisted.

I rolled my eyes and hoped she wouldn't take it personally. I just didn't know how to explain *why* I had a boy's ring and wasn't dating him. Finally, I explained, "I'm just holding it for him. I don't want to lose it so I just put it on my finger so I know where it is. Besides, I don't want my mom to find it either." I finished. I wasn't really lying about that. If my mom decided to go snooping through my room again and found a boy's class ring, a boy who was four years older than me, she'd probably freak out. Keeping it on me was the best answer. I kept it in my pocket at home.

Mandy looked at me skeptically. Smiling at her bewildered stare I suddenly wondered how she knew whose ring it was. When I asked, she smiled, "Well, I dated him last year for a little while. He never gave it to me to wear, but I always griped when he'd hold my hand because it hurt my fingers."

I looked at her and felt a sudden let down. Mandy Manson was one of the popular kicker girls. She had long, auburn hair and freckles. If Rick had dated her, I knew there was no way he'd truly want to go out with me. I began to feel my whole *'I'm nobody'* syndrome when I found out that Rick and Mandy had dated. The rest of the day I walked around down in the dumps. Even rehearsal didn't give me my usual mood boost.

As I walked into the door that night, my mom asked me if I knew someone named Rick. I looked at her feeling a little weird. I didn't trust that she hadn't been going through my stuff again, even though I'd quit keeping a journal, and I hadn't written Rick's name anywhere. I was truly curious why she would ask. "Why?" I asked, haltingly.

I saw my mom point to the kitchen counter. Sitting there was a small basket with chocolate kisses and balloons tied to it. I'd never received a balloon arrangement before. I walked over to the basket and on the tiny card written in neat print I read,

DeLaine,
Sorry about Saturday. I'll make it up to you.
Rick

My back was to my mom so she couldn't see the huge smile playing across my face. Now I would have to tell her. I'd never brought a boy to meet my mom before. She'd met Kevin, but only because he'd been there when I got hurt in 7th grade.

"Rick's just a guy I met a few weeks ago that's all," I was smiling as I turned to face my mom. I was grateful she was in a good mood for a change.

"So, what does he have to make up to you?" my mom asked me.

"Um, he told me he was going to the dance and he didn't. I guess he thought I'd be upset because I think he likes me," I told her, uncertain how I was supposed to explain him to her.

"Does he go to school at Calvin?" Mom asked.

I dreaded telling her how much older he was than me, but I was 17 now so it wasn't like it was that big of a deal if he was 4 years older. "Uh, no he graduated already." I shrugged my shoulders.

After a few more inquiries about the mysterious Rick, my mom finally let the matter rest when she declared, "Well, if he wants to go out with you, he has to pick you up and come in to meet me. He better not just drive up and honk his horn thinking you are going to come running like some *hussy*!"

I snorted and began to chuckle. I could just see him honking from some gigantic truck that only a giant could get into and me running out, needing a ladder just to get into it. I told her I'd be sure to keep that in mind if he ever asked me out. I just didn't know how soon it would be that he would ask.

I decided since she was in such a good mood I'd spring the whole dance lesson for Scotty in. She appeared genuinely pleased that I'd asked her to help out my friend. She told me that would be great. So we agreed that Saturday, if Scotty could spring it, she would teach both of us how to two-step. I laughed because I figured I would be hopeless, but agreed. Maybe Rick would actually ask me to a dance and I needed to know how to at least look like I knew what I was doing. I kissed her on the cheek, grabbed my balloons and rushed to my room to call Scotty to come to my house that Saturday.

The next day in VOE, Mandy whispered to me while we worked on a data entry assignment, "Hey, DeLaine, Rick called me last night and asked if I had your phone number. I told him I didn't, but I had a class with you. He wants to know if you'll go out with him this weekend."

I felt my face scrunch into a truly incredulous look. "What? Are you serious?" Mandy smiled and nodded her head. "Why did he call you?" I asked her feeling a little weird that a girl who had dated a boy who was interested in me was asking me out for him.

"We're still friends. It's not like he's an asshole or anything, we just didn't really click right. He's too old fashioned for me." Mandy was smiling.

I sat there for a minute and then replied, "Tell him if he really wants to go out with me he needs to come up here in the evening, while I'm at rehearsal. He can ask me then and I'll give him my answer."

Mandy shrugged and said she would. I wondered if he found where I lived to have the balloons delivered, why he didn't find my phone number too. I thought it was odd he had found out where I lived. Things with Rick were weird it seemed. I wasn't sure exactly what it meant.

Walking to my car that night, in the front parking lot of the school, I kept my head down to avoid the chill of the wind blasting through. All the teenagers leaving with me were walking and talking together. I still felt myself tending to come out as a loner. I wondered if I'd ever feel like I fit in somewhere. When I got to my car, I heard Pete Mulligan holler my name. I looked up and he was grinning broadly at me.

"What?" I hollered into the wind.

"LOOK!" Pete yelled back to me and swept his hand across the line of cars beside mine.

Written across the windshields in white shoe polish was

D-E-L-A-I-N-E- (first car)
W-I-L-L Y-O-U (second car)
G-O O-U-T (third car)

W-I-T-H M-E? (fourth car)
T-E-L-L MM (fifth car)

I stood there staring at the five cars totally bewildered. One of the windshields assaulted had been Pete's. I looked at him and he exclaimed, "I think this guy deserves a chance!" He was the only one who wasn't upset about having his brand new silver Camaro written on, as we all tried to find something to wipe it off so they could see to drive home. After apologizing profusely and helping everyone wipe the shoe polish off their windshields, I climbed into my car feeling like a popsicle. I was frozen and my fingers were burning.

The next day the whole school was buzzing about the date proposal written on five cars. By the time I got to VOE, Mandy knew and was anxious for my answer. I told her to give Rick my number and wrote it down for her. I also told her to tell him yes and he needed to call me that evening at 9:30 *exactly.* I had never gotten out of rehearsal later than that and I didn't want the phone ringing any later. I didn't want my mom upset. Mandy smiled and promised she'd let him know.

Thankfully, I got home in plenty of time to get Rick's call. I felt funny with a boy calling the house. Chance had called when Mom and I had our wreck, but Rick could be a potential *real* boyfriend. His voice sounded even deeper on the phone. He was also just as impossible on the phone as he was in person. I felt myself blush more in the phone call than I'd blushed in long time. By the time we hung up after talking for about 20 minutes, I was grinning like an idiot.

Mama knocked on my door. I hollered for her to come in, she poked her head around and smiled at me. "Well, are you going to go out with him?" she asked me.

Smiling at her, nodding my head. "After the way he asked me out, I really didn't have a choice, did I?" I told Mom about the shoe polish on the cars as a means to ask me out. She thought it was funny. I loved it when my *real* Mom was around and not the anger fueled alcoholic that came out for no reason.

I'd noticed Mama had been acting peculiar and went back and forth from either being exceptionally angry and violent to being almost weepy with sentiment. I wasn't sure why she was acting that way. When I tried to dance around the topic of her moods it usually led to her getting into a dark one, so I rarely talked to her about what was wrong.

I'd agreed to go out with Rick that Saturday because I knew it would be my last free Saturday evening for the next two weekends. We were performing our play for our first audience on the following Thursday so we had to make all the final preparations to our sets. We would perform on Thursday through Saturday nights for two weekends. I was nervous and excited to finally perform before a real audience. After our last weekend of performances, we would be getting out for Thanksgiving break so there was a ton of activity going on at school.

On Friday before my date with Rick, I was called out of my Accounting class and had to go to the counselor's office. When I walked in the secretary smiled at me and handed me a white envelope with my name on it. I asked her what it was and she said it was a letter for my mom and I needed to take it to her, and not to open it. I couldn't begin to imagine why they were sending a letter home to my mom, but I'd learned the hard way about surprises with my mom. When I got to my car after school, I opened it. If it was something that had to go into an envelope, I could go find another one, but I wanted to know what the letter said.

I scanned the letter that explained to my Parent that I'd been chosen to be in the National Honor Society. I didn't have a clue what it was, but the letter went on to explain that there would be an induction ceremony the next Tuesday evening in the auditorium. I wondered if Mr. Magnus knew and if our rehearsal was being cancelled that day. He hadn't said anything in class.

I sat there looking at the letter and wondering if I should give it to my mom or not. There was nothing for her to sign or for me to return. I thought it was weird that they wanted me to take it to my parent and have them read the letter first. Then I thought about all the other kids who probably got the same letter and how their moms and dads would read it and be so proud. They'd celebrate by going out to dinner or something. I knew my mom was proud of me, but she was just so unpredictable. I decided that depending on how she was when I got home was whether I would hand her the letter. It didn't say anything about it being sealed so she'd never know that it had been in an envelope if I did give it to her.

As I turned into our driveway and clicked the garage door opener, I could hear Willie Nelson singing "Whiskey River". I knew that was a bad sign. If I could hear it before the car shut off, it meant that she was totally bombed and probably depressed or mad. I sighed as I grabbed my homework and purse and went inside. I had just an hour to eat something for dinner and change my clothes to get to rehearsal. I hoped I got to do that without a huge scene since I could hear ol' Willie out in the garage.

Opening the door into the living room I looked around and didn't see my mom and knew Ray wasn't home because his car wasn't there. I walked in quietly, hoping to make as little noise as possible. Sometimes if I just ghosted my way through, my mom would mutter to me and I could escape her wrath. I prayed she wouldn't pull this on Saturday when Scotty came for his dance lesson or even worse, when Rick Geist came and picked me up.

I went into my room and changed clothes. I came out to find her sitting in the dark at the table. "Hey Mom," I greeted her agreeably.

She swung her head around to look at me as if it were made of cement on a swivel. I saw her deep, dark brown eyes that looked red from either drinking or crying or both. She swung her head back and looked down at the large tea glass she had in front of her with V.O. and water as well as a couple of ice cubes. If truth be told it probably had no water by now because she counted the ice cubes as water too as they melted. She flopped her hand up in some kind of pathetic wave. I stood there uncertain what I should do. I asked if she was okay, waiting for her to answer in the way she used when she was exceptionally drunk, on the verge of either passing out or flipping her demon switch on. Finally, after almost two minutes of no words passed between us, I told her I needed to go to rehearsal. She just nodded her head. I turned around and got into the '73 Thunderbird as fast as I possibly could.

There was nothing for dinner and I didn't want to take the chance of her flipping out on me. I pulled out and got to the small shopping center that was right before the school. I pulled in and parked. I took my wallet out of my purse and checked how much money I had. I decided to go through the drive-through at the fast food taco place and get a combination burrito and a coke. They actually had good crunchy ice there like Sonic's. I was starving and knew I needed to eat something.

When rehearsal was over and I got home, I was relieved to see the house was all dark and Mama was passed out in her room. I noticed that Ray wasn't there and figured they must be arguing and he decided to go to his lake house at Lake Mathis. I tiptoed into my room with the rest of my coke I'd bought before rehearsal and sat on my bed to begin my homework. I grabbed my purse to find my black pen and as I dug through the purse the letter for the NHS induction ceremony fell out. I looked at the letter and was glad I'd looked first before giving it to her. I would just tell her I had rehearsal and wear a dress to school that day. I wished I could give her the letter, but I knew that it was best not to chance some things. Just the fact that she knew about the play and was planning to attend one of the performances worried me to death.

Chapter 5

Scotty showed up on Saturday at 10:30. Thankfully, Mom had just poured her first beer and tomato juice right before he knocked on the door. That meant she was still good for a few more hours, but of course worried me for later when Rick got there. I had to hope fervently that she took it slow.

Mama stood Scotty and me in the center of our large kitchen and after she was satisfied with how she positioned us and our hands, she began pushing us and explaining each step. We laughed and giggled with almost every one we took, but by the time noon rolled around we were dancing effortlessly through my entire house. Mama had us begin in the kitchen but eventually she had us dancing through the dining-room, the living-room, down the hall and back to the kitchen over and over. When Scotty left at a quarter til one, I walked him to his truck and he hugged me tightly. Thrilled that he wouldn't look silly trying to dance with Sara. I just hoped she didn't treat him badly. I had to admit, Scotty was quickly becoming someone I really cared about. If possible, he was becoming the equivalent to how I felt about Levi Parker when I was in 8th grade. He was becoming my best guy friend and I was a bit surprised to realize that as I hugged him close.

When I pulled back, I looked into his blue eyes. He was a bit taller than me, and had reddish brown hair and freckles, and in all honesty didn't look much like Chance at all. They favored enough you knew they were brothers, but where Chance had perfectly straight, toothpaste commercial worthy teeth, Scotty had one tooth that was a little crooked. I thought it gave him an endearing smile though. Again, I wished I could feel something for him like I had his brother. I shook the thought from my head as I thought about Rick Geist and remembered I was going on my first date with him just as

Scotty was taking Sara on their first date the same night. I grinned and kissed Scotty on the cheek. "See you at the dance!"

I quickly turned to run into my house to hug my mama. Thankfully, she'd been too busy with me and Scotty to drink even that first beer with tomato juice. I was hopeful she wouldn't be stupid drunk when Rick got there!

My date with Rick Geist came around and my mom thankfully wasn't smashed either! She was just her normal amount of inebriated, without going overboard one way or another. My mom was a hopeless flirt though and was actually flirting with Rick. I groaned inwardly and hoped he wasn't too uncomfortable. I was plenty uncomfortable for both of us.

We went to the dance in Orange Grove and I couldn't believe how much fun I had. I'd never been to the dance hall there before. I was shocked that he was such a good dancer, since Rick was a bear of a guy. I wasn't nearly as good a dancer, but was grateful I'd let my mama teach me that morning, along with Scotty. I told him I wasn't that great because I watched as some of the people on the dance floor twirled and whirled all over the place. I was worried that if Rick danced like that, as hopelessly klutzy as I was, he'd try to twirl me and I'd fall flat on my face.

By the time he got me on the floor he waited until they played a really slow and steady country song, and he danced with me smoothly. Gone were the days of wrapping your arms around a boy's neck, like we'd done in junior high at the sock hops at Skate Whirl in Wichita Falls. Now I had to actually dance like a grown-up. He asked me if he could ask other girls to dance, from Calvin, and I nodded my head smiling. I was happy when I realized that he was actually being easy with me, as I watched him dance a Polka with Mandy Manson. They whirled and twirled and I got dizzy just watching them.

I finally spotted Scotty standing on the edge of the dance floor while Rick was dancing with Mandy and jumped up to go see how his date was going with Sara. When I reached him, I noticed he looked extremely pathetic. "Hey Scotty! Where's Sara?"

Scotty Cahill turned to me and looked almost like he was going to begin crying. Alarmed I grabbed his arm. "Please tell me she didn't stand you up!" He shook his head. He nodded his chin towards the dance floor and I turned to see Sara out polka dancing. "Oh no! We only learned the two-step! Is she dancing with someone because she wanted to polka?" I asked curiously. Rick was dancing with Mandy, but I didn't know how to polka, so I was hoping that was the case with Scotty and Sara. Sadly, I didn't think it was by the look on his face.

"Not so much," Scotty sighed. Finally he looked at me and I could definitely see tears in his eyes. "As soon as we got here she ran over to the table full of Calvin kickers and began dancing with that guy. That was an hour ago. She hasn't come back over to me since then."

"What?" I demanded hotly. "Are you fucking kidding me?" I was livid. How dare that horse-faced bitch treat Scotty so badly. He was possibly the sweetest boy I'd ever known. He deserved a girl who would adore him just as he did her. This whore didn't deserve him and I basically said that as I let out one of my infamous strings of expletives. "I am going over and having a little talk with her," I stated angrily.

As I was about to walk away, Scotty grabbed my arm. "Just leave it alone, DeLaine," he pled. I looked at him confused. How could I leave it alone when he was so obviously hurt? I stood there uncertain what to do. "She's not worth it. Besides, you're on a date with Rick. You don't need to fight my battles." When I began to protest, Scotty shook his head again and told me to let it drop and go back to the table with the other Calvin kickers. I didn't want to sit at the same table with Sara Barker knowing how heartbroken Scotty was over her actions.

"I am not sitting at the same table as that skank!" I huffed.

"You have to. That's where you were already sitting with Rick," he pointed out. Because the table was so long, I hadn't even noticed Sara way down on the very end. It was three extra long tables pieced together. Rick and I had been on the opposite end. Since there was no way to talk with anyone other than those immediately next to us, I'd completely ignored the other end.

Finally, I looked at Scotty and hugged him tightly before I turned to go back to the Calvin table. I would eventually say something to Sara Barker. Scotty was a senior at Midway. There was no way for him to know if I approached the bitch at school. I felt a determined look cross my face as I watched Sara walking back to the table as well. I really wanted to kick her ass. She would know my name by the end of the week I knew without a doubt. Just as I got to the table, Rick met me and swept me up to his side and smiled down at me. I quickly forgot how angry I was when I looked up into his cat green eyes. He was really handsome.

While the band was taking a break the song "Islands in the Stream" came on the jukebox and Rick jumped up, grabbing my hands to go onto the dance floor. His eyes were lit with mischief and I found myself laughing even though I kept pulling against his strong grip. I knew the song was fast and I was terrified the whole klutz factor was about to come out! I knew I'd be mortified. Even though he was larger than life, and had a loud personality I was surprised that he could sense my fear because once we got onto the floor, he swept me up into his strong embrace and we danced *slow* to the song's beat. When I craned my neck to look up at him, he smiled down at me. I could feel my blush beginning and there wasn't anywhere to turn my head except to put my cheek against the western shirt he was wearing. Thankfully I didn't step on his toes more than twice.

I drank my usual coke and Rick only drank three beers, which made me happy. I wouldn't have been surprised if he drank six or eight. Thankfully he seemed to be on his best behavior, I decided. Surprisingly, I felt good sitting at the long table with a bunch of Calvin alum and current Calvin kids. I felt a part of the crowd, even though I didn't know any of them very well.

Rick proved to be a really sweet date and I hadn't felt so good going out with a boy since I'd been with Jax and Kevin. Even though Rick wasn't my boyfriend, and Kevin hadn't been either, I still felt that sense of security with him that I never felt when I'd messed around while I was drinking or getting stoned at the Game Room.

We pulled up to my house right at 12:15. I felt suddenly a little self-conscious sitting in his old, green truck. Rick turned to me, "I'm going to kiss you goodnight."

I'd never had a boy tell me that before so I felt a little weird. Finally, I replied, "Um, okay."

"Are you going to let me?" Rick asked me seriously.

I cocked my head to the side, "Well yes, I figured if you said you were going to kiss me and I said okay, then we were most likely going to kiss."

Rick smiled at me, "You know you are a really hard girl to read sometimes, right?"

I furrowed my brow. I wasn't sure how to respond to that statement. Finally, I explained, "I don't try to be." I was relieved when Rick smiled at me. Thankfully he didn't say anything else, he just leaned across the seat towards me and our mouths met in the cold, dark of his pickup. I felt strange kissing him since I hadn't been partying this time after coming home. Kevin had been the only boy I'd been with, except for Chance's thwarted attempt the first time I went to his apartment. I liked Rick's kiss. It was warm, soft and tender. I was surprised in many ways because his size made me think he would be as forceful as he was in his pursuit of me.

As we pulled apart, I felt a warm flush go through me as I opened my eyes and saw the piercing, cat eyes looking at me intently. "What?" I asked curiously, once my eyes were open and meeting his gaze.

"I knew kissing you for real would be wonderful. You are so beautiful, DeLaine. You don't even know it though. I don't know where you learned how to do that, but I want to kiss you again. I want you to get inside the house on time though, because I want your mama to let me take you out again. So, I'm going to give you a little kiss this time. If I kiss you much more, you won't get in there on time, because I won't be able to let you go." Rick whispered.

Not sure what to say to him, I just smiled and nodded my head. He leaned back in to me and his mouth met mine chastely. He still felt warm and comforting though. Even in the cold, November night, sitting next to this bear of a young man, I felt no chill. This time we parted much quicker and he told me that he would walk me to the door. It was a strange feeling sitting in the truck waiting on him to come around to open the door. I'd realized earlier that evening that he was extremely old fashioned when it came to opening doors and being a gentleman though. I didn't really know how to respond.

Once he deposited me at the front door, again kissing me softly. I unlocked the door and slipped into the sleeping house. When I closed the door, I leaned against it and smiled a silly grin. Had I found the *real* boyfriend I was supposed to find? If so, then I was happy it was Rick. He wasn't Kevin and he wasn't Jax. But he also wasn't Chance Cahill. He was everything I'd hoped to find in a boyfriend. I heard Rick's truck start up and drive off as I stood there leaning against the front door. I felt silly still, but I just couldn't stop standing there grinning.

I didn't hear my mom as she came walking into the living room. When I finally realized she was there, I immediately froze because I was afraid that I had gotten in a few minutes late or something. I didn't want to have a bad end to such a fun night. Thankfully, Mama whispered, "Did you have fun?" I looked at her and smiled. nodding my head. Mama smiled at me lovingly. I was so happy to see that it was *my* Mama and not the drunk that I hated. “I’m so glad! I like him. He seems like a sweet boy.” I smiled even bigger. If my mama liked him, then she wouldn’t be a hard-ass about me going out with him.

Finally, I stood up straight and began walking away from the front door. As I began to pass my mom, she reached out to me and we hugged. I was surprised, but happy that my mama liked him and was being loving. I missed this side of her. I knew it was inside of her when she didn’t drink, but she couldn’t seem to not drink every single day. I was so afraid of becoming like her. I knew then as she held me that if I went back to drinking like I had been, I would be that way quicker than she had been. I decided that I didn’t *ever* want to be like that! No matter what, I wasn’t going to party like I’d done in the past. I was finally feeling happy inside of my own skin again, and I didn’t know how that feeling had come about. It seemed to have snuck up on me which was surprising. When my mom let me out of her embrace, she kissed me on the cheek and told me she was sorry about how she’d been the day before when I got home. I smiled at her. She always apologized after a bad drunk and sometimes lost days from the benders.

Nodding my head, I whispered, “It’s okay, Mama. I love you. Goodnight.” I wasn’t sure what else to say to her. I wanted to tell her about the National Honor Society induction ceremony when she was loving and sober, but I never knew if she’d show up sober. I decided to keep the ceremony to myself still. It was always better to be safe than sorry. Things seemed a lot better at school now. I had people I sat with at lunch now. I was becoming friendly with other people just by being in Theater Arts and VOE. I didn’t want anyone to know that my mom was a drunk. I didn’t want them to reject me because my mom came up there cussing everyone out if she came drunk.

When I got home Monday, Mama told me that before I went to rehearsal, she wanted to talk to me. I put my books up and changed my clothes and came back into the living room. Mama looked at me with deep hurt in her eyes, “The counselor from school called me today and wanted to know if I would be taking part in the induction ceremony of the National Honor Society. I didn't know what he was talking about. Seems you got a letter last week and I was supposed to *R.S.V.P.* so they could make arrangements for the parents of the students being honored."

I looked at her feeling like a cornered rat. I had seen the R.S.V.P. and a phone number at the end of the letter, but I didn't know what the initials meant. I'd been caught and there was no way out. Finally, I said, "Oh yeah, I got the letter. I didn't really know what that was. I figured you wouldn't want to mess with something stupid like that. I don't even know what it is."

"It's an *honor,* DeLaine! That's what it is. That's why they are doing a ceremony. I told him I'd be there. I *always* want to go to things that are special for you honey." Mama stated quietly, with tears brimming in her eyes.

My heart was breaking as I saw the tears filling her eyes. I was afraid of my mom's other personality, so I didn't want to include her in anything. I was terrified on a constant basis that she would show up drunk, and I would be mortified. I didn't know how to tell her that, so instead, I whispered, "*I'm sorry, Mama.* I just thought it was some *lame* thing for my grades or something."

"Well, your grades had a play in it, but you have to be *chosen* to be in that. Obviously, you have teachers who thought you deserved it. If you don't *want* me there though, I won't go." She declared, sadly.

Rolling my eyes and feeling exasperated now, I groaned, "Geez, Mom, *I'm sorry.* Yes, I want you there. Go ahead and come. We aren't having rehearsal obviously since they are doing it in the auditorium, but you can come. You already told the counselor you would." My mom just turned her head away from me and nodded her head. I stood there waiting for her to say something more. After what felt like an eternity, I finally whispered, "I gotta go or I'm gonna be late for rehearsal. We only have this full-dress rehearsal and one more on Wednesday before the play opens on

Thursday. *I'm really sorry Mama!* We'll go to the ceremony tomorrow evening *together*, okay?"

My mama got up and went into the kitchen and murmured an okay to me. After a few seconds I decided that there was nothing else I could say, so I turned and went out into the garage to get into my car. As I pulled out of the driveway, I felt like a total heel. I didn't know how to make it up to my mom. I hoped that the next day she'd be fine. All I could do was pray.

When I got out of rehearsal, I found a red rose with a ribbon and a note under my windshield wiper on my car. I knew it had to be from Rick and when I hurriedly opened the small piece of notepaper I saw the same neat print that said,

Little Bit,

This rose only wishes it was as beautiful as you.

Will you go out with me again this weekend? I decided to just trash your windshield this time but with something beautiful instead of shoe polish.

I will call you tomorrow night.

Rick

I grinned and began to blush. I was grateful it was dark and I had on my stage makeup still. I couldn't believe how thick the makeup was I had to wear onstage, but I had to look like a middle-aged woman. Humming on the way home, I wasn't expecting the chaos I walked into. I had gotten comfortable by avoiding being around my mom and her drunken rages. Usually by the time I got home from rehearsal, her raging had burned itself out and she was passed out. This night she had waited until I left to really begin drinking heavily.

When I opened the door, I was shocked to see every light on in the house. It was usually quiet and dark by the time I got home. Ray was usually asleep and Mom usually was too or on her way. This time though, every light burned brightly, and even appeared harsh to my tired eyes. Mom came storming out of the hallway with her face twisted in fury. "You want to keep me *out* of your life? That's fine by me, you ungrateful little bitch!" Mom exploded. I stood there shocked into silence. I knew it was best to not even try to engage with her when she was in this mood, but it was hard sometimes, because she wanted answers. She didn't disappoint this time. I didn't want to say anything and she kept after me, "You're *embarrassed* of me is that what it is, you ungrateful brat?"

I shook my head and began to walk towards my bedroom. It was always best to try to get out of her way. Finally, she jumped in front of me and grabbed me by the arms. I outweighed my tiny Mama by at least 20 pounds and was a good two inches taller. When she was drunk though, she was stronger than ten men. Her grip on my arms was crushing and when I finally winced, she seemed happy that she was going to get a response from me. Instead, I just tried to walk around her. She wouldn't let go. She was hanging on to me like a dog with a rag doll.

"Let go of me," I finally growled in a low voice.

"Why? So you can walk away from me like Ray? Not a fucking chance young lady! I'm sick to death of neither of you appreciating a *damned thing* I do around here. I do everything for you two and neither one of you can appreciate a fucking thing I do!" She screamed into my face.

I looked at her as my heart thumped hard inside of my chest. I could tell my rage was going to build as well if she didn't let go of me and quit screaming in my face. "Mom, I appreciate everything you do! I really do. I don't know why you don't think I do." I began to plea. I felt her grip on me loosen a little and she looked down at the floor and it seemed as if all the steam went out of her.

"Whatever, it just doesn't matter anymore," my mom muttered.

"Mom, I love you. I appreciate everything, *I mean it,*" I began to cry. She let go of me and walked around me giving me a clear path to the door to my room. I noticed that her room she shared with Ray was already closed so I assumed Ray had gone to bed in order to get away from her. I'm sure she didn't let him lay there peacefully though. I sighed quietly and walked slowly into my room. I took off my clothes and went into my bathroom to wash all the makeup off of my face. I could hear the record player and Mom was listening to George Jones sing "He Stopped Loving Her Today." I didn't know what to do for her. I wanted to help her. I wanted her to know that I loved her and appreciated her, but I knew that where she was now, I wasn't going to be able to get through, so I walked back to my room to begin my homework.

Since Mom knew about the ceremony, I didn't wear a dress on Tuesday. I had to go home and change because all the girls had to wear a dress and the boys had to wear slacks, dress shirts and even ties. I was surprised by the whole tie business, but everyone except me, were popular kids. I was surprised when I found that out. Most of the kids in that crowd were all rich kids, so I figure they already had fancy clothes. I decided I was going to wear my black dress. It wasn't too dressy, but it was nice and looked good on me.

When I walked into the house, I saw there were no lights on and it was quiet like no one was there. I looked around and was surprised when I couldn't find mom. I walked through the entire house and when I got to her room, I was surprised to see her lying in her bed.

"Mom? Are you okay?" I asked.

Sleepily, my mama replied, "I don't feel good, DeLaine. I'm not going to be able to go tonight. I'm sorry. I know it's a big honor. Congratulations honey."

Standing there I felt stunned. After all the drama of the day before and now she was too hung over to even come to the ceremony. Nodding, I turned out of the doorway, and went into my room to begin getting ready for the ceremony. I knew I'd be the only one there with no parent. I thought briefly about not even showing up, but knew that if I didn't it might spark a whole different war with her.

Thankfully, the induction ceremony wasn't too extravagant. When they announced our names and asked us to come on stage, they introduced my mom also, who was supposed to come to the stage in order to pin the NHS pin onto my dress. I felt my face turning a deep plum color when I got up on the stage by myself, with all the bright lights glaring down on me. The teachers who were involved with the NHS, including Mr. Magnus, all looked at me. I saw their eyes sweep past me and down, wondering where my parent was. I didn't know if I should tell them she was sick or what. I knew everyone was looking at me and thinking what a loser I must have been.

When I got to the center of the stage, I felt a huge relief as Mr. Magnus stepped up out of the chair he was sitting. He came forward to take the pin from the principal as I got up to the tiny cluster of people. Mr. Magnus smiled at me and then pinned the tiny NHS pin to the collar of my dress. He took the certificate from the principal and shook his hand as if he were my parent and handed the certificate to me. I felt such a tremendous relief just having him that close by. I walked off the stage on the opposite side and kept my eyes down because I didn't want anyone to see the tears in my eyes. I went back to the seat I had to sit in next to the other inductees. I kept my head down until the tears dried up in my eyes. I finally looked up and finished watching the rest of the ceremony.

Once everything was over and everyone went into the side hall for punch and pastries, I slipped out to get to my car to go home. I didn't want to go over there with everyone and their parents. I felt conspicuous enough without a parent as it was. I didn't need to stand by myself drinking punch and eating a dry piece of fried dough.

As I was unlocking the door to my car, I heard Mr. Magnus say my name quietly. I jumped because I had not heard him walk up behind me. I turned around and looked up at his lean form. His head seemed too large for his body. His large glasses, much too thick, made his eyes appear too large for his face. He could get some scary looks on his face, but right now he had one of the kindest looks I'd ever seen. I knew he had those kind looks, because for whatever reason, he gave them to me before. "Um, hi, Magnus," I whispered, quietly. I felt a little sheepish ducking out after he had stepped in acting as my parent when I went up without one.

"I wanted to give you this pin for your mother," Mr. Magnus stated, handing me a small pin.

I looked at the tiny pin he held in his long-fingered hand. It was a pin for the parents of NHS members. That was why they were asked to be a part of the ceremony. I nodded my head and reached out and plucked it with two fingers from his outstretched palm. "Thank you," I whispered.

"I'm sorry your mother wasn't feeling well enough to come tonight. I do hope she is feeling better soon," he smiled at me calmly.

I nodded my head as I looked at him somberly. Finally, I remembered my manners, "Thank you Mr. Magnus for stepping in and pinning me. I didn't know what to do." I looked down feeling a little embarrassed.

I was surprised when Robert Magnus pulled me to him in a strong hug and laughed a large, booming laugh, "My dear, it was *my honor*!" Mr. Magnus let me go and held me out looking into my face. "DeLaine, you are a talented and smart young woman. It is my *delight* to be a part of your journey."

I smiled at the teacher that so many didn't appreciate and nodded my head. "Thanks Magnus," I replied, getting a little bit of my sauciness back into my voice. He brought out the bawdy edge I had. I felt free to be my jaded, sarcastic and sometimes caustic self around him. I had been feeling full of melancholy and sorrow. I also felt embarrassed by the fact that I was the only one without a parent, so I had wanted to hide. Mr. Magnus knew that. He had made sure to let me know that I was okay no matter what. I was forever grateful to him. I got into my car and waved at my theater arts teacher as I drove off to go home to an unknown situation.

Walking into the darkened house, I felt myself relax knowing that everything was hopefully going to be quiet. I went into my room and saw that it was almost 9 o'clock. I took off my clothes and put on a night shirt. As I settled on my bed to begin my homework, the phone rang. I grabbed it on the first ring.

"Hey Lil' Bit," I heard Rick's deep, rich voice on the other end of the phone. I smiled before I said hi back. "So, would you like to go out with me this weekend?" Rick asked me without any preamble.

"I'd love to, but our play is opening on Thursday and we're going to be doing shows on Thursday, Friday and Saturday nights." I responded, disappointedly.

"Well, I'll come see you and then take you out after," Rick stated, resolutely.

I felt bashful. "You don't want to come to a high school play," I was a little self-conscious about him seeing me acting like a middle-aged matron.

"Why not? I used to be in choir. I like the arts. I used to do musical numbers in choir. I was pretty damned good if I say so myself!" Rick's big voice boomed on the phone.

I laughed, "Yeah, but if you watch me, you might not want to go out with me anymore."

"IMPOSSIBLE!" Rick boomed. "Are you playing the *"Elephant Man*???"

Laughing, I quipped, "Well, no!"

"So why would you think I wouldn't want to go out with you then?"

"I play an evil, middle-aged, British housekeeper," I was still chuckling.

Rick was now laughing too, “Ooh, I think older women are kinda sexy!” We both began to laugh then. Finally, he admitted, “There’s nothing wrong with that!”

“But I really look old and crappy! No pretty dresses or anything for me in this play!” I groaned a little mournfully.

“There’s *no way* they can make you *ugly*!” I laughed and he insisted.

“Okay, you just wait and see! I’ll have to ask my mom. Which night? Friday or Saturday?” I asked.

“Yes” Rick replied.

“What?” I asked him, uncertain what he meant.

“Yes,” he stated again.

“No, I meant, which night,” I was trying to clarify what I was asking him.

Rick respond with a laugh in his voice, “And I was saying ‘yes’ to BOTH of them.”

“OH!” I said quickly. “Um, you mean you want to go out BOTH nights?” I was a little unsure if I understood correctly.

“Yep!” Rick affirmed.

“Um, okay. Well, uh, I’ll have to ask her. Do you know what you want to do?” I asked him feeling a little silly.

“I figured I’ll go to your play both nights then Friday we’ll just go hang at Sonic a little afterwards. Saturday I’ll go to your play again and afterwards we can go out to the dance for a little bit if you want.” Rick explained.

Sitting on my bed shaking my head as if he could see me, I finally agreed, “Okay, I’ll talk to her tomorrow and call you when I get home from rehearsal, if that’s okay.” Rick told me it was and we got off the phone so I could do my homework.

Once we were off the phone, I sat there wondering what all of this meant. I felt silly, but I also felt a little giddy at the prospect of maybe having a real boyfriend for a change. I remembered what it had felt like when Jax and I had been together in 8th grade. Smiling I thought about all the great memories of our time together. We had a lot of them. I remembered our times babysitting my step-sister Lisa and our time together at his Uncle's place when he took me riding horses. I thought about the small clump of brush where we'd gone parking and where I'd let him undo my shirt. I felt myself begin to blush at that memory. Then I thought about the last time we'd been together in the tunnel at the playground and how it had ended so badly. We'd been so drunk and I'd been so mad. We'd eventually made up, but I was sad that our intimate times together ended on a sour note. I shook my head as if by doing that it erased that time and tried to remember another good time. I immediately began to think about the cold nights we would go out to the lake with Bailey and Levi and sitting there looking across the water at the big full moon, wrapped in horse blankets, wearing his letter jacket.

I wondered if I started going steady with Rick, if it would feel the same. I liked how it felt to go steady with Jax. I felt safe and secure and as if I belonged finally. Not really like I belonged *to* someone, just a sense of belonging. I laughed to myself and decided I was getting a little too far ahead of myself. Rick and I had only gone on *one* date. I still had to ask my mom. I had to focus on getting through the play. I thought about my mom and about how she'd suddenly been too *sick* to go to the NHS induction ceremony and her tantrum the night before. My life was never dull that was for sure. Sighing, I pulled my copy of *The Great Gatsby* out and settled in to try to finish reading it. I needed to finish so I could complete the report on it before the following Monday.

Chapter 6

The next day, as I was walking to VOE, I happened to run into Sara Barker who was talking with Mandy Manson. I still had a bone to pick with her. I walked up with what I hoped was an amiable expression. The two girls turned and smiled at me. "Uh, I need to talk to Sara a minute," I smiled sweetly, hoping Mandy understood I wanted her to get lost. Thankfully, she did and hurried into our vocational office education classroom. Sara looked at me completely unaware that I was not nearly as friendly as she thought I would be.

"So, I hear you had a date with Scotty Cahill," I began. I saw Sara immediately stiffen in posture. She nodded her head and maintained her agreeable smile. I smiled wickedly and said to her, "The next time a boy asks you on a date, you may want to be sure and actually stay on the first date instead of running off with some other guy and shaking your fuckin' ass around," Sara began to interrupt me, but I held up my hand to her face as I stepped closer. I wanted to make sure she heard me without raising my voice even a notch. "No, you cunt, don't say a fucking word to me until I'm finished. Scotty is my friend. He really liked you and you used him to go to Orange Grove to meet up with that guy you were hanging all over. Don't you ever even look in Scotty's direction again. I will fucking beat your ass so fast, you'll wonder what happened. You are a fucking whore and Scotty Cahill is much too good for your skank ass! Don't you dare cross me on this, because I promise I will rearrange your fucking face where no one will ever ask you out again. Do I make myself clear?" I demanded. When she began to speak, I shook my head angrily. "No Bitch, just nod your fucking head!"

After she nodded, I stepped away and told her she better never cross my path again. She looked at me with naked fear and turned to quickly get away. I knew that I could intimidate when I wanted to. This week had already proven to be rough on me and I was damned sure going to use it when I could to intimidate Sara Baker. I didn't care if she told on me or not. I could lie and say she was crazy and I knew that chances were I'd be believed. I was becoming quite the actress in all things. I'd had to become one in order to survive. Sara had no idea who she was messing with if she dared to cross me. I had enough repressed anger I would literally enjoy beating her.

I didn't even get to come home after school because it was our last full dress rehearsal before our first performance. We were basically in performance mode and doing the play for a few of the school board members. I was actually shaking when the curtain went up, but was grateful for Pete Mulligan. He led me through the entire play. When I completely blanked out in one of our critical scenes, where we got physical, he carried me until I remembered my lines.

When we were getting ready to leave, he came up to me and gave me a huge hug. I whispered, "I'm sorry I screwed up so bad!"

"What are you talking about?" Pete asked me smiling.

"You know! I totally blanked out!" I replied.

"Oh shit, that wasn't anything! It happens! You just roll with it! You'd do the same for me! It's theater! Just remember, if someone does something like that you just pick up the lines until they remember where they're supposed to be. You'll do it someday for someone else. Hell, maybe for me tomorrow night, who knows!" he was smiling.

I looked at him shaking my head. "I doubt that!"

"Did you know the lines?" he asked seriously.

"Well, yeah," I agreed.

"Point made. We all do it sometimes! Don't worry about it!" Pete stated emphatically. "See you tomorrow!" I smiled and waved, as he ran off.

When I got home, I hoped that my mom was still awake. She hadn't gotten up that morning when I got up for school, which was unusual. She usually woke me up and made me breakfast and sat and drank coffee and read the paper while I ate. She had scrambled me some eggs and gotten me up but had gone back to bed after I came to the table.

I walked in after our rehearsal and found only the kitchen light on. I sighed and wondered how I was going to answer Rick about the weekend. As I began to walk across the living room to get to the hallway and my bedroom, I heard my mom's voice. "How was rehearsal?"

Jumping I turned to find her sitting in her chair, in the darkened living room. "Oh, you scared me, Mom! Um, it was okay. I kinda messed up, but Pete helped and we did okay." I replied, conversationally.

"That's good." She whispered.

"Why are you sitting in the dark?" I asked.

"Just thinking," my mom said quietly.

"Are you okay?" I asked, feeling a little worried the longer I stood in the darkened room talking with her.

My mom reached over and turned on the lamp sitting on the end table, next to her chair. I could see her sitting there in her robe and nightgown. "Yes, I'm just sad." She responded.

I walked over to her and sat on the ottoman at her feet. "Why?" I asked her sincerely.

"You won't understand, DeLaine."

"Try me, Mama," I murmured, quietly.

My mama looked down and then reached for her cigarettes and took one out of the pack and lit it. How I wished I could do the same, but I still hadn't told my mom I smoked, so I couldn't. "DeLaine, you're growing up. You're 17 now. You're going to be leaving home soon. I'm just sad. I feel like I've missed out on so much of your life. I feel like you're already gone and I don't know how it happened," my mama choked off tears.

I reached out and grabbed her hand. "Oh Mama, I'm not going anywhere! I'm still right here! I still have a year and a half of high school. It isn't like I'm going away to college or anything!" I felt bad because I still dreamed of leaving some day. I wanted to move back to Wichita Falls and get an apartment with Bailey. I hoped to go to Midwestern State University and become a teacher. I had hopes of me and Kevin eventually having our chance together. I was excited about Rick right now, because I'd told Kevin I'd find a boyfriend for this school year, but my heart would always belong to him.

My mom sniffled, "I'm just going through the whole empty nest thing I guess."

I wasn't sure what that meant. I smiled at her as I held her hand. I wanted to reassure her because I felt somehow responsible for her depression. If I had only told her about the stupid NHS thing then maybe she wouldn't be depressed. I was a horrible daughter I thought. This whole bout of depression was because I'd been too selfish to tell her about something stupid at school because I was frightened she wouldn't act right. She knew to act right at school, didn't she? I mean, she never came to anything at school acting stupid, right? She *had* come to Woodway and called Mrs. Gonzalez Godzilla, but Mrs. Gonzalez was a bitch and had deserved it! I couldn't really hold that against her and I hadn't had anything else she'd ever had to come to. So why did I think she would embarrass me at a school function? I felt really shitty.

"Mom, *I'm so sorry*." I had tears brimming in my eyes now.

"Why are you sorry?" My mom asked me curiously.

"Because I should have told you about the stupid NHS thing. I just didn't think it was that big of a deal. If I had you wouldn't be sad like this," I shrugged my shoulders as the tears finally escaped my eyes.

My mom leaned forward and grabbed me to her. "No honey, it isn't that. I love you. I understand you thought it wasn't any big deal. I'm just being a silly mom. I'll be okay. Really. Don't worry about me." We sat there embracing each other for several minutes crying. I didn't really understand why we were both crying and holding one another.

I was crying because I felt lost. I was crying for the mom that I felt was lost inside the woman I held. I wondered if the woman I held was crying for the same thing. For whatever reasons, we continued to hold one another for a long time and cried. Finally, we parted and my mom cupped my face in her hands, "DeLaine, I love you. I'm *not* angry with you. I'm sorry about acting so stupid. I don't know why I do that. I'm so proud of you. Please forgive me." I looked at her sadly and felt the lump in my throat grow even more because I wanted to sob out loud. I wanted to say so much, but instead said nothing, and just nodded my head. Finally, my mom instructed me, "Go wash your face sweetheart." I got up and began to walk to the hall bathroom.

When I got to the entrance I turned around, "Mom when I get done, I need to come talk to you okay?" She smiled as best as she could and nodded her head. I did the same.

Once I had wiped a cold wash rag across my red face, and held it to my swollen eyes, I came back out to the living room and sat in the black, leather recliner that Ray normally sat in when he was watching television. Mom sat across in her orange and brown, crushed velvet chair. I told her about Rick wanting to take me out after the play on both Friday and Saturday and she told me she was fine with it as long as I was home by curfew. She seemed excited about the prospect. We talked a little about Rick. She told me she liked him. I saw it was getting late and told her I needed to call him really quick to let him know. Mama stood and leaned over to kiss my cheek.

"Call him and tell him he can take you out afterwards but if he is going to the play on Friday, he has to sit with me." She declared.

Laughing I replied, "Okay, I'll tell him!" Mama left telling me goodnight. I picked up the princess phone that set on the end table and called Rick's number that I already memorized. I hoped it wasn't too late since it was almost 10 o'clock. I knew he had to go to work the next morning.

When he answered he sounded like he was almost asleep. I felt a little alarmed, but as soon as he heard my voice he seemed to perk up. I told him that I could go out and he was happy to hear that. When I told him what my mom had said about him having to sit with her on Friday, he told me he'd do one better and pick her up and take her and be her personal escort. I told him she'd probably flirt hopelessly with him and he reminded me he liked older women. I laughed and then we got off the phone. After hanging up I worried about whether she'd be drunk or not and then decided that there wasn't a lot I could do about it if she was. Sighing, I got up because I had to finish *The Great Gatsby* tonight!

Our opening night, I realized, was really just to warm us up for our weekend performances, because there weren't that many people out there. I was grateful because when Friday night rolled around, I peeked out the side of the stage curtain to see if I could find Rick and my mom. I was shocked to see that the auditorium was packed. I looked at Pete Mulligan as he went through his pre-show ritual of some sort of meditation chant. I felt my whole body begin to quiver.

By intermission I had become my character. Mr. Magnus came backstage during the intermission and sought me out, "Mrs. Case? You are absolutely TERRIFYING! *Everyone* in the audience is wondering *who* is playing that *evil* woman. No one can recognize who you are! Signs of a *true* and GIFTED actress my dear!" I felt a million things at once when he told me that. It was amazing the rush of emotions that were playing out inside of me just realizing that maybe I'd finally found my niche in the world with theater.

When the play ended, we all came out and took our bows. Pete was holding my hand and the leading lady's hand. I saw people coming up to the stage with flowers and I didn't understand who they were for. I thought they must be for the girl who had played the leading lady. Pete ran down to the edge of the stage and when he came running back up, he brought a bouquet of six red roses and handed them to me. I looked at him and wrinkled my forehead. He laughed and just nodded his head. He turned and ran back and he grabbed a smaller bouquet of three and came back and gave it to the other leading lady. We all took another bow and then the house lights came up. The entire cast began to break apart and go down towards the edge of the stage. I wondered who had given me the large bouquet of red roses. I saw Rick standing a full head above the rest of the audience and smiled thinking they had probably come from him.

Kneeling at the end of the stage I realized there were other parents and students who wanted me to sign their programs. I laughed and smiled and obligingly signed them. I was surprised when out of the blue one of them would hand me a rose or a carnation. I took the flowers and thanked them surprised that people I didn't even know were handing me flowers.

Finally, Rick and my mom were in front of me and I leaned down and let my mom hug me. I was so happy to smell the cigarette smoke and perfume on her and only a hint of her V.O. which told me that she wasn't smashed. She gushed about how wonderful she thought I was and handed me a bouquet of beautiful pink roses. I was surprised that she had brought me roses. I now had an armful of flowers. She stepped out of the way and Rick walked up and handed me a bouquet of yellow roses. I hugged him and wondered where the six red roses that Pete handed me had come from if Rick just handed me a dozen yellow ones. I could smell all of the roses and carnations and their sweet smell was heavenly.

I pulled away from Rick's hug and said as loudly as I could manage over the din of the crowd that I had to go change. Afterwards, I would drive to the house and meet them there. They agreed and offered to take my armful of flowers. I smiled and nodded. My mom had her camera out with the flash cube on top and I smiled as she took a picture of me kneeling on the stage with all the flowers. She told Rick to lean over for one and she got a picture of the two of us together. I thought about how I would have a photo of myself with two boys now. I wondered if I would look at this photograph as many times as I'd looked at the one of me and Kevin. Once she was happy with the picture taking, she and Rick left and I was happy to see that she was acting reasonably.

I stood up and posed for some other photos with other cast-mates and finally was able to go change into my street clothes. I was grateful when I was able to get out of there and get into my car and back to my house. I wouldn't get to go out with Rick for a long time but at least I'd get to go out for a while. I hoped that my mom had behaved herself while she'd been alone with Rick. I felt bad for thinking like that while I drove through the red light that crossed the highway to get to my neighborhood just down the road from the high school.

Once I got home, I was happy to see that Mom was still acting fine and Rick didn't look distressed. I couldn't believe how many flowers I had. I looked all over our kitchen counter and smiled as I saw that Mom had put all of them in vases and was trying to count them all. As if she could tell what I was doing Mom said, "You have three dozen roses and half a dozen carnations!"

My mouth fell open and I said, "WHAT?" My mom smiled and nodded her head. "WOW!" I breathed out. I looked at the pink ones she gave me and the yellow ones that Rick had brought to me. The others were all red. She had put the red ones all together and then broken apart the other two colors into their own vases as well. I hadn't ever gotten that many roses at the same time in my life. I remembered all the flowers I'd gotten in the hospital when I'd almost died when I was 13, but it wasn't anything like this. I didn't really know what to think as I looked at all of them.

"You kids need to get going," Mama said smiling. I looked at Rick and he stood up dwarfing my mom and me.

"Mrs. Reynolds, thank you so much for letting me be your escort tonight," Rick stated, seriously, to my mom.

Laughing in a flirty way, my mom touched his arm and exclaimed, "Oh honey, call me Rita and really it is me who needs to thank you for escorting me and picking me up! I'm so grateful you offered to take me and sit with me. I really do appreciate it!" I noticed Rick looked a little embarrassed and almost seemed to blush. "You kids have a good time and just be home by 12:30, DeLaine, okay?" I nodded my head and Rick and I rushed out the door to his truck.

I got in Rick's truck on the passenger side while he opened the door for me. I smiled at him after I was safely inside and he closed the door. He ran around and jumped into the driver's seat. After he started it he turned to me and smiled. His green, cat eyes seemed to glow in the dark. "You were so awesome up on that stage tonight!" He was full of admiration.

I ducked my head down. "I was playing a bitch," I admitted.

Rick grinned. "Yeah, you were playing an evil one! You scared the shit out of me in a couple of those scenes! I hope you aren't like that in real life! If you are, I might be in real trouble!"

I started laughing. "Well, I don't know. I'm sure I can be if I needed to be."

"Well, remind me to keep you happy *all* the time," Rick said as he leaned over and kissed me soundly before we pulled away from my house.

My weekend was a heady one between the performances of the play and getting to go out with Rick afterwards. He was continuing to treat me like a princess and I was feeling so happy I didn't know quite what to think. On Saturday night he brought me another bouquet of roses except this time he brought me lavender ones. I was thrilled with them. I didn't get as many flowers, but I still got several. I was surprised that I still seemed to get more than the leading lady and wasn't sure why that was, but I didn't want to make a point of asking anyone. I just accepted them and smiled graciously.

By the time the weekend was over, I was happy and tired and ready for the Thanksgiving holiday. It was still a whole school week and two more school days away. Rick and I talked every night and Mom let me go out with him the following weekend both nights again, after the last two performances of our play.

I felt a little bittersweet after the last curtain call. It was the end of something that I had put so many hours into. I could recite my lines in my sleep and often woke myself up saying them. Pete Mulligan gave me a big hug after our last performance and told me how awesome he thought I'd done for being a newbie to the acting world. I felt myself blush because I thought highly of him and his talent.

As I drove to my house to change, I thought about how different I was now. I was so much more involved. I was busy and it felt good. I never seemed to have time to do anything except spend time at school. I wondered if that was why my mom was feeling depressed because I wasn't around the house as much. Her moods had been even more unpredictable. She was being so great most of the time, but then just as I thought she might be okay she'd go off the deep end just to keep life interesting. I was still terrified she would pull that crap and Rick would be around to witness it, but so far, she hadn't done it around him.

Rick had been a total gentleman, which was a change for me as well. I was used to Chance who was always trying to have sex or get a blow job. Rick liked to kiss me and was affectionate, but he was never trying to undress, me which made me happy. I was so tired of fighting guys.

Kelly and I had begun to fight a little bit more and weren't hanging out a lot either. Of course, between the play and now Rick, I didn't have a lot of time for her. I also wasn't drinking and partying any more either, and she still was. Before I started going out with Rick, if I was hanging out with Kelly at Chance and

Lonnie's and she got drunk, I was always the one who had to drive her home. I felt like I was outgrowing her and felt a little sad about that.

I wasn't writing to Bailey as often either. I couldn't understand what was going on with me and my friends. The real friends who meant everything to me, I seemed to be too busy for. I wondered if life would always be that way, or if I was just going through a phase. I used to write Bailey at least twice a week and now we wrote only twice a month. Our letters were taking on a less personal quality too which bothered me, but I didn't know how to say something without sounding like I was griping at her for not being friendly enough. We weren't really talking about anything important in our lives.

She had broken up with Donny right after I'd left Wichita, which I was happy to hear and she started going with a new guy named Casey. I didn't know him, but she seemed to really like him. Her brother Jason and his girlfriend had to get married because she had gotten pregnant. I remember thinking that was so weird because Jason was the high school pot dealer. I laughed when I thought about it because Jason was actually 20 now and hadn't really been a pot dealer in a couple of years. He worked at PPG, and was making good money from what Bailey had told me. I felt sometimes like we were drifting apart and it frightened me.

The Friday after Thanksgiving I thought life was going along great when everything began to crash down around me. I went with Rick to his grandmother's house in Orange Grove for the afternoon. His family celebrated Thanksgiving twice. They had one on Thanksgiving Day, and then went to Orange Grove on Friday afternoon and had another one. I felt funny going to a family event, but it got me out of the house and even though we still hadn't said we were going steady, I felt like we were.

His younger brother was a year younger than me and even though he wasn't as tall as Rick, he was still a big guy too. When I was standing in the small house his grandmother lived in, I felt squeezed in with all the large men crowded around the table. His family was kind and funny, just like him and seemed to like me, which I was glad. I was so nervous to meet them. His grandma was hilarious and was what I thought the word bawdy had been invented for. She spoke her mind and didn't mince words at all. She was tiny, but she didn't mind knocking those big men around when any of them got out of line. It cracked me up to see them all cow down to a tiny 4'11" woman.

When he brought me home, he kissed me gently. I wanted so much to ask him where exactly this was going. We'd been seeing each other for a few weeks and it felt like things were just rocking along with no real sense of urgency. I wasn't used to that. I was too afraid if I asked him what *exactly* we were doing he'd get freaked out by my need to have a label put on us that he'd cut and run. I just kept my mouth shut and left it alone. He smiled as I closed the door. Little did I realize that I was closing the door on my own sense of sanity for a while.

Chapter 7

As I began walking to my room, I could hear the familiar sounds of Mama and Ray yelling at one another. I stopped in my tracks and wondered if I could retreat and sneak back out without them knowing I was even home. It was still daylight. They might not hear me and think I was still with Rick. I could stay out until curfew at 12:30. Of course I wasn't sure where I'd go until then or how I'd get anywhere unless I walked, since Rick had already dropped me off. He was leaving to go hunting with his dad and brother. I didn't have to worry long, while I was contemplating my choice, the door to my parents' room slammed open and Ray came tearing out, trying to get away from my mother's wrath.

"Rita, leave me the fuck alone! What the hell is wrong with you? Won't you just shut the fuck up and go lay down or somethin'? I mean, I said, shut up! Let it go woman! Dammit! You need some kind of fuckin' help, Rita! I'm not living like this anymore! You either get some fucking help or I'm leaving for good and I mean it god-dammit!" Ray bellowed.

I stood there listening to him yell at my mom. I was shocked to hear him say that since he was a huge drinker himself. I couldn't believe he was telling her to get help. Didn't he realize if she got help he wouldn't be able to drink in the house? I knew I'd been spotted and I froze where I was standing. I didn't know what to do. Finally, Ray glanced over his shoulder towards the open bedroom door and then back to me, "I'm going to the lake kid, you need to get your old lady some kind of help! I can't live with her shit anymore! Either she gets some kind of help or I'm gonna be gone for good this time!"

Standing there, I looked at him, unsure quite what I was supposed to say. I heard my mom in her room crying bitterly. I felt so sorry for her. I wanted to go inside of their room to comfort her, but knew that it wasn't the thing to do at that particular moment. Ray walked past me with a small bag and was out the door in less than a minute. I was left standing in the middle of the hallway listening to my mom's sobs. Sighing, I pushed my feet to move forward into her room.

I opened my bedroom door as I got to my mom's room and threw my purse inside. I only had to take a little side-step to go from my room to being back on track to my mom's. When I crossed the threshold of the master bedroom, I found my mom lying across her bed weeping loudly. I walked over and sat down gingerly. My mom didn't say anything and I wasn't really sure what to say to her. I'd never heard her sob so bitterly. She'd been extremely depressed lately and I didn't understand it. Her moods were *more* unpredictable than ever. If she wasn't raging, she was bawling. I reached out and stroked her hair to try to soothe her.

Finally, after several minutes her sobs began to lessen and she finally looked up at me with swollen, red eyes. I could tell she'd been drinking heavily, but she was also something else, which I'd never seen before in her. I couldn't really describe the look I was seeing on her. It was almost as if she was ready to give up on living. She had reached an end to something. "What can I do?" I asked her quietly.

"DeLaine, *I need help*," my mama whispered in a broken, mewling voice.

I sat there staring at the woman who was my mother. I loved her so much and yet I despised her and was frightened of her as well. I couldn't believe that she was actually telling me that she needed help. I felt my heart leap up into my chest. The one thing I had truly wanted since I'd moved to Corpus was happening. I thought it would be easier though. I thought that she would realize that she shouldn't drink and would just quit. I had no clue that we would go through years of raging, screaming and physical attacks. I was shocked that this is how my dream was finally going to happen.

I took a deep breath because I wanted to say everything right and not screw this up. "What do you mean you need help, Mama?" I asked, quietly.

"I have to quit drinking, DeLaine," my mama moaned, as she began sobbing again. I nodded and she instructed, "Look in the phone book and see if there is something under alcoholics or something like that. I've got a problem and I don't know how to stop."

I smiled weakly at her, trying hard not to jump for joy and maintain my empathetic posture. I got up and grabbed the phone book. I wasn't sure what to look for so I went to the Yellow Pages first and looked under "A" and found Alcoholics Anonymous. There was an 800 number and I called it. I told them my name and the situation and they took down my phone number and told me that someone would contact me within the next 15 minutes. I hung up the phone and told my mom. She nodded and got up and went into her bathroom and began to throw up. I jumped up to go hold her hair and get her a wash cloth. It wasn't the first time I'd held her head while she puked. I hoped though it would be my last.

Within 10 minutes, the phone rang. I shot out of the bathroom to answer it. I heard an older sounding woman on the other line. She told me her first name and I said mine. I explained the situation as best as I could. She asked if my mom was able to talk with her and by then my mom had managed to come out of the bathroom and was once more lying across her bed. When I asked her if she wanted to talk, she sighed deeply and took the phone. She began talking to this woman and after she'd been on the phone for over 15 minutes, I got up and went into the kitchen to make me a coke. I was uncertain what the next move was. Everything felt so surreal.

I walked back into my mom's room several times to see if she was off of the phone, but each time I walked back there she was still talking on the phone. She went from lying on the bed to sitting up, to standing, to sitting in a chair. I wasn't sure what all the other woman was telling her, but I hoped she would tell Mama how to quit drinking. I thought if she just quit drinking everything would be so much better for all of us. We'd all find some kind of happiness in the house. Finally, I went into my room when Mama stayed on the phone for over 30 minutes.

An hour after the woman from Alcoholics Anonymous called back, my mama came to my open doorway and said that the woman was coming to pick her up and take her to an AA meeting. I looked at her curiously. "What's an *AA meeting*?"

Mom looked at me and shrugged. "I'm not really sure. I just know I need some help and this lady thinks that I can get some by going to one of these. She goes to them all the time. She's been sober for 12 years. She seems really nice. I have to do something, DeLaine. I have to learn how to drink where I don't push everyone away from me. Right now when I drink, I don't even know half the time what I do. I can't do that anymore or else I'm going to lose Ray completely, and in another year and a half you will be gone. You won't ever want to see me again either."

"Mom, that's not true," I whispered, hoping that I wasn't lying.

"It is true. I know it and you know it." My mom whispered quietly.

I looked at my fingers as they plucked invisible lint off of my bedspread. "How long is the meeting?" I asked.

"I'm not sure. I'll probably be home by 10 is what she said."

Nodding I stated, "Okay. Well, I'm not going to go out tonight. Rick is hunting with his dad and brother. I'm tired. I'll go out tomorrow night."

My mom tilted her head and looked at me curiously. Finally, she nodded her head and went into her room. She only washed her face. She didn't put makeup on or change her clothes, which was unusual for her. She always wore makeup and fixed her hair if she was going out. She didn't like not looking her best.

The lady from AA showed up and they were out the door within a matter of minutes. I stood in the middle of the living room as they left, wondering if this whole AA thing would work for her. I hoped so, but I didn't know how any of this stuff worked. Would they teach her how to drink like a normal person? Would they tell her she couldn't drink again? I thought if they did that she'd probably tell them all to go straight to hell. I felt at a loss as to what to do. I had walked in the door feeling so great after spending the day with Rick's family and then walking into the hellish nightmare, that was mine! I was left alone, wondering what the hell to do with myself yet again. Finally, I went into my room and closed the door.

I got out my stationery set that I wrote all my letters to Bailey on, and began writing an in depth, bottom of my heart, soul wrenching letter to my best friend. I needed to lay bare everything inside of me somewhere. I knew if I did it on a piece of paper and mailed it, at least it wouldn't be sitting in my room for my mom to find eventually. The safest person to leave it with was Bailey Rains.

The next day when I got up I found my mom sitting in the kitchen drinking her coffee and looking clear eyed and determined for the first time in a long time. She didn't appear hung over or depressed, which she had been so much for the last several months.

I had gone to bed surprisingly at 11, when my mom still wasn't home. I didn't know when she got in. I was surprised to find out she hadn't come in until midnight. She had gone to have coffee with a group of people from the AA meeting afterwards to learn more about it and how to get sober. I sat down and listened as she told me what all she learned and how she knew that she couldn't keep living the way she had been. I felt like jumping up and down for joy, but managed to contain my glee while listening to her talk. She explained that she had reached what is known as a 'bottom' and that in order for her to get sober she had to reach it and when she reached it the only way she could go is up and that is what she was doing by going to AA.

Listening to my mom's excitement over everything she'd learned the night before was infectious. I felt the same buoyant joy inside of me that she seemed to feel as well. For the first time in years, my mama finally seemed to be somewhat the way she'd been when I was little. I was hopeful that maybe life was about to get a lot better for all of us. I thought about all the good changes that were happening in my life. My mom was going to get sober. I had maybe found a real boyfriend in Rick, and that was a good thing. I felt a slight pang of sadness when I thought about it being so great, though. Briefly my mind skipped over the thought of Kevin.

My mom and I talked for a long time about AA and how she was going to make changes in her life. I listened and asked what I needed to do to help her. I wanted to make sure that I did everything I needed to do to make sure she stayed sober. I would do everything she needed me to do.

She left later that afternoon with the lady from AA whose name was Judith. She was in her 50's and wore lots of powder and really red lipstick. Her hair was dyed a strange brown color and teased into a bee-hive style. She smelled like an old lady perfume, but I didn't know the name of it. She was nice enough and my mom seemed to relate to her. She smoked like a freight train like my mom and had a gravelly, smoker's voice. They were going to meet some other people for coffee and dinner and go to another meeting. I wondered how many of these meetings my mom would have to go to before she wouldn't want to drink anymore.

Once they were gone I was alone again in the house. I wondered what I should do. I was supposed to go out with Kelly and Robin later, but I was alone for the rest of the day. I was restless and didn't want to just stay around the house. I decided to take my car and wash it. While I was out I dropped the letter off I'd written the night before to Bailey. I knew if I kept it at the house I would eventually decide against mailing it to her because I'd laid myself so bare in it. I hadn't done that in a long time but the night before I had felt so conflicted and vulnerable.

When I got home later that afternoon I felt good that I'd gotten something done and began to get ready to go out with Kelly and Robin. There was a big dance and I was sad that Rick was out of town hunting. I was going to try to have a good time. Even though we weren't going steady, I felt like we were, so I wouldn't be hooking up with anyone else.

I got home several hours later, after an uneventful night at the dance hall, to a still empty house. I felt so lonely and wondered what my mom was doing out so late. I hoped Ray would come back tomorrow. I knew he was really upset when he left on Friday. I had been happy to have Mom decide to quit drinking, but for some reason I felt strangely depressed at the changes happening around me. I didn't even wash off my makeup before going to bed. I just got out of the smoke filled clothes that I had worn to the dance that night, and threw on a fresh smelling nightshirt. It smelled of fabric softener and bleach. I realized its clean smell made me think of Kevin briefly. I felt a slight pang when I began to drift out into a sea of dreams, but none of them proved to be memorable.

Very early the next morning my mom came into my room and told me that Bailey was on the phone. I raised my head and looked at her sleepily. "What time is it?"

"It's 7:30," my mom answered, yawning.

I looked at my mom curiously and she pointed to my phone. I saw her shadowy form go down the hall towards the kitchen. I rolled over and picked up the phone on my night stand. "Hey Bay!" I muttered, groggily.

Bailey was sniffling loudly into the phone when I picked it up. I sat up in alarm. "What's wrong?" I demanded, without waiting for her to respond to my initial greeting.

"Lala! Oh Lala! It's bad! I had to call you! I knew you'd want to know!" Bailey wailed and started crying again. I couldn't begin to imagine what had happened. I thought immediately of Kevin and felt my heart stop in my chest. I wondered if I could die at 17 of a stopped or broken heart.

I took a deep steadying breath and asked in a deathly calm whisper, "What's bad, Bay?"

Bailey cried into the phone softly and finally she got out one word, "Jax."

"What?" I managed to strangle out of my throat.

"Hang on," Bailey cried.

I sat there trying to keep myself calm, but I couldn't do it for long. "Dammit Bailey! What happened to Jax? Is he okay? Is he….is he dead? Oh Jesus! Bay! What the hell happened?"

"I'm sorry, Lala! I'm still so freaked out by it. I was there and it was just so crazy! I was right there and I couldn't do anything to help him. I was at the hospital all night with him and Levi is just crazy. His new girlfriend wouldn't even go to the rodeo with him and oh Lala, it's just so bad." Bailey babbled, in a jumble.

"Wait, what? I'm confused. Whose girlfriend? What happened? Tell me what the hell happened to Jax first!"
I was frustrated.

Bailey took a deep breath, "Last night there was a rodeo. Like a last rodeo of the year thing. Jax was riding a bull and…oh Lala, it was bad." Bailey whispered.

"Oh fuck!" I groaned, through clenched teeth. "What happened to him?"

"Jax got gored by the bull. He's in critical condition right now in ICU, Lala!" Bailey whispered, as a fresh set of tears threatened to take over the cool, aloof girl who never seemed to let much trouble her.

"What does that mean Bailey?" I asked, as I felt my own hot tears now spring into my eyes.

"Jax got bucked off. He stood up and when he did he was trying to get away from the bull and was running towards the fence. They were trying to get the bull to run the other way, but he was pissed and went straight for Jax. As Jax was climbing up the side of the fence, he ran at Jax and rammed him in the back with his horn." Bailey took a breath as she seemed to gather strength to finish her tale of terror. "Everybody started screaming. Levi was sitting on the gate and he jumped down in there after it happened and was the first person to get to Jax. I was standing right there, talking to Levi when it happened. I was in front of that side of the fence where it happened."

I was sitting up in my bed hugging my knees to my chest. I wasn't really sure what this meant. Was Jax going to be okay? Was he going to be messed up forever? Finally, I asked, "Bailey is Jax going to be okay?"

"I don't know, Lala. He was in surgery all night. They had to cut him from his back to his front. The bull punctured his lung. He could die, Lala. They said that the next 48 hours are going to be very critical for him. They have a tube down his throat helping him to breathe."

"A tube?" I asked.

Bailey explained that the tube pumped air into his lungs while he was asleep. I sat there uncertain what to think about all of it. I didn't understand it and I wasn't sure I wanted to. "Bay what happens next?" I whispered not sure what I was supposed to do. Jax was the first and so far the only *real* boyfriend I'd ever had. He'd also been the one boy who confused me and caused me much consternation between him and Kevin.

"I dunno, Lala. The doctor said that if he does okay, in the next 48 hours, that hopefully they can take the tube out of his mouth and try to make him breathe by himself. They have him in a coma with medicine right now. They said he could be this way even longer though, but for sure at least 48 hours because this is a critical time." Bailey explained.

"Bailey, do you think he's going to be okay?" I asked my best friend wanting her to give me a magic answer.

Listening to the silence on the other end of the phone did nothing to make me feel any better though. Finally, Bailey whispered, "I honestly don't know, Lala. It's *really* bad. I've never seen anything like it before. *It was awful*!"

I sat there imagining Jax scrambling up the wooden and metal fencing of the arena, with a huge bull ramming him from behind, full force. "Does he have a girlfriend now?" I asked softly, wondering if there was some girl sitting in the hospital right now crying for the green eyed cowboy who stole my heart in 6th grade.

"No, he's been dating a couple of girls off and on this year, but nobody really steady," Bailey replied. "Why?"

I felt silly. "Um…no reason, I guess I just wondered if there was anyone up there worrying about him."

My best friend started giggling. I was shocked! "Oh Lala! He has people up there. His mom and sister were up there when Levi and I left. Some of the people from the rodeo club were up there, but Levi and I stayed all night. Casey is pissed at me for even going to the rodeo, but he went out of town with his family. I told him I was going with or without him. He doesn't even know about this yet. When he hears I was up at the hospital all night with Jax, and Levi was there with me, he's gonna be really pissed, but I just don't care. Levi was a real mess, and well, I couldn't let him be by himself. He was *so freaked out,* Lala. He was crying and screaming out in the middle of the arena before the ambulance attendants got in there."

I sat there for a minute feeling completely out of touch with everything that was Wichita Falls and Samson High School. I usually still felt somewhat connected, but I really felt removed from my hometown completely now. I suddenly felt sad for more reasons than just being scared about Jax being hurt. I knew many of the kids in the rodeo club, but there were many that I didn't know. I realized that Levi was now dating girls I didn't know and so was Jax. Even Bailey was dating someone I didn't know. It was no longer just the four of us or the four of us, plus Kevin. Suddenly the miles and the two hometowns became more certain and more permanently *divided.* My two lives were slowly and silently slipping away from one another. I sat there thinking that I was watching it happen and not able to pull the two pieces together anymore. The only problem with that though, I thought sadly, was I still didn't feel as connected to Corpus as I had felt to Wichita Falls. Now I felt like I didn't belong in *either* place. I wanted to know how to make myself belong in at least one.

Bailey and I talked about Jax and she told me about what happened and how it happened at least three different times and different ways. I sat there listening to every word envisioning everything and trying to put myself there with them. Trying to remember the way it used to be, when it was the four of us all together. It was strange because the memories of those times were becoming dimmer, and I hadn't really realized it. They seemed to have happened to someone else even though I knew they had happened to me.

While I sat there and listened to my best friend I knew that no matter what we would always be best friends. I could never imagine caring about anyone else the same way I cared about her. Even the way I felt about Kelly and Robin Stubbs wasn't the same. I just knew that even if she was my best friend *forever,* I was afraid that my life in Wichita Falls might never be able to be retrieved. I wondered if I did move back after graduation, would any of the people I'd hung out with in 8th grade still be around. I realized that thinking things would ever go back to how they'd been before was just a silly dream. That was a *closed* chapter in my life.

I realized for the first time that Kevin was the one who knew that. That was the reason he'd insisted that I not contact him for the whole school year. He knew that the life I'd had there was *over,* but I hadn't figured it out yet. I sighed and Bailey stopped talking. I realized I hadn't really been listening to her for the last couple of minutes. She asked me if I was okay and I told her I just had a lot on my mind. I told her I'd just written her a long letter and mailed it the day before and now this shit with Jax happened. My brain was working over-time right now. Quickly I told her what had happened with my mom over the weekend.

"Lala, do you think your mom's gonna stay sober?" Bailey asked me quietly.

"I guess. I mean, she seems serious about it. She's going to these meetings and she's meeting with these people and talking to them about how to get sober and shit, so I think she means it. I hope so Bay, 'cause I dunno if I can last much longer with her and the insanity around here! When she's drinkin' it's so bad. She's been so *unpredictable* lately," I chuckled a little bitterly and then said in a hushed voice, "Even *more* than normal!"

The girl with the aqua, green-blue eyes that I thought was the coolest girl in the world admitted, "I wish I could make things better for you, Lala. *I always have*."

I sat there with tears still on my face from crying for Jax. Now my eyes were moist again. "Bay, that means more to me than you'll ever know."

"*I love you, Lala,*" Bailey declared, softly.

I held the phone close to my head and tried to gather myself before I spoke again. Finally, I pleaded, "Bay, please call me again if you can. I really want to know how Jax is doing. I'm goin' to worry about him 'til I know he's out of the woods."

"Glenda already knows that I'm gonna call you every day, Lala, don't worry! I promise! I'm gonna call you every day when I get home from school. Oh wait, you have rehearsal still or is that over?" my best friend asked.

"No, the last performance was last Saturday. No more rehearsals. We won't be doing anything until the first of January,"

I explained, shrugging my shoulder as if my best friend were in my room and could see the motion.

"Okay, then I'll call you around seven every night, so I can have time to go by the hospital after school and get an update for you." Bailey now changed her tone to one of brisk efficiency. She wanted to go back to her cool, aloof manner. I knew from past experience that she went into this way of behaving when she wanted to regain her composure, after having been in a vulnerable or emotional state. I smiled when I thought about all the odd little things that I knew about the girl who I thought could never be best friends with someone like me.

We got off the phone shortly after agreeing to the time she'd call. I quietly set the phone into the cradle on my night stand. I sat there thinking about Jax and quietly cried some more. I was terrified he'd die and I'd have to go to *another* funeral. I couldn't stand the thought of walking up to a casket and looking down and seeing Jax's still form lying there. I imagined the beautiful green eyes never opening again and the sobs I'd been holding in began in earnest. My mom pushed my door open after hearing me crying and sat softly on my bed.

"What happened?" She asked me, alarmed.

I looked at my mom and was so grateful she was sober because if she'd been drinking she'd probably have a smart-ass comment to make about Jax, and it would just piss me off right now. "Jax got hurt really bad last night, at the rodeo, Mom!"

"Oh shit, what happened?" she asked me.

I explained everything that Bailey had told me. I broke down several times as I tried to relay the story because I thought about the pain he must have been in. Then I wondered if he'd ever even realized what happened after the initial attack. I wondered if he'd ever been conscious. I realized I'd never even asked Bailey. I would have to try to remember to ask her. When I finally finished telling my mom what happened, she held me while I cried some more. Finally, when I was cried out my mom pulled away from me and told me that she would be there for me no matter what. I took that to mean that if the worst possible thing happened, she wouldn't stand in my way of getting to the funeral. I felt a sharp pain in my heart when I thought about Jax in a coffin like I had seen Kevin's little sister, Donna's tiny body. I pushed the fresh round of tears I felt coming on down, because I didn't want to make my mom have to stay in there any longer than necessary. I knew she had things she needed to do and she didn't want to be tied up with me and my crybaby shit.

Finally, my mom got up and trying to cheer me up, she asked if I wanted her to make pancakes and sausage for breakfast. I smiled and nodded my head. I loved pancakes and sausage. She got up smiling and walked out of my room. I sat there thinking about how strange my life felt right now. I wanted to feel like I belonged *somewhere*. I wanted to know that I was good enough to have others around me. Right now I still seemed surprised when I realized that others *wanted* to be around me. I had been that way about Bailey for our entire friendship. I never understood why she loved me and wanted to be my friend. I knew that we had some unspoken connection that was almost like a weird psychic bond, it seemed, at times, but the more obvious reasons still seemed much less so. Now I was with Rick. I still didn't understand what exactly I was with him. I realized that I was going to have to talk to him and find out, because even though it seemed like something unspoken I needed to know for certain because at the moment I wasn't really certain about anything in my life. I hoped it wouldn't mean that I would lose Rick by making him tell me exactly what was happening with us, but I had to know something.

Chapter 8

That evening Rick came over to tell me all about his hunting trip. He was full of life and warmth. Little did he know what an emotional wreck he was going to get when he came to see me.

My mom came to my room late in the afternoon, while I was trying to finish the last World History report Dr. Vandergriff said he'd require until the first of the year. I was really glad because he expected much more from me and only a couple of other students in his class. It was like he separated the smart kids and gave us extra work, on top of the regular stuff. I didn't like it in the beginning, but now I realized that I was enjoying it! He was making the history of the world come alive for me where the other teacher was making me answer junk I read in a book. I wouldn't remember anything from his class, but even with the added work in Dr. Vandergriff's class, I would never forget about Caesar's rule or any of the other wonderful stories he brought to life every day.

"DeLaine," Mama knocked on my bedroom door, "Rick's out in the living room for you."

"What?" I exclaimed. "Oh shit! I don't have any make-up on or anything! Dammit! Can you stall him for a couple of minutes for me?" My mom smiled at me and nodded her head. I was so glad she understood. I jumped up and scooted over to my desk and turned on my make-up mirror. I looked deep into my dark brown eyes and saw how red the rims of them still were from my break down over Jax that morning. I didn't know how to make the swelling go down, but I could at least put a little powder on and maybe some lip gloss. I just didn't want to scare him completely away. Finally, after getting irritated with not having enough time to do anything with my unruly curls I ran to my dresser and pulled out a bandana. I'd just have to tie one of these over my head. I'd tell him I'd been cleaning my room. I stopped to look at myself in the mirror and decided it was the best I could do. I hadn't been expecting him to just stop by. I thought he'd probably call, but not drop in.

When I came walking out into the living room, I found Mom sitting there talking with Rick. He seemed to be enjoying their conversation. I was surprised, but then I remembered that she had been really sweet with Kevin when I was in the hospital too. I realized if I'd give her the chance, she might surprise me. I physically shook my head a little as if I was trying to clear out any confusing thoughts about my mom being an alcoholic. Kevin had to come to mind and of course once I thought about Kevin I immediately thought about Jax and found tears coming to my eyes completely unbidden. I stopped just as I got into the room, when I felt the surprising tears. I reached my fingers up and rubbed my eyes quickly, hoping that the water wouldn't keep coming out.

"Hey, DeLaine!" Rick called, as he pulled his large frame off our earthy colored sofa. I tried to smile at him and hoped it wasn't a grimace.

"Hi, Rick," I responded, smiling. I really didn't want to see Rick, I realized, as soon as he was towering in the middle of our living room. I had been looking at my photo album most of the afternoon when I wasn't working on homework. I wanted to see the pictures of Jax, Bailey and Levi. I didn't spend nearly enough time looking at them any longer. The ones I looked at the most still were the ones of me and Bailey, and me and Kevin, the first two photographs I ever had of each of them. I felt twisted and confused inside of my head. I was happy, but I was horribly sad too. I didn't know what I was supposed to feel about Jax being hurt, and then my mom getting sober had me confused too.

"I just thought I'd come by and see if you wanted to ride up to Sonic and grab a coke," Rick announced, sweetly. I noticed he almost looked like he was about to blush. I smiled at him and looked over at my mom.

Mama smiled at me, "I already told him it was okay with me if you didn't have too much homework. I knew you were in there working on it this afternoon." She looked at me and I realized she was giving me an excuse if I didn't want to go to Sonic. I was grateful to her, but I thought maybe if I got out of the house I'd feel a little better. I smiled at my mom and told her that I'd just finished the big History report I had to do, and thought getting out of the house for a few minutes might be nice. "How long do you think you'll be gone?" Mom asked while she looked at Rick.

I looked at him also and he realized that he was the one who needed to answer. "Uh, I guess maybe an hour or so?"

My mom smiled sweetly at him and told him that she wanted me home by 6:30. It was just a few minutes after 5 and it was almost dark. Rick told her he'd have me back by then and I ran to my room and grabbed my jacket and purse. I came back out and gave my mom a kiss on the cheek and went out the front door into the cold, late November wind. I realized I hadn't been outside all day long.

When we got to the end of my street Rick turned to me and asked, "Why do you look so sad Lil' Bit?"

I was surprised that he noticed. I thought I was hiding it well. "I didn't realize I was looking that way," I murmured, quietly. I looked over at the large boy-man sitting next to me with the cat green eyes. It dawned on me I was thinking about a different pair of green eyes. Rick gave me a little bit of a perturbed look. I tried to smile my way out, but realized he wasn't going to be charmed either.

Sighing I rolled my eyes and finally admitted, "I've just had a really strange weekend. There's been a bunch of shit with my mom and Ray and well, just some complicated shit," I concluded weakly. Finally, I looked at my hands in my lap and explained, "I got a call this morning from my best friend in Wichita Falls, and my ex-boyfriend there was gored last night during some kind of end of the year rodeo. It was some kind of special holiday thing. He's in the ICU and has some kind of breathing tube in his mouth and they gave him something that has him in a coma. They don't even know if he's going to live yet. The doctor's said the first 48 hours are the ones to really watch him. So, I mean, I guess I'm kinda worried about him too," I shrugged my shoulder and turning my head to look out of the passenger side window.

Rick didn't say anything and I wondered what he thought. We drove the rest of the way to Sonic in silence. I didn't know what to say and I wanted to defend myself so badly. Finally, when he didn't say anything I just gave up and sat in the passenger side. I didn't even understand why I felt the need to defend myself.

We pulled into a slot at Sonic and Rick rolled down his window of his dark green pick-up. He ordered our drinks and I continued to sit there silent. Once the car hop brought our drinks out, Rick rolled the window up and turned to me. I'd already cracked my window and lit a cigarette. I needed something to keep me busy since he was being silent. I didn't like the silence. I missed the loud and boisterous side of Rick, I realized, as I sat there blowing the cigarette smoke out of my mouth into the crack of my window.

"So, are you in love with this guy or what?" Rick finally asked me quietly.

I snapped my head over and looked at him surprised. "What?" I asked him shocked that he'd even said it.

"Are you in love with this cowboy up there?" Rick asked slowly as he looked out the windshield.

I sat there not believing we were even having this discussion. I sighed deeply, "Jesus, Rick! He was my boyfriend in 8th grade! I'm just sad because we stayed friends. I would be sad if anybody I knew up there was hurt like this!"

Sitting there silently for much too long, Rick finally admitted, "Look, DeLaine, I like you a lot! I like you more than I've liked just about anybody. I'm not gonna lie and say you're the first girl I've ever dated or that I haven't ever been in love with someone else before. I guess I'm just a little crazy not knowing much about your life in Wichita Falls. You sometimes seem so *closed off*. You are funny and opinionated and you aren't scared by me, which I think some girls are sometimes just 'cause I'm so big." He paused a minute and looked at me. He finally finished his thoughts, "I don't know what we're doin' and I'm always scared to ask you 'cause you seem *skittish* if I try to get too close."

I sat there feeling a little surprised at his description of me. I didn't think I'd been that closed off to him. I'd told him about my life and then I realized I'd only told him the *top layer*. I'd told him the stuff I only let everybody in the world know. I still kept all my secrets from him. I'd been too afraid to tell him the realities of my life. He knew I was from Wichita Falls. He knew my best friend lived there and I went up there in the summer. He knew my mom was *complicated* and he knew I was smart and was in theater arts. Other than that I'd been pretty closed off.

"Rick, I'm sorry. I've had some…well I've had some *bad* things happen in the past that make it hard for me to trust people. I guess because of that I don't just tell *everybody* my personal stuff." I looked at the plastic top of the coke, sitting between my jean-clad thighs. I ran my finger along the raised ridge of the lid afraid to look up into the glowing, green eyes that had first intrigued me in a Circle K parking lot only a few weeks earlier.

After sitting there for a few minutes Rick asked, "DeLaine, do you remember the night I gave you my class ring here at this Sonic?" I nodded my head mutely. "I gave it to you because I honestly believe in love at first sight. I think I fell in love with you when I was drunk and got into your car! I saw you pumping gas and you were standing there with no one around you and you looked so pretty. Your face was so smooth and your eyes were looking so far away. I knew I had to come tell you how beautiful you were. I'm not a real smart guy and I probably drink too much. I'm a little rowdy, but I can love you if you let me."

I looked at him shocked that he'd said that to me. I'd wanted Kevin to tell me easily that he loved me. I had to drag it out of him, even though he showed it to me. I realized though that I *needed* to hear it. Here was a boy who was telling me without me ever even trying to get him to. Finally, I whispered, "So, what *exactly* are you saying Rick?"

Shaking his head he laughed a little softly. He explained as he looked at his own cup, "I'm saying, little girl, that I fell in love with you the first time I saw you. Giving you my ring that night here in this very parking spot, at this Sonic, was my way of trying to get you to be my girlfriend. I thought if you had my ring, then when you went out with me, you wouldn't need to give it back to me. You still have it and you've been goin' out with me." Rick looked uncomfortable and then he set his drink on the dashboard. He scooted more to the middle of the bench seat, of the pickup, so he was closer to me. "DeLaine, *I love you.* I want you to be my girlfriend. I guess I thought you would be my girlfriend if you'd just go out with me, but I didn't realize how hard it was going to be to get close to you. If this guy getting hurt is what it took for us to finally talk, then I'm glad he got hurt. I'm not *really* glad, but I'm glad that it gave us the chance to talk. I want to know everything about you! I am gonna love you no matter what."

Rick was really telling me he loved me. He was telling me he wanted me to be his *girlfriend.* He was doing it in a strange way, but then I realized that the only other boy who'd been my *real* boyfriend had asked me to go steady in 8th grade. I didn't know how a boy asked a girl to be his girlfriend when they got older. I wondered briefly about Bailey and how she and Donny, and now Casey, had started going steady. Shaking my head I looked at Rick and smiled slowly. "Rick, I *want* to be your girlfriend. I, uh, I don't want to just say I love you because *you* said it. I'm not really sure how to just let go and love people. I mean when I do, I *really* love them. I'm not saying I may not be in love with you. Shit this is getting all twisted up." I felt tongue tied. Finally, after rubbing the side of my face, I turned to look at Rick whose face seemed unbelievingly close to me now, "Look, I want to let you know me better. Just know that it is going to take a little while. I have 17 years of *shit* to catch you up on. I can't just tell you everything in an hour. I don't know if I believe in love at first sight or not, but I'm willing to see where this goes. Just be patient with me, okay?"

Watching the smile begin slowly to spread across Rick's face, he nodded his head. Finally ever so slowly he leaned over and kissed me softly. His size sometimes belied the gentleness he could use with me. When he pulled away he commanded,
"Okay, *girlfriend*, you put that ring on and you *leave* it on. I'm gonna marry you one day, you know it, DeLaine Reynolds. *I mean it too*!"

I laughed softly and shook my head. I couldn't believe it that I was sitting there with this crazy and larger than life person and finally had my *real boyfriend*. I only wished that I felt happy about it. I kept thinking that if it had happened on a different day it might have been different. If this had happened on Friday maybe I could be happy about it, but instead it happened after an emotional weekend with my mom and then on the heels of Jax's rodeo accident. After having all these things rattle through my still emotionally saddened brain, I leaned into Rick and kissed him passionately. I hoped that by doing that I'd feel everything begin to click into place. When I pulled away from a slightly surprised Rick, I realized that even though it had been passionate, warm, and felt nice, I didn't feel the same for him that I felt for Kevin. I *knew* that I loved Kevin. I hoped that I could *eventually* fall in love with Rick too. I was willing to try. "Please don't tell me you love me all the time and think that I'm just going to say it back, okay?" I suddenly said.

Rick looked at me and after a few beats he nodded his head. "DeLaine, I'll do *whatever* you want. I want you to love me and *when* you tell me I want you to *mean* it. If that's what you need then okay, that's how it'll be." I nodded and he leaned in and kissed me again quickly. He glanced at his watch and said, "Believe it or not, it's time to get going!" I nodded my head and was happy to be going home and to the safety of my room. I wanted to be in my space *alone*. I wanted to think about everything we'd talked about.

Chapter 9

After the Thanksgiving holiday, I went back to school with a newly minted boyfriend. It seemed a little strange to me to know I had a real boyfriend now, as opposed to just making out with a guy at the game room or messing around with Chance Cahill. It was even different than knowing I had Kevin in Wichita Falls still. It wasn't like when I was in 8th grade and was going with Jax either, because we'd been in the same class. Rick was already out of school and working at one of the refineries. He worked a real man's job. It wasn't just an after school job or a summer job, but a *real* one that he might work at for the rest of his life.

Mom continued to go to AA meetings, and it felt odd seeing her clear eyed every afternoon when I got home. Ray came home and I could only guess that their relationship was different. I still felt a little *off* by a sober mom as opposed to the demon who inhabited her when she was drunk. I had gotten so used to the drunk devil, that the sober saint was a little off putting to live with as well. I at least knew the drunk devil. The saint was a whole new creature to learn.

We seemed to be able to talk a little easier now that she was sober, but I still felt guarded with anything I told her that was significant. I was always afraid she'd use it as a weapon later down the line, so I still tended to keep things close to me unless I *had* to tell her. I knew that I would have to tell her that Rick and I were going steady, but she seemed to really like him, so I didn't think she'd be too upset by it. I wasn't wrong either because when I got home that Sunday evening and told her, she reacted as if she were Bailey by jumping up and hugging me tight. I felt like I was living a lie in some way because my heart wasn't into how excited she seemed by it all. At least now though I could wear his ring without keeping it in my purse or pocket like I'd been doing since he gave it to me before we ever went out on a date.

School was full of all the pre-holiday excitement that any school year holds. The usual round of choir concerts and band concerts were happening. Since our play was over and we wouldn't be starting anything new until January I thought we'd have a fairly easy month in Mr. Magnus's class, but I was wrong when he came in and made us begin doing duets. I was shocked when Pete Mulligan jumped up and ran to me when we had to pick partners. I usually never got picked for anything and here was the best actor I'd ever met running to my side to partner with me. I was excited to still be acting though. I had actually dreaded not doing anything.

The year before, when I had started going to Calvin, I had found out that they had a Winter Ball every year. It was a small school dance where they announced the favorites of the class and each club as well as Mr. and Miss CHS were announced. They were honorary titles that I didn't know much about. I hadn't ever really been in a club before. Since I was in theater arts and had been in the fall production, I was officially part of the theater arts club and of course VOE and Office Education Association which was the class that Mrs. Davis taught. We all voted for our favorites in each class and handed our ballots into the teachers the Friday before the dance.

I wasn't going to the dance because Rick was going to be out of town hunting again. I didn't want to go by myself. Tina wasn't going to go and I really didn't hang out with anybody else. When I went to theater arts though, everybody was excited about the dance. When I received my ballot to vote for the drama club favorite, I of course picked Pete. I knew that he'd won it for the last two years in a row, but he was really a great guy and a great actor. I thought out of all of us, he deserved it the most, plus he was a senior.

Mr. Magnus had given us that Friday as a free day. He had a lot of things he was doing to help prepare for the dance because he'd been elected as part of the planning committee. He wasn't exactly happy about it. He loved being the head of the English department. I could tell that in the joy he had in discussing the different novels I was reading in the accelerated program I was finally a part of now. He didn't seem to be the type of person though who played well with others sometimes. Not everyone seemed to understand him, and that even went for the teachers. I found that a little odd even though none of them ever once said anything bad about him. I just knew that some of them were irritable when he would make a stand on a student's grade and whether their grades made the difference between a team being able to play or not.

The new *no pass, no play* rules were hurting a ton of the schools and their sports programs. Sometimes I would think of Kevin when I heard others talking about it. I wondered sometimes if that rule had been in effect when we were younger if maybe Kevin would have been pushed a little harder academically. I knew he was very intelligent. Talking to him told me he was smart. He had never had a teacher take any real interest in his academic achievements though, because he was such a jock. Most of the time those guys were green-lit all the way through so they could play whatever sport they were involved in.

While I was in theater arts that Friday, before the Winter Ball, I was talking with a couple of the girls I'd gotten closer to that were all seniors. When they asked if I was going to the dance I shook my head, "Nah, I mean, Rick's out of town on a big hunting trip to Colorado, so I'll probably go hang out with a couple of friends from Woodway and try to get some of my homework done.

I was shocked when one of the girls, Carrie, who was usually quiet around me exclaimed, "DeLaine you HAVE to go Saturday!"

"Why?" I asked her perplexed.

Her best friend, Shellie, who was a funny, heavier girl, who rarely was quiet, popped off, "Yeah, c'mon man! There's a bunch of us going! You can hang out with me and Carrie. I looked at Carrie Martinez. She was so pretty with sharp features and a cool blonde streak bleached into the front of her hair. I looked at Shellie Macintosh then and told her I'd think about it.

Right before the bell rang Pete came up to me and stated, "Hey, you should come to the dance. I'm gonna be there! We all know you wanna come see me, right? I mean, as President of the Theater Arts Club I'll be presenting the award."

I laughed at him, "You shouldn't even bother. You know you're going to get it, right?"

Shaking his head he said, "Nah, not this year. I got it for two years. It's someone else's turn now! C'mon and say you'll show up! It's not like it's a formal or anything. Just wear that killer black dress you have with those gray heels. You'll look great!"

"Why Mr. Mulligan, how in the world do you know what my wardrobe consists of?" I asked Pete in a silly Southern Belle drawl.

Winking, Pete laughed, "Well, shit woman, I'm not *blind*!" I felt myself blush at that comment and told him I'd try. He told me he'd be really disappointed if I didn't come at least for a little while. I smiled and told him I'd *try*!

I almost didn't go to the Winter Ball, but I was restless. I wanted out of the house and away from my now sober mother. I thought it was so wrong of me to want to be away from her. I'd wanted her to be sober for so long, and now she was, and I wanted to be away from her still.

Sitting on my bed most of the day, listening to my records and reading, I glanced into my louvered closet door and spied the black dress that Pete had mentioned the day before. I smiled when I remembered what he said. I was still trying to get used to the attention of the boys around me. I seemed to get lots of attention now that I was back to a size 7. It seemed since Rick and I had made it official that we were going steady there wasn't as many boys flirting, but Pete still flirted with me and that made me feel good.

About an hour before the dance started I got up and went out into the living room where Mom and Ray were watching TV. "Hey

Mama, can I go to the dance at school tonight? It starts in about an hour. I probably won't stay for the whole thing, but I'd kinda like to go long enough to see who all gets picked for favorites."

Mom smiled at me and nodded, "Sure, DeLaine. You can stay as long as you want as long as you're home by 12:30." I turned around and went into my room to get ready.

While I was putting on the last of my eye makeup, the phone rang. I didn't answer it. I was hoping maybe it was actually a call for my mom, but less than a minute after it rang I heard the soft tapping on my door. I hollered for her to come in and she opened it up enough to poke her head in. "Honey, Bailey's on the phone."

I jumped out of the old, straight backed, kitchen chair that sat in front of my desk with my makeup mirror and jerked my phone off the cradle. Bailey had been so good to call me every other day after she'd called to tell me about Jax. I felt my heart slamming around inside of my chest because she'd called me just that morning.

Jax had made it through the first 48 hours, but the damage was severe and he had to have another surgery. The doctors kept the ventilator on him for over a week and when they finally took it off of him he stayed in a coma. This coma though wasn't because of any medicine they gave to him. They weren't sure how long he would be that way, but they still felt like he had a good chance at a full recovery.

"Bay, what's wrong?" I breathed heavily into the phone.

"HE'S AWAKE!!!" Bailey yelled from her phone almost 500 miles away.

I felt my legs give way, and I slid onto my queen sized bed. "*Seriously*?" I whispered.

"SERIOUSLY!" Bailey crowed.

I sat there and looked at the photo of Jax that I'd set on my night stand. I'd taken it out of the photo album I had and looked at it every day. I talked silently to God every night before I went to bed begging Him to let Jax live. I usually ended up falling asleep with tears streaking into my ears and my nose stuffed up. I wasn't even sure what I should ask Bailey. The important thing was he had woken up. That must mean he was fine I thought. I felt myself crash back to the ground though after I'd said that to my best friend.

"Lala, he's been in a coma for almost *3 weeks*. He's gonna be out of school for a long time. He's probably gonna have to go to summer school just to be able to graduate on time. He's awake, but he's in a lot of pain now that's awake and can feel it. Levi just called me. He's practically been living at the hospital with Jax's family. He calls me every day so I can give you an update, but I thought this was a big deal!" my sweet Bailey stated softly.

I felt so stupid. I just expected he would get over everything so easily. "I'm just really excited," I replied feeling a little chagrined.

"Lala! You *SHOULD* be excited!" Bailey said sweetly to me. "This is HUGE NEWS! He's gonna just keep getting better now! I truly believe that!

I held my head in my hands as I cradled the phone to my ear. I wasn't surprised that there were tears all over my freshly made face. She went over everything in her list of reports now that he was awake. He was awake, but they had him heavily medicated for the pain. He had been in ICU this whole time, but hopefully being awake meant he'd be out soon. I couldn't help but feel my heart leap at that news. I knew that he was going to be fine. I felt it in the core of my being.

After I had hung up the phone when Bailey and I were finished talking I sat on the side of my bed. I looked at the picture of the cute, meadow-green eyed boy who smiled out at me. I realized that he was older now than he'd been in the photograph I had. I hadn't seen him the summer before like I normally did. I wondered if he'd changed a lot. It seemed boys were the ones who were changing the most by getting taller in high school. I felt a huge sense of relief. I finally took a deep breath and got up off of my bed and walked slowly over to my desk and blotted the streaks left from the tears and wiped the eyeliner that had bled a little with my tears and once everything was fixed I finally began the arduous process of putting on my pantyhose and slipping my dress on. I grabbed my gray high heel shoes and my small gray clutch handbag.

When I got to the school, I saw all the popular kids were mainly there. I felt a little weird walking in by myself, but I had timed it to where I would get there only a few minutes before they did the "Favorites" presentation. I found Carrie and Shellie and said hi to them. I drifted off a while later, feeling a little strange being there and seeing others as couples. Some of the prettiest girls had corsages that their boyfriends or dates who were part of the popular crowd had given them. I suddenly felt a little silly being there all by myself, with no flower on my wrist or dress. Thankfully, I was able to go into the auditorium fairly quickly after arriving so I could sit down anonymously.

As each club and group named their favorite for the year, I sat there watching the same kids walk up on the stage over and over. I wondered why I'd even *cared* to come. I was feeling a little silly for even bothering when I saw Mr. Magnus get up on the stage to introduce the Theater Arts Club favorite. I saw Pete sitting on the stage because as the senior class president he had to announce certain winners.

I heard Mr. Magnus clear his throat and then he opened his mouth and out of his cultured and exceptional speaking voice came the words, "Our theater arts club has chosen this year for its Drama Club *sweetheart* ...Miss DeLaine Reynolds!"

I felt like everything began to move in slow motion. I wasn't sure if I'd heard that right and thought I must be dreaming it at first. I had been watching Pete on the stage because I wanted to see his reaction when his name was called. When my name was called instead, it took a few moments for it to sink in that *my* name had been called. As if he'd known exactly where I was sitting Pete had turned to look directly at me as Mr. Magnus began clearing his throat to announce the favorite in the class. Once my name was called Pete jumped up and yelled, "*Yes*!"

Finally, the boy sitting next to me gave me a push, "Get up there and get your award!"

As if snapping out of a dream, I stood up on now shaking legs. I kept my eyes trained on Pete as I walked up the stairs and was surprised to see him at the side of the stage, extending his hand towards me. I reached up and took his hand and let him escort me the rest of the way. He tucked my hand into his folded arm and walked me over to Mr. Magnus. For the second time in one school year, Mr. Magnus was standing in front of me handing something to me. I bowed slightly as he slipped a white satin sash over my head and shoulder that read "DRAMA CLUB". Pete turned me around and picked up my right hand and slipped a dainty gold bracelet onto my wrist. "What…" I began, but my voice faded off. I looked up at Pete's mischievous grin and he winked at me. After he finished clasping the bracelet onto my wrist he leaned over and kissed me on the cheek and then I was walking off of the stage as the students and staff sitting in the auditorium clapped. At the end of the stage, Mrs. Davis was standing there to tell each student to go to the bulletin boards after the ceremony to have our photos taken for the year book. I smiled at her and just floated out of the auditorium.

Pete was chosen as Mr. CHS for the year and also made the senior class favorite for the year. I was happy to see that. While I was waiting to have my photo taken I took a few minutes to look at the small, gold bracelet. It held a small round charm that had engraved on one side, "DeLaine Reynolds" and "Sweetheart" and then the opposite side said "Drama Club" and "1983-1984". I traced the letters with my fingertip still feeling a little shocked. I would never have thought I'd have been called for anything and had mainly come because I wanted to see *Pete* named as the Drama Club Favorite.

As if he knew I was thinking about him, Pete came up behind me and goosed me. I jumped and turned to find him smiling broadly. "I told you I wasn't gonna be it this year!" he was laughing at my surprised look. "I told Magnus to take me out of the running!"

Looking at him defiantly I chided, "See, you would have gotten it if you hadn't done that!"

Shaking his head and still grinning like a loon he admitted, "Nope! You beat me fair and square no matter what!"

"What?" I asked incredulously. Pete nodded his head and then it was my turn to go and have my photo taken. When I came back out of the room Pete was standing beside the girl who had been voted Miss CHS and there was no one out there waiting to talk to me. I smiled his way and waved my hand at Pete and then slipped out of the school with no one else to notice if I had been there or not.

My mom had been thrilled to find out that I was chosen as the Drama Club Favorite. I knew that she was probably disappointed that she didn't know so she could have been there, but I hadn't known. Rick even seemed to be excited for me when he came back home from Colorado. I went to school the following Monday feeling so much different yet still felt invisible. I felt a little confused because I'd basically won something for being the most popular vote in a club and yet I didn't feel popular at all.

Bailey continued to call to update me on Jax. By Christmas he had gone home and was expected to make it back to school by the middle of January. I was so glad to hear that. I realized that there was a part of me that was aching for Wichita Falls again. I was also aching over Kevin. I wanted to be able to talk to him so badly. I knew if I asked my mom if I could call him she'd probably give me a lecture about not leading Rick on if I had feelings for another boy. When I would think about that it never failed to make me chuckle silently. My mom had never really told me anything about leading a boy on or not. I hadn't ever really had one to talk about with her when she was sober before.

It seemed that the Christmas holidays came and flew by and it felt strange actually trying to shop for a gift for Rick. I didn't know the first thing about shopping for boyfriends. I had bought a St. Michael medal for Kevin years ago and had gotten Jax a present way back in junior high. Rick was a *man.* He was a young one, but it wasn't like he was a little kid like Jax had been so long ago. Eventually my mama finally took me to go shopping for Rick and I found some cologne that he liked. I got him that and I found a nice leather wallet at the Western Wear store that I could afford. I hoped it didn't seem too lame to him.

We exchanged our gifts and I was surprised that he had given me some solid gold heart earrings. He told me that he wanted to give me something extra special for Valentine's Day so he hoped I didn't mind such a small Christmas gift. I tried to keep my mouth from falling open when he told me that. I kissed him quickly and told him how much I loved them.

For New Year's Eve we went to a party at his family's house. I was surprised at how insanely drunk everyone seemed to get except me. He kept trying to drive me home and I was glad when his mom gave me his keys and told me to drive his truck to my house. I could bring it back the next day. When I left at 2 a.m. I was probably 3 hours past when I would have liked to have come home. I just had little patience for drunks any longer no matter what their age.

January 1st was the first really big argument Rick and I had. I got up early and took his truck to his house. When I got there, I stood out on the porch and rang the bell three times and knocked twice. Finally, I stooped and placed his keys underneath a planter that was by the front door. I was pretty mad by then. I struck out walking down the old street in Annaville that led to Chance and Lonnie's house they were renting now. They'd gotten too many complaints at the apartments for too many parties.

I knocked on the door and saw that there was a variety of beer cans and even a couple of whiskey bottles in the yard. The front door opened up into a darkened front room. Scotty Cahill's Auburn head poked out around the door. He smiled when he saw me. I asked if I could come in until Chance woke up. Scotty let me in and I told him that I was hoping that Chance might give me a ride home when he got up. I could tell that Scotty was severely hung over, but he was trying to be sweet. We sat on the couch in the living room and turned on MTV while I looked around noticing a lot of different passed out teenagers in the room.

While we sat there with music videos playing softly in the background, I told Scotty about Rick getting drunk and how I had taken his truck back and no one answered the door. He asked if Rick knew where I was and I shook my head. Scotty looked at me and grinned, "Shit, don't tell him where you got the ride from! He and Chance have almost gotten into it a couple of times at the dance hall."

I looked at Scotty surprised. I hadn't known that. No wonder Chance had been a little strange about me and Rick dating. He hadn't said anything to me though to his credit. I was just glad that my mom hadn't really given me a time to be home by. I knew she'd want me home at a reasonable time. Of course, she assumed I was going to be with Rick. I hoped she didn't try to call me at his house because he'd freak out too and probably be pissed at me as well.

Thankfully my mom didn't try to call me. I got home right before Rick showed up on my doorstep trying to find me. My mom had gotten just a brief reason why Chance Cahill brought me home and not Rick. I was grateful she didn't pester me too much about it. I just wanted to go into my room and hide. I was mad at Rick, but I didn't know how to tell him that without him breaking up with me. Then I felt like such a baby. I had gotten so brave when I had been around Bailey and had been dating Jax. I hadn't let him bully me, when he had tried. Now I acted like Rick would be the only boy who would ever like me.

Rick was banging on the glass storm door. I knew it was him without looking outside when I heard the pounding. I sighed deeply as I got up off of my bed and opened my bedroom door. I shouldn't make my mom have to deal with him being mad at me. I needed to deal with it. I was surprised when I got into the front foyer and he was standing there talking amiably to my mom. She excused herself and I walked out, expecting him to follow me. Thankfully, he could tell I wasn't exactly happy with him either, in the insistent way he'd been banging on our front door.

"I've been crazy trying to figure out how the fuck you got home, since my mom told me she gave you my keys. I didn't know *what* could have happened to you, until I looked inside the truck and found the note in the seat that told me where you'd put the keys. I thought maybe someone had kidnapped you from the front yard when you were leaving!" Rick huffed.

Rolling my eyes I said facetiously, "I'm *not* that great of a catch, Rick! Not worth millions to anyone, so I doubt I'd be stolen from your front yard! I feel like I'm pretty safe there!"

"Dammit, DeLaine, you don't know! You don't know what kind of sickos are out there now days! You could have been down under Nueces River bridge raped, and your throat sliced," Rick growled.

Before I could stop myself, my sharp tongue retorted, "Thank God that hadn't happened or else you'd *just now* be making it to tell my mom. The damned murderer would be all the way to fuckin' Mexico by now, if I was waiting on you to come save me!" Rick grabbed my arm as I turned to go back inside and slam the door in his face. When he did, I jerked my arm out of his strong grip. My former stepbrother, Geoffrey had grabbed me one too many times and made marks on my arms for me to take kindly to anyone else grabbing me that way, other than my mom. I yelped in pain and when I jerked away Rick's hand let go suddenly and caught my mouth just right in an offhanded backhand. I grabbed my mouth shocked. I knew that he didn't mean to hit me, but it was still a shock. I'd been my step-brother's punching bag a lot, so being hit by someone else came as a huge surprise. I stepped away from Rick as my fingertips rubbed my lips. I was more hurt from the shock than the actual hit. My mom had hit me way harder and I'd stood there and stared at her silently begging her to do it again. This time though I wasn't going to stand there and endure it.

"*Oh shit*! DeLaine!" Rick began.

Shaking my head, I looked at him, yelling, "Don't!"

"Honey, *I'm sorry*! I'm hung over and I was worried. I honestly didn't mean to hit you." Rick began.

"So fucking what! You don't have any right to grab me like that and then to hit me on top of it! Leave Rick! I don't want to see you anymore!" I growled angrily.

"DeLaine, honey, I'm so, *so* sorry!" Rick was almost crying as he pleaded. I shook my head and told him to leave. I told him I needed to calm down. When I was calmer I'd call him and we could talk. I watched as the giant man-child got into his truck and he drove away sadly and slowly.

My mom tried to get me to talk to her, but I was crying and told her I'd talk to her later. I went into my room and closed the door softly and flung myself across the bed. I sobbed into my pillow. I reached over and grabbed my stuffed puppy that Jax had given me for my birthday when we first started going steady in 8th grade. I hadn't cried into the soft fur in a long time. For some reason it just felt right to cry into his fur. I ached, wanting to call Bailey and tell her all about what had just happened. She was the only one I felt like would understand how much I was hurting. In the end, I finally cried myself out and went into my bathroom to wash my face. I went back into my room and went to bed early. I didn't want to talk with my mom or anyone else that I could talk to in Corpus. I just wanted to escape into sleep.

The next day I was out of school for one more day. I floated through the house not saying much to anyone. I knew my mom wanted me to tell her what happened, but I didn't want to talk about it. Later in the afternoon the doorbell rang. My mom came knocking on my door after a few minutes. When I told her to come in I saw a large balloon arrangement coming into my room. I sighed because I knew it was from Rick. A part of me was thrilled in a way that he was sending it to me, but another part of me just wanted him to get lost. I was still angry.

Mama walked in and smiled at me. She set the arrangement on my desk and sat on my bed. I looked at the basket and Mom asked me if I wanted to talk. I sighed and then told her briefly what happened on New Year's Eve and then the day before. I told her about Rick being upset because I'd left his truck there when no one answered the door. She listened and tried to be understanding. She told me that she really liked Rick and thought that he meant well, and he'd just messed up. She explained that it was sweet that he was trying so hard to make up to me. I rolled my eyes. I didn't know *why* I had to accept his apology. I didn't tell her about him accidentally hitting me in the mouth because I was afraid she'd go ballistic on him. I was still angry enough about it.

"DeLaine, I think Rick might actually love you, honey," my mom was trying to explain to me how he felt.

"Mom, I don't know what love's got to do with it at all!" I replied angrily. "Bottom line is if he loved me, he wouldn't have acted like that."

My mom sat there quietly, "I know you think that he can't love you and act like a jackass at the same time, but I've acted pretty awful sometimes. I still love you and you still love me.

"You're my *mom* though," I whispered.

"Doesn't mean I can't still love you," she replied, quietly.

"Mom, I just can't deal with him acting so stupid. I mean, if he wants to be with me, he can't treat me like that," I whined.

My mom smiled at me and told me to give him another chance. I finally nodded and she encouraged me to go over there and at least thank him for the balloons. After she got out of my room I walked over to my desk and looked at the basket. It was huge. It had Hershey's kisses and a huge teddy bear. It was funny because Rick reminded me of a big teddy bear. Inside that was a card. I opened it up and it simply said, "I'm so sorry…*please forgive me*!!!" I sighed and sat in the chair at my desk and began to put on a little makeup. I was in my car within 45 minutes and on my way to his house.

I pulled into the driveway of his parents' home, knowing that he had just gotten home from work. I wondered if he would be in the shower or not. I thought about him being in a shower and felt myself begin to blush. I was still surprised that he hadn't really tried *anything* with me. I'd had my share of boys who were extremely *grabby,* but Rick wasn't one of them. Sometimes I even wondered if he *wanted* to be with me. I worried that maybe I wasn't attractive enough to him to want to be with me. I shook my head as if to clear my thoughts and got out of my car.

When his mom saw me she smiled and apologized for getting so *tipsy* on New Year's Eve. I told her it was okay and she told me that Rick was indeed in the shower. I sat at their kitchen breakfast bar uncomfortably, waiting on him to get out of the shower. I watched his mom walk towards the back of the house to tell him I was out there waiting on him. I looked at the large room with the huge high ceiling and thought about how masculine the whole feel of the home was. His mom was the only female in a house full of men. I wondered what that was like to live with men who were so extremely rugged as far as being avid hunters and fishers. They were all about being outdoorsman.

Within five minutes Rick was out in the kitchen, with wet hair and no socks on under his jeans, and long sleeved shirt. He looked like a young giant. His green, cat eyes glowed in the darkened hallway. He held his hand out for me to take. I hopped off the barstool and walked towards his outstretched hand. I placed my much smaller one into his and let him lead me down the hallway to his room. I'd been in there only a couple of times and only for a few minutes each time. It was the same room he'd had since he was a kid, but it wasn't like a normal guy's room. It was fixed up like an adult's, which impressed me.

Rick sat on the side of his bed and pulled me towards him. He was just a little bit shorter than me when he sat on his bed. I walked up to him grudgingly. I didn't want us to just kiss and make up without talking about what happened. He reached his large hand up to my cheek and gently traced the curve of my face. I wanted to feel the things that Kevin could make me feel, and yet I still couldn't with Rick. I didn't understand it. I didn't know *why* I couldn't feel for him what I could so easily feel for Kevin. Rick was every bit as gentle and loving as the boy who won my heart when I was only 12 years old. Sometimes he was even more so. I felt odd thinking about Kevin and tried to focus as Rick spoke.

"DeLaine, I'm so sorry! I *never* meant to hit you in the mouth! I wouldn't hurt you on purpose for *anything* in the world! I'm sorry that I didn't take care of you on New Year's Eve. I shouldn't have gotten that drunk. I was acting stupid. Please don't break up with me. You have no idea how much I love you," he concluded softly.

I gently swept a lock of hair off of his forehead. I smiled at the dampness. I looked into the beautiful, glowing green of Rick's eyes and saw so much kindness and warmth. I knew that I could do a lot worse and that he *really* seemed to love me. I hoped that eventually someday I would love him just as much. I leaned down and kissed him gently and told him I wasn't going to break up with him. He seemed so relieved. I couldn't understand what in the world he could possibly see in me. I wished that I could understand it.

Things went back to the way they had been for another couple of weeks until our next argument. That one began because Rick told me I needed to tell my mom that I smoked. I told him that he didn't understand a lot of things about my mom. I hadn't told him everything about my mom or what I'd gone through with her. I still hadn't told him much of anything about me or my life before. I didn't want him to know how screwed up I was because I thought that if he knew, then he might not want me any longer.

When he began to tell me I had to tell my mom about my smoking, I got angry at him for telling me what to do. He told me that he was giving me until that Sunday and then he was telling her if I didn't. I was so angry that he would try to control anything about me or my life. I had been controlled by Geoffrey and Clarice for so many years that having someone else try to do it angered me.

I told my mom I smoked that Saturday afternoon. She wasn't really surprised. She said that she wasn't angry with me and it was no big deal. I didn't tell her I'd been smoking since before she caught me smoking at the game room, way back my freshman year of high school. After I talked to her I went into my room and picked up the phone and dialed Rick's number. When he got on the phone I growled, "She knows. You can call her if you want. I don't give a shit, but don't *ever* threaten to do something like that again," then I hung up the phone.

We began to bicker and makeup more than we seemed to get along. I was sad most of the time which seemed so stupid to me. I should have been ecstatic since my mom wasn't drinking, and I had a boyfriend. Instead, I was more miserable it seemed than I'd been in a long time. I wasn't drinking either. I wasn't getting stoned anymore. I was keeping my nose clean all the way around, but I was just so unhappy. The only time I was happy was when I was at school. I was so excited to go to school every day that I usually left early just so I could get out of my house.

By the end of the month, when the auditions were held for the Spring production, I was so excited I couldn't see straight! Mr. Magnus had decided on a play that had been made into a movie a couple of years before. I just *knew* that Pete would get the lead role! I didn't know if I'd get a role or not because there were only *three* female parts. One wasn't very big, and one was the part of the mother of the lead character. She was a real bitch. I thought I had it down playing a bitch! The only other part was that of a teenage girl, and I thought it was funny because *that* was the one role I didn't want to play. It was the one that I truly had *no clue* about playing. I had no clue how to be a happy, teenage girl. I didn't know how to have hopes and dreams like most teen girls. I was beginning to think that there were no hopes and dreams for me. Just unhappiness and pain seemed to be what I had to look forward to. I felt sad when I realized that.

After the auditions, Mr. Magnus came around to my English class once again, and pulled me out of class. I knew that he couldn't possibly be coming to change my schedule again, so I was curious what he wanted to discuss this time. I was shocked when he asked me which role I liked the best. I told him that of course I liked the mother's role the most. It was a meatier role and she was a strong character. I liked that. She could be all the things I wanted to be, but didn't know how in my own life. He asked if I was worried I'd be typecast into only being able to play that type of role. I had to think about that question.

The next morning when I got to school, I rushed up to the bulletin boards to find the cast list. I knew I'd find Pete's name at the top, so when I saw another name my mouth fell open. I couldn't believe that Pete's name wasn't listed as the lead. Instead it was a boy named Mattie Maldonado. I saw Pete's name as one of the supporting characters, but not as a *lead.* I couldn't believe that Magnus would do that to him. I read further down the list and saw that the mother's part had gone to Mary. I felt a huge wave of disappointment wash over me because I had really wanted the part. Then I remembered how much Mary had wanted the role I'd won in the Fall production, and decided that maybe it was fair. I wondered then if it meant I was the next stage manager, so when I got to the 5th character and saw my name I was surprised. The part of the teenaged girl had been given to me.

The one part I *didn't* know how to play was the one I'd been given. I went down to Magnus's classroom and found him sitting at his desk grading papers. When he saw me in the doorway he waved me inside. "DeLaine, I trust you found the cast list on the bulletin board?" he asked me pleasantly.

"Um, yeah, that's why I'm here. I'm not sure I'm right to play the teenaged girl. I mean, I know I'm one, but, Magnus, I'm not sure if I know *how* to play one." I responded, shyly.

Looking at me curiously through the thick lenses of his glasses he smiled, "Why DeLaine, *of course* you know how to play her."

I looked down at my feet and shuffled them a little before I replied, quietly, "No, you don't understand, Mr. Magnus. I'm not as good of a person as the girl in the play is."

Mr. Magnus's gaze was intent upon me, but I was too embarrassed to look at him. Finally, after several seconds I looked up at him and his face began to slowly break into a beatific smile. "My darling DeLaine, you are just as nice of a teenage girl as the character in the play. I think that you might actually be *nicer* than she is. See, I can say that because while the play allows us to think that we know the character, in all reality I don't know *her*. But *you,* I do know. If you are unsure how to play her, then she is the perfect role for you my dear. As an actor, you should play roles that leave you a little uncomfortable. You should always do someone who will stretch you as a person and make you delve deep within to understand their character. If you do this role, I think you might find you have more in common with her than you realize. And if you don't, then it might do you some good to really reach deep down and figure out how to be a teenager every once in a while. You might be surprised."

Nodding my head I lowered it again and as I was walking out of his room I stopped and turned back around and asked him before I lost my nerve. "So, in the play it says my character and the main character kiss a couple of times. You're not *really* going to make me kiss a guy are you?"

Big booming laughter came out of his throat from deep within. He smiled at me warmly. "Well DeLaine, tell me, what do you think I'm going to say to that?"

I shrugged my shoulder up, "Probably that there is no reason that we would need to change that part of the play. If it is written that way, then that is the way you are going to have us perform it."

Mr. Magnus smiled at me and nodded his head. He told me he would see me later in the day and before I walked all the way out I turned one more time, "Why didn't Pete get the lead?"

My teacher looked at me curiously, "Because I thought that Mattie would be more believable as a tortured, young man. Pete is too arrogant and brash. I don't know that he can show the depth that Mattie will be able to."

"Pete's the *best* actor in this whole school though," I whispered, horrified.

Smiling at me Mr. Magnus slowly shook his head. "No my dear, that is where you are wrong. He is an exceptionally talented young man. I agree with that, and I've enjoyed working with him all these years. I have another student who is by far above and beyond more in just raw talent alone. That person has no clue they are, which makes them even more talented in my opinion. I think that it is time for Pete to let someone else have an opportunity to shine a little bit."

Nodding, I waved silently at Mr. Magnus and ambled back towards the bulletin boards. I saw Pete standing up there and could see the displeasure spreading across his face. I felt awful for him. I thought he would have done a great job at the lead. I wondered why Mr. Magnus didn't think he was talented enough to find the depth of the lead character. I thought Mattie Maldonado had done an okay job, but I sure didn't think that he was *that* great. I turned off before getting to the bulletin boards. I didn't want to be face to face with Pete. I felt awful for him but I didn't want to make him uncomfortable. I still had to figure out how I was going to explain to Rick that I was going to have to kiss another boy on stage.

The days after the posting of the cast for the play were fraught with Pete and Mr. Magnus's struggle over Pete feeling snubbed at not getting the lead in the last play of his high school career. By the end of the week, Pete had transferred out of Theater Arts and Mattie had transferred in. I was sad to lose Pete from our class. He was the one who made me feel so good when I was in Mr. Magnus's room.

Rick was also upset over the play. I told him about getting the part of the teenaged girl and he seemed happy until I told him about the scenes where I would have to kiss Mattie Maldonado. His face seemed to cloud up when I told him about that. I was uncertain how to deal with his unhappiness. I didn't want to quit the play because my boyfriend was upset, even though I was nervous about having to kiss a boy on a stage. I wasn't about to quit doing something that I had found made me so happy. Being in the play in the fall made me realize I was sad I wouldn't be in more plays. I wished I'd found theater my freshman year, but since I hadn't, I wanted to make the most of the two school years I had.

The weekend after finding out I was about to start the grueling hours of rehearsals, Rick took me out to a fancy dinner. I was surprised when he told me to get dressed up for our date that Saturday night. When I asked why, he smiled mysteriously and told me he wanted to take me somewhere *special*. He told me to wear a dress and heels. I thought about my black dress and gray heels but chose another ensemble, even though the black dress was my best one.

When we pulled up in front of the restaurant, I was shocked. It was one of the most expensive ones in Corpus Christi, down on the bay front. Rick came around and helped me out of the truck and we walked into the quiet, dimly lit restaurant. I still didn't understand what the big deal was, but Rick kept telling me I was going to be happy when the night was over.

We sat there and Rick ordered for me. I was a little surprised because I wasn't sure if I'd like what he'd ordered. He also ordered a bottle of wine. The waiter brought two wineglasses which surprised me at first. Then I remembered I didn't look 17 and Rick certainly looked well over 20. Rick took the bottle and poured wine into the glass sitting in front of me. "I don't really like wine, Rick," I stated quietly.

"Just *try* it tonight. You might like it. You never know," he insisted, winking.

"No, I DO KNOW! That's why I said that," I replied tightly, trying not to get upset. I knew that he was trying to do something sweet, but I was feeling constrained by him constantly telling me what he wanted me to do, or just assuming I was going to act a certain way because he said to.

Rick smiled and picked up his wineglass. I noticed that he mercifully didn't put as much in my goblet. Holding the fragile stemmed glass in the air slightly, Rick declared, "*Happy Anniversary!*"

I looked at him with my brows furrowed slightly. I wasn't sure what to do. What did he mean anniversary? "Um, *anniversary*?" I asked.

Nodding his head he said, "Yeah! I fell in love with you three months ago."

"*What*?" I heard myself squawk.

"Three months ago I fell into your car and fell in love with you," Rick was still smiling.

I groaned inwardly hoping the sound didn't reach out into the air. I hadn't even paid attention to how long we'd been seeing each other. "Um, three months? Are we supposed to celebrate an anniversary already?" I asked quietly.

"We can celebrate our anniversary every day, week or month if you want. I'm so happy I saw you that night at Circle K. I don't know how I would have lived my life without loving you, DeLaine," Rick declared earnestly.

"Um, okay," I replied, uncertainly. I still had not told him I loved him. I enjoyed our time together. I enjoyed the few times we'd made out, even if it had been a lot more chaste than I ever had been with someone I was involved with seriously.

"DeLaine, I want you to *marry* me," Rick explained, quietly.

I choked on the wine I had just tried to sip. "*What*?" I sputtered.

"I have a good job. I want you to *quit school* and *marry me*," Rick stated seriously.

"*Quit school*?" I squawked. "Rick, I'm *not* quitting school!" I noticed the fallen look cross his face. "I mean *maybe* one day we will get married, but I'm not quitting school! It's important to me! My mom didn't graduate! I promised her a long time ago that I would. I want to go to college!"

I watched as my boyfriend looked into the wineglass he had so happily raised only moments earlier and finally noted, "You can still go to school and be married. I know someone who did that."

"*Are you serious*? I'm only 17! I'm not even *legal*!" I croaked, still unbelieving that I was having this conversation.

"Yeah, but you can get married at 17. My mom did," Rick grumbled, now beginning to sound just a little sullen.

"That was a completely different *time* than now! This is the *'80's* Rick! Nobody gets married at 17 just because they *want* to. Usually it is because someone is pregnant! I'm not pregnant Rick!" I said trying to calm myself.

"I hope you aren't," Rick sniffed. "That isn't the *only* reason to get married you know!"

I rolled my eyes. "Rick, I know that people get married for other reasons, but not when they are 17! I'm just a junior in high school! I am not quitting school. I'm sorry, but I'm not quitting school for *anybody*!"

"I just told you that you could still go to school and be married," Rick retorted.

I sighed deeply. "Rick, I'm *not* getting married right now. I'm sorry. I don't want to hurt your feelings, but I'm just not doing it." I looked at the cloth napkin in my lap. I felt horribly uncomfortable now. "Will you take me home; I don't really feel like eating now?" As soon as I said that though the food came out and Rick looked at me as if he didn't know what to say. "Never mind," I whispered and began to pick at the food on the plate. We ate silently and when I couldn't pick my plate over any more Rick got the check and we left.

When he pulled into my driveway he put the truck in park and scooted towards me on the seat. Taking me into his arms quickly he drew me to him and kissed me passionately. I was surprised. "DeLaine, I know you think that we shouldn't be married right now, but I want you to marry me. Will you? Not right now, but soon!"

I looked at Rick unsure what I needed to say. Finally, I whispered, "Rick, I need to go in. I'll talk to you later." I slipped out quickly and went into the house. I realized I couldn't stay with him if he insisted on me marrying him. He seemed to be so insistent that we get married, I didn't understand it. My mom was surprised when she saw me home so early. I didn't want to talk to her about what had happened so I walked by her and told her I wasn't feeling very good, so I came home early. She of course wanted to know if she needed to do something for me. I shook my head.

The next day Rick called me and asked if I wanted to come over and hang out. I really didn't, but I didn't know what to tell him in order to get out of it. When I got there we went into his room. He wanted to hang out alone. I felt a little odd since we'd never been extremely physical. He had his TV on and was watching a movie on HBO. For the first time ever, I lay down beside him and nestled into his embrace. I felt a little strange at first. I was glad when things finally seemed to relax and the awkwardness from the night before finally dissipated.

When the movie ended, Rick began speaking softly, "Look, I thought that you would be happy that I asked you to get married. I guess I thought girls wanted that."

"I *do* want to get married one day, Rick, but not right now. I want to graduate from high school. It's important to me." I stated quietly.

"I just thought maybe if you agreed to marry me, and became my fiancé, you'd quit that play or at least have Mr. Magnus change it since you were married, or engaged." Rick explained, with a wry grin.

I looked at him and tried to hide my shock. After a few minutes I asked, "Are you kidding me? That's the reason you want to get married? So I don't do that play?"

"No, no, I *want* to marry you! I told you that when I first got to know you that I wanted to marry you some day. I still do. But I have to admit, I'm not real crazy about you being in this play." Rick declared, shrugging one of his shoulders.

I sat up and looked at him still disbelievingly. I couldn't imagine that me doing a stupid stage kiss with a guy would make my boyfriend get so stupid. "Rick, you need to step back a little bit. I'm not quitting school and I'm not quitting the play. I know that you think you love me, but I don't think you do. If you did, you wouldn't ask me to do either of them. You would trust that I'm with you and not out trying to be with anyone else. I don't even party for God's sake. I'm not going to get all stupid over a dumb kiss with a guy I don't even know or like. He's just some guy in a play! That's all!"

Rick sat up too and I knew he was going to try to explain himself to me. I didn't want to hear any more. I stood up and shook my head. I walked over to the chair and grabbed my suede coat my mom had given me for my birthday. My boyfriend stood up and his impressive height and size seemed to swallow the small bedroom. "DeLaine, I'm sorry. I just don't seem to be able to say the right thing."

I sighed deeply. Finally, after a few seconds, I turned around and looked at him. "Rick, this isn't gonna work. I really care about you, but I can't keep doing this. I don't want to be *married* and I don't want someone to tell me what I can and can't do. Telling me to quit the play…look, there's not a lot that I've got in this world that truly makes me happy, but since the fall and the last play I was in, I know that I'm *good* at this and I like it. If you can't trust me, then we need to break up. I'm sorry, but I just can't keep feeling crappy. Lately that is all I feel when I'm around you."

"You don't mean that, DeLaine," Rick whispered sadly. "Valentine's Day is only a couple of weeks away. I want you to give me another chance. Give me until Valentine's Day. I swear we'll work through it.

I thought about it briefly. I hated seeing him look sad, but I also knew that I couldn't keep going like this. I had hoped that I would eventually fall in love with Rick, but knew that I never would. I loved Kevin still. I missed Kevin and wanted him. I didn't want to be serious about Rick. I wanted a real boyfriend, but Rick was almost too serious and too real for me. Finally I replied, "Rick, if I give you until Valentine's day you're going to spend way too much money on me, and I can't be bought. I don't want to hurt you and waiting until Valentine's Day is just prolonging it. I'm sorry. I need to leave." I set his class ring on his dresser, walked out of his room and didn't look back. I didn't want him to see the tears in my eyes and think that he could talk me into staying.

When I got into my car, I drove down the road, pulled over and began to cry. I had hoped that Rick was the answer to everything that Kevin wanted of me for the school year. I knew I didn't just want to screw around with Chance Cahill anymore, but I didn't want to be smothered until I couldn't breathe any longer either. I'd been smothered by Rick since we'd first begun seeing one another. I felt sad that it seemed like I couldn't even have a regular boyfriend in high school. I thought that Rick was my answer to everything. After a few minutes of serious snot and tears, I finally ran my hand across my face trying to wipe it as best as I could.

I went home and found my mom sitting in the living by herself. When she saw me she smiled sympathetically as if she knew that something bad had happened. I walked in and sat on the couch. "You okay, Sugar Bug?" My mom asked me.

I started to nod my head and before I could say I was fine, the tears betrayed me as they began to slide down my cheeks. I looked at my mom heartbroken and unable to speak. I didn't know what exactly to tell her. She was going through her own crap and my stupid stuff was probably not what she needed right now. My mom got up and came over to the couch and held me while I cried my eyes out. I wasn't even that sorry that things had ended with Rick. I knew I wasn't in love with him. I was in love with Kevin. I had always been in love with Kevin. I had tried to make myself feel something that was never there in the first place. I wondered if I could ever love someone besides Kevin.

Rick had been perfect. He'd been sweet, gentle, caring and a handsome guy. He'd been generous and had adored me. I didn't know what else I could hope for. He was everything I ever wanted and yet I didn't feel for him what I wanted to feel. I cried all of this to my mom and she held me and stroked my back as she crooned loving words of support. I was so grateful she no longer drank. I *needed* her so much. I just didn't trust her. I didn't trust *anyone* anymore. I wasn't sure if I even trusted Kevin now. He was the one who had sent me on my way to this fiasco. I was doing everything for *him*. I didn't feel like I was doing anything for myself except for theater. I was so tired of doing everything for everyone else and nothing for myself. I wondered if that would ever change. I felt like I'd done nothing but take care of everyone and made sure everyone else was happy. The only one who was never happy was *me*.

Chapter 10

We began rehearsing and I threw myself into the play with a passion. Mattie Maldonado was nice, but not Pete. When we had to do our first stage kiss, I was grateful that Magnus did that scene with just the two of us the first time. I was nervous and Mattie seemed to realize that. He was really quite a goody two shoes. He was cute, but not someone I would ever be interested in. He was a big Preppy and in with the whole popular crowd. I was still a pretty big *nobody* even though others knew me. I thought that it was entertaining when I really thought about it that I'd been picked to play the pretty and popular teenaged girl in the play. After our first couple of stage kisses, it became a little boring to kiss him. We weren't sticking our tongues down each other's throats, which I was grateful for. It was already great fodder for everyone in school that there was a play that was going to have a kissing scene in it. Thankfully, his girlfriend wasn't threatened by me. She would actually tease me about kissing her boyfriend. She was a hugely talented singer in the choir, so she understood the desire to be on a stage.

As the talk about the play gathered momentum though, the school also knew the news of my break up with Rick. It was through the school before the end of Tuesday, after I'd broken up with him. I was grateful he hadn't sent any more balloons or flowers. He hadn't called me at all either.

I was positive that Mandy Manson had seen the ring missing first and was probably the one who had called him and asked him if we'd broken up. I wondered if he had talked badly about me? She never asked me anything, even though when Rick and I had first met she was all over me with questions. Now she smiled politely in my VOE class, but never talked more than was necessary.

A couple of weeks after I broke up with Rick, I went to Chance and Lonnie's house with Kelly and Robin. I was still pretty depressed. For the first time, in a really long time, I realized I was getting drunk before 11 o'clock. I was surprised when one of the guys in mine and Kelly's class at Woodway came up to me while I sat outside on the hood of my car. His name was Shannon Hanks. He was a really handsome guy who looked much older than he was. He had longish, blonde hair and blue eyes. He wasn't very tall, but he was built nicely. There were a lot of girls who liked him and even Kelly had messed around with him. She'd messed around with several guys by then, and it seemed we all managed to eventually date the same people at some point in the small suburb.

Shannon sat outside with me and we drank beer and smoked cigarettes while the rest of the people were mainly inside the house. He was related to a couple of the guys we knew also, as it seemed happened out there as well, I noticed. If you didn't date or mess around the same people, then you were related to one of the families.

When I got ready to go that night, Shannon kissed me goodnight. I felt warm and happy kissing him. He was so good looking. I didn't feel any pressure to feel anything for him except the basic carnal instincts my teenage body was already feeling all the time. I realized that Rick had been such a gentleman, but to the point where I hadn't really felt *desirable*. At first it was nice to not have someone pawing all over me constantly, but after a while, I wondered why he never tried more than just kissing me. I had begun to think that while I might be okay to date, I must not be the type of girl that a nice guy wanted sexually. I had begun to think that maybe he viewed me as not good enough if he had heard about my history of drinking and making out with guys. Maybe he heard that I'd been one of Chance Cahill's conquests.

Kissing Shannon made me remember how nice it was to feel wanted and desired. I felt strange, but I also felt deeply satisfied knowing that I was okay too. He asked me for my phone number. I wondered if he would really call me or not. He waited until late the following week, but he called me finally. We made plans to see each other again, and I felt excited for the first time in a long time about a boy.

We had less time to prepare our play because we had to also make it ready to take to the One Act Play contest for UIL. I was excited about a lot of things during that time. I hoped that we would do well, not just during the performance, but also at the contest too. I was really nervous about the play because while I had learned the lines and become comfortable with Mattie, he was still no Pete Mulligan. I was missing Pete's infectious energy. Mattie had a strong work ethic, but he was *very* serious. He also told me I couldn't smoke before rehearsals or the play because he didn't want to kiss me if I'd been smoking. I got angry with him about that so I would do it just to spite him right before we began our performances. I sometimes wondered if Pete would even come to see it. He'd told me that he had gotten a role at the playhouse down by the Harbor. Robin and I went to see it.

I went out with Shannon Hanks a few times, but it was never anything serious. I had gone to his house the third time we went out. We went into his room after talking briefly to his parents and before I left he became my next lover. I knew that there was no future with him, but he was like a summer breeze. It was warm and fun and sexy as hell. I realized that Kevin wasn't the only boy who could bring me to orgasm either, which was a wonderful finding.

We did our performance before Spring break so we could begin rehearsals for the One Act Play as soon as we got back. Magnus had already cut the play down and gave us the shortened version to begin learning over our break. On opening night, I was surprised and happy to see Pete Mulligan standing at the edge of the stage with a bouquet of roses. I noticed they were red ones. I remembered briefly the red roses I got on opening night in the fall and then wondered if they had been from him. He didn't wait for normal stage protocol, and give them to me when we were done taking our bows. He let us take our first round of bows and ran out to give them to me and kissed me on the cheek. When we came back out for our second curtain call, I noticed when the house lights came up that Pete was gone. I smelled the red roses and smiled, grateful that he'd come to the play that had broken his heart and ended his high school career as an actor.

During Spring break, I went over to Shannon's house a couple of times and was always so surprised that he had sex with me so easily with both his parents in the house. I was always nervous they would come in, but he laughed and told me that they never came in to his room. I enjoyed our time together and when he asked if I wanted to go in town to a party in his old neighborhood I smiled and agreed. I knew my mom would be mad if she knew that I'd driven into town, but Shannon's car was in the shop, so I would have to drive us. I decided to not tell her where the party was going to be held.

When I picked him up, I was surprised to see that he was already half drunk. I had gotten pretty lit the first night we had kissed, at Chance and Lonnie's, but I hadn't drunk since then. Shannon seldom seemed to drink when I saw him out, so when I figured out that he was already drunk I was surprised. We went into Corpus Christi and he had me going places I'd never been before. I didn't know the neighborhoods so when he had me running all over the place, it didn't take long to get me lost.

I wasn't exactly comfortable at the party we went to, since I didn't know anyone. I was shocked when Shannon came up to me and whispered in my ear, "Let's go! There's another party I wanna go to!" I nodded and got up. We walked down the street to where my car was parked. He gave me directions and we were at another house in no time, that seemed to have teenagers and 20-somethings all over the place. I did notice though that there weren't very many white kids there. They were mainly all Mexican kids. I felt a little strange, because I didn't know if Shannon actually knew these people. He didn't seem to, but he walked in and started drinking like a fish. I stood off to one side hoping that no one got into a fight or the police got called, because if I got caught, I was a little afraid what my mom would do.

While I stood off to one side, watching everyone, I wasn't aware that Shannon had gone into the house. Before I knew it, he was getting pushed out the rickety screen door. I jerked my head to the sound of the screen, and Shannon's yells. I realized he was starting some kind of trouble. I ran up on the porch and told him to get out of there. I looked at the other people and apologized as I pulled an extremely intoxicated Shannon Hanks off the porch, towards the street where my car was parked. I wasn't sure if I was mad or just afraid of Shannon. I decided to take him home and maybe even though I'd had some great sex with him, I should just cut ties and move on. It wasn't like I was *in love* with the guy. I was beginning to realize that I didn't have to love someone to have *sex*. Sex felt just as good with someone you didn't love as it did with someone you did. I was finally beginning to get it! I thought maybe I should feel guilty about feeling like that, since I really shouldn't be having sex *unless* I was in love with someone, but I didn't.

I didn't know how to get back to the highway to get back to our side of town, and was relying on Shannon to give me directions. He had grown up on the South side and hadn't moved to the Annaville area until high school. He had a built in group of friends though with the cousins he had out there. I was hopelessly lost, and he seemed to be taking some kind of twisted pleasure in that fact.

The more I drove though, the more it seemed as if I were driving out of the city limits. Finally, I pulled over on the side of a small country road and told him to tell me how to get back to Annaville. Shannon seemed to leer at me from the dark, "Only after we go someplace I wanna show you out here!" Sighing, I agreed, and he gave me directions until I was driving down a caliche road, in the middle of a big field. The night was so dark that my headlights seemed to slice through it eerily.

As I was getting further down the gravel road, Shannon asked me if I knew that Corpus had Devil worshippers. I looked over at him nervously, and told him I'd heard about them. He smiled and it seemed as if his teeth glowed in the light from my dashboard. "What would you do if I told you I was one?" Shannon asked me, seriously.

I licked my lips nervously and looked straight ahead. "I'd say you're full of shit, and just trying to fuck with my head."

Shannon laughed and then I noticed the whole tone of his voice was changing. It somehow began to take on a deeper tone. "When the devil worshippers are out here they do sacrifices. They've done some human sacrifices, but they aren't done as often as other sacrificial rituals. Most of the time we use animals like goats, but we've had to use cats before too. Goats are preferred because they have cloven hooves."

"Shannon, you've scared me enough, let's get the fuck out of here and go to Annaville," I growled, testily.

He laughed loudly and deeply. "What? We'll miss all of the fun if we do that!"

I began to feel my arms get goose bumps. I suddenly felt extremely terrified. I was afraid of the boy who was sitting next to me. He outweighed me by about 50 pounds and he was bigger and stronger than me. I was afraid I'd made a huge mistake in judgment with this whole night. I wondered how I had done that. I'd usually been a fairly decent judge of character. Shannon hung out with me, Kelly, Robin and all the rest of the kids I hung out with from Woodway. He was well liked, popular and respected, but right then I was feeling *very* afraid.

I slammed on the brakes. "Dammit, Shannon, I'm turning the fucking car around! I'm scared and you are scaring me worse!"

Shannon looked at me and it was like a totally different boy sat next to me. "Oh, c'mon, DeLaine! I'm just messing with you! There aren't any devil worshippers out here, *tonight.*" I felt my shoulders begin to relax. I looked at him seriously and he smiled at me with a big, toothy grin. I began trying to back up and turn around on the narrow gravel road to get out of the field we were in. Shannon began to slide over towards the middle of the seat and even though he seemed like his normal self, there was something screaming in my head that he was a wolf in sheep's clothing. I kept looking at him and thought I was being silly with seeing a cartoonish wolf, with a fake lambskin on, in the middle of a flock of sheep. He was beside me quicker than I realized and he leaned over to kiss me. I kissed him back at first, hoping that I would be able to tell if he was just teasing me.

While Shannon Hanks kissed me in the dark field, inside of my Thunderbird, I was surprised when I felt his large hand begin to grip the back of my neck. Soon the hold he had on me began to hurt and I tried to pull away. He held onto my neck firmly. When I finally bit his tongue to make him let me go, I pulled back to see someone else in my car than the amiable Shannon Hanks from Woodway High School.

The boy sitting beside me looked maniacal in the hard way his eyes glittered as he looked at me, as if I were no more than a bug he was about to step on. "You fuckin' bit me, *you bitch*!" he spat at me.

"You're hurting me," I yelled back angrily.

"I've only *begun* to hurt you," he leered at me. I felt my blood begin to pump furiously in my veins, but the blood didn't feel warm at all. I felt like I'd suddenly developed ice water inside of me. Shannon grabbed the steering wheel with his right hand while his left remained clamped onto my neck. He stuck his left foot over the center hump and stepped onto my foot on the gas and my car rocketed forward towards a grove of trees. As we got closer to it I was screaming at him to stop. He whipped the wheel around and my car threw up gravel and rocks as it fish tailed around a couple of the trees. "*Shut your fuckin' screamin' up!*" the strange boy barked, while holding me in a death grip.

I quit yelling. I tried to bring my left foot up to slam on the brakes. I just knew that Shannon was going to wreck my car with us inside of it. Before I could get my foot all the way over, he moved his foot off of mine and slammed it onto my brakes. The car careened crazily and I saw as the lights threw crazy shadows all over the place, including a gate or fence that had some old animal bones on it. I screamed when I saw them. I began to seriously wonder if I'd ever see my mom again. I thought about Kevin and Bailey and wondered if my last moments in this world were being played out right in front of me.

Once the car was still, he threw the gear shift into park and grabbed the keys out of the ignition. He threw them in the back seat. "In case you get any ideas of leaving before I'm ready, you'll have to work to get to those keys right now."

"Shannon, I don't know what the fuck you are doing, but I'm done with this shit," I shouted, with the most false bravado I could muster. He just laughed at me and crushed his mouth into mine. I didn't want to kiss him, so I fought him at first. Finally, he pulled away from me and told me it would probably be better on me if I just cooperated. I felt myself gulp, "What does that mean?"

"It means, DeLaine, that you are going to do *everything and anything* that I want you to do. If you do, then maybe you won't become the next human sacrifice out here, okay? If not, then I'm afraid you will probably disappear, and no one will ever know what happened to you. You'll drop me off later at my house and I won't know where you went after you left my house. Do you understand *what* exactly I'm saying?"

I felt myself begin to sweat and quietly nodded my head. "*Shannon, please, don't hurt me.*" I pleaded.

"That's all gonna depend on you, DeLaine! If you don't do what I tell you to do, well, I can't promise that you're going to go home to your mom." Shannon's eyes looked like two, bottomless, dead wells in the dark of the night. He bent over me and began to kiss me. When I didn't seem to kiss the way I'd done before, he pulled away from me, demanding, "Dammit! Kiss me like you've been so anxious to do the last few weeks you've been coming to my house and fucking me. Quit acting like you're such a fuckin' *prude* now, DeLaine! I know better! You're just like all the other bitches out there. You can't wait for me to fuck you, until I want to show you something personal about me."

When he began to kiss me again, I felt my body sigh involuntarily as I thought about all the tricks that Magnus had taught me and Mattie when we first began to do our kissing scene. I held my breath and made myself quiet my mind. Finally, I was kissing him back and trying to be as passionate as I'd been when I'd been happy to be making out with him and having sex. I tried to go outside of my body as he slammed me back and when he began to shove me down onto the seat of the Thunderbird. I whimpered as he shoved me into the seat belts, along the the front seat, as if he were breaking my back and maybe even some ribs. He held my neck much the same as Geoffrey had. I felt the tears as they slipped down my cheeks, as I lay back on the leather bench seat.

Shannon was no longer the generous and hot lover he'd been only days before. Now he was greedy and hurtful. He didn't care if he was hurting me or not. I began to cry and it seemed the more I cried, the more he found some perverse pleasure in the soft mewling sounds I was making unconsciously. When what we were doing wasn't providing him with the release he was craving, he pulled me up by my hair and leaned back against the passenger door as he jammed my head into his lap. I knew what he wanted, but I couldn't do it. I began to cry in earnest and he grabbed my hair again and jerked my head up as he leaned his face into mine and hissed, "Either do it, or else I'm going to give you something to cry about. I'm going to get off *with* or *without* your help. Either way, *you* are going to give it to me, one way or another!"

I nodded my head as I tried to do what he wanted. I couldn't calm myself down though and continued crying. I was truly terrified now. I'd been beaten and hurt by Geoffrey badly, but this was worse than anything he'd ever done to me. I honestly was terrified that Shannon was going to kill me and leave my body out there for some weird sect of Devil worshippers. Finally, frustrated with my lack of ability to help him, Shannon grabbed me by my hair and jerked me up and turned me around bringing me to my knees in front of him.

When I realized what he was about to do I began to cry and begged him to stop. I told him I wouldn't tell anyone, but he didn't need to do what he was trying to. The Shannon I knew was no longer inside the body of the person who was hurting me. The being that inhabited that body was something I wasn't familiar with.

After what felt like hours, Shannon was finally done with me. He opened the passenger side door and tumbled out backward and came around to the driver's side. I was trying to gather myself when he jerked the door open and leaned inside. He told me to move over because he was driving us back. He reached into the back seat and grabbed the keys he'd thrown there. I felt bedraggled and as if I'd never quit hurting both emotionally and physically. I scrambled over against the passenger door, as he turned the car on and got behind the wheel. With just a few turns, he had us back out on the back roads to Annaville and I sat in the passenger side of my car with tears streaming down my face.

I wondered what I would tell someone about what just happened. I had not wanted to do what we'd done and had tried to talk him out of it, but since I'd already had sex with him before, I didn't think that I could really cry *rape* if I'd participated in it. I felt like I had no choice in the entire thing except to keep my mouth shut. I knew that once we got back to Annaville I never wanted to see or speak to Shannon again. The more I sat there though I kept trying to figure out if I had *willingly* participated or if I'd really just been raped. I knew that I'd never go to the police like they showed on TV shows. I could never go through all of that. Annaville was much too small for me to ever have a life there again if I did. I knew I'd never get to move back to Wichita Falls until after graduation. There was no sense in even pretending like that would happen before. I didn't want to go back home like that either. I didn't know that I could tell even Bailey about what just happened. Would she think that I deserved it since I'd already screwed around with Shannon? I tried not to sob as I hugged the door all the way to his house.

Shannon drove like a maniac and kept turning the lights off as he sped over 100 miles per hour on the back roads. I stayed down in the passenger seat praying I'd get out alive. Shannon looked at me and laughed, stating he knew he wouldn't die on this night because he'd been promised to live until the age of 36 when he pledged his soul to the devil. I actually believed him. I however had no such knowledge of my time on Earth!

I was over two and a half hours late getting home. I wondered if my mom knew and if she did would I be grounded. I had never been that late before. I'd come in a few minutes after curfew and been terrified she'd wake up. Now I was almost three hours late. Was my my mom sitting there freaking out? Had she called the cops? When they saw me would they know? I kept having all of these things run through my mind, as I sat in the passenger seat feeling dirty, numb and disgusted. Shannon pulled up in front of his house. I got out to walk to the driver's side. He stopped in front of me briefly and grinned at me evilly. I couldn't believe he was behaving this way.

"G'night DeLaine! Hope you had a good time, *I know I did*," Shannon leered at me again.

I felt goose bumps prickle on my arms and I hurried away from him like a scared, little puppy. I slid into the seat gingerly, feeling every bruise that he'd inflicted on my body. I felt everything below my waist screaming out in protest at being abused the way it had been. I wanted someone to talk to. I wanted to tell someone something. I hurried home and prayed there were no cops and no freaked out mom waiting on me. Thankfully when I opened the door from the garage, I was met with a quiet, dark house. I tiptoed down the hall and went into the safety of my room. I threw my purse onto my bed and grabbed clean clothes out of my dresser. Immediately I went into the blue tiled bathroom and ran the hottest bath I could.

As I lowered myself into the tub, I tried not to cry out, feeling the scalding hot water on my skin. I hurt and burned in places in the lower part of my body that I didn't even want to think about. The water just added insult to injury, but I felt it would be the only way to feel clean. I felt nasty. I felt myself shaking from the inside out. I thought about the weird way Shannon had begun talking about the devil worshippers and how he alluded that he *was* one. He talked about things I'd never heard anyone talk about before and I prayed that God would just keep me from having a demon child. I also worried that the way he had manhandled me would show up as bruises I wouldn't be able to explain.

I held my face in my now wrinkled hands and cried softly. I didn't know how this whole thing couldn't be my fault. I'd had sex with Shannon in the past. I'd gone out with him on a date, fully anticipating having enjoyable sex again. I surely *must* be at fault, I thought. He must have thought that he could do whatever he wanted to with me since I'd been so easy before. I sat in the water replaying everything for a long time. It was only when my shaking turned from terror to being cold that I realized I'd been in there for too long. I pulled the drain and hoped Mama wouldn't wake up hearing it gurgle down the pipes.

After I dried my body and inspected myself as best as I could, I could see that I had more bruises on my body than Geoffrey had *ever* given me in one beating. I was black and blue from my shoulders all the way to my legs. I only had a couple of small bruises on my arms which I was grateful for. I could hide everything else with clothes, but my arms weren't going to be hidden as easily. I felt a bruise even on my tailbone. I was truly tender both inside and outside physically. I slipped my night shirt on and shoved my towel into the hamper. I still wiped tears off of my cheeks every once in a while throughout all of my ministrations to my drying off and dressing. When I got into my room I closed the door gently and slipped into my safe and warm bed. I pulled my Velveteen Rabbit that Kevin had given me and held him tightly, as I cried myself to sleep.

The next morning my mom asked if I'd taken a bath during the night. I told her that I had woke up from a really bad dream and couldn't go back to sleep so I got up and took a warm bath hoping it would help. She smiled at me lovingly. I marveled at how quickly and fluidly I lied to her without batting my eyes even a tiny bit. She noticed I was walking slowly and asked if I was okay. I was glad that it had begun raining that morning because I could blame the rain. I told her that the knee I banged up in the wreck, along with my neck and shoulder were aching. It wasn't an unusual occurrence since it had happened several times since our wreck, during my sophomore year. My mom thought I was just getting arthritis early because of it. I didn't know, but it was another great lie to use instead of actually telling her the truth.

Shannon never called me again. The next time I went to see Kelly and Robin they were teasing me about him. I told them I never wanted to talk to him or see him again. When they asked me why I decided to try the truth to see how they responded. "Because he *raped* me," I replied, vehemently.

Kelly started laughing, "You can't rape the *willing* dumbass! You know you *wanted to."*

I stared at my best friend, shocked that she said that. Finally, I realized that they both knew I'd already had sex with him. Of course if they thought that, then no one would ever believe he'd really raped me. I was right in telling myself that it was really *my* fault, I thought. I sighed and told them he tried to make me do stuff I didn't want to do and we got into a fight. I wasn't seeing him anymore. For some reason they both thought it was funny, and teased me about it. They had no way to know that their words were like sharp barbs every time they said something. I was glad they finally changed the subject. I held true to my word in not ever going around Shannon again, willingly.

He was actually good friends with Kelly and Robin and their mom thought he hung the moon. I went over to their house a couple of weeks afterwards and he was sitting in the living room. I felt myself stiffen immediately, as I saw him sitting in their home. I wanted to burst out crying, but instead I told them that I realized I had to go take care of something. I hurried out of the house. Robin ran after me and caught up to me at my car.

"DeLaine! Wait a minute! Are you okay?" she asked me.

I already had tears escaping when I hurried down their front stairs. I felt myself wipe my cheeks quickly and turned to smile at her. I hoped it was a decent smile and was believable. From the expression on her face, I realized I was failing miserably at looking *fine*. "Yeah, I'm fine! I um, I just didn't know you guys had him over here. I *can't* be around him Robin," I finished in a whisper.

"It's cool. I mean, I understand. I mean, okay, I *don't really* understand, because what you said he did, I just can't believe Shannon would ever do. I believe that something happened between ya'll and you don't wanna see him again though. It's cool. I hope you aren't telling anyone besides me and Kel that he *raped* you. I mean, *no* one else in Annaville is gonna believe that shit. He'd *never* do it, ya know." Robin responded, quietly.

I looked at her. I knew that she believed what she was saying. She wasn't trying to be mean to me. I numbly nodded my head. "I gotta go Rob…see ya later!" I slid inside my car, where Shannon had *indeed* raped me, in a remote and frightening place. I smiled grimly as I pulled out of their driveway and went home. I hoped that I wasn't going to keep running into him or else I was going to quit going out.

Chapter 11

Thankfully I still had the play going on. Now we were working hard to get it ready to take it to the District UIL meet. I was shocked when we won first place. We got home late that night and all of us were extremely pumped at our win. I didn't know until we went to the contest that if we won at District we would get to go to Regionals, and if we won there, we'd go to State. All I knew was it meant I got to keep on going to rehearsals. That kept me out of the house and kept me involved with something at school, so I didn't have to think about how miserable I still was inside. I felt stupid for that too because everything I wanted was happening. My mom wasn't drinking, school was going okay. I even had a couple of girls I considered friends now besides Tina Murphy at Calvin. I was doing good with my grades as well. My life was looking better, but for some reason I was horribly depressed and messed up.

When we lost at Regionals a couple of weeks later, I felt completely crushed. That weekend found me drunk once again at Chance and Lonnie's. I didn't know what else to do. I was angry at myself for drinking, but I was so tired of *feeling*. I just wanted to be numb for a little while. I knew I couldn't get away from all the things that were making me miserable.

I still woke up in a sweat sometimes from dreams that Shannon had me out at the Devil worshipping grounds, and this time there was no doubt in my mind that he raped me. I wanted to be with Kevin. I wondered if he would *know*. I wondered if anyone could tell, by having sex with me, about Shannon. I knew that there was only one way to find out for sure.

It took little for me to entice Chance into his dark bedroom. He was surprised at first. Since we'd last kissed when he was living in the apartment with Lonnie, before I began dating Rick, we'd only been friends. He acted strange sometimes when I brought up Rick before, but since I'd broken up with him, Chance had been flirty a lot more lately. I got another beer into me and went into the house and began to play quarters. Before long, I was sitting on Chance's leg. I was surprised since he normally didn't like to show personal attention to me, even though I noticed he seemed to give it to Kelly easily. After about 20 minutes of playing quarters, Chance reached up to whisper in my ear. When I smiled at his question, I saw the toothpaste commercial smile light up his face. After about two more minutes, I quietly got up and went to his bedroom.

I was surprised that kissing him still affected me the way it did. I still lit up like a Christmas tree. It was almost like being a silly and stupid freshman again, even though I was nearing the end of my junior year of high school. I'd grown up a lot since then. I wondered if he could make me orgasm too while I
was hungrily kissing him helping him to undress me. I thought I must now surely be a whore because I'd been with too many boys sexually and had orgasmed with *two* of them. I figured I couldn't be any worse of a person than I already was, and at least Chance was just someone I was *revisiting.* I had no doubt that I had been asking for Shannon to do what he did. I must have given off some kind of weird vibe that I *wanted* that, even though I truly hadn't. Now here I was about to have sex again just to see if a boy could tell that Shannon had hurt me horribly. I had to know though if Chance could tell.

Happily I found out that Kevin and Shannon didn't own the corner on orgasms and the more I did it, the more I was realizing how my body responded to certain things. It was strange to feel myself waking up to my body. I wondered if it was normal that I could have sex with someone again after what Shannon had done to me. Chance was someone I knew already, quite intimately, so I thought maybe that was why I had a level of comfort being with him. I wished that he would hold me afterwards. I wanted to be held so badly. I didn't realize that I was missing that more than anything. Rick had been good about holding me. He'd never tried to have sex with me, but he comforted me in other ways. Right now I was missing that.

After we were done, I stood up to slip my jeans back on. While I was finishing dressing and was buttoning my blouse, Chance whispered, "Um, you know, let me leave first and then you come out a few minutes later so no one knows we were in here, you know?" I felt my fingers freeze on my buttons. Once again Chance wanted to play the whole no one knows what we are doing game. I realized I didn't want him to start all of that over with me.

"Um, you know Chance, about that, I'm gonna go out through the window if it's all the same with you," I replied, nonchalantly.

"*What*?" Chance asked as he jerked his head up to look at me in the dark room.

"Well, you know, I don't really want everybody knowing I just fucked you, so I figured I'd just go out the window. That way neither one of us has to walk out of here feeling *ashamed*, you know?" I retorted, as I shrugged my shoulders up. I was hurt, but I wanted to hurt him too. I knew that to get angry with him wouldn't bother him, but if I was embarrassed by being with him, I hoped that maybe he might feel a little bit of how he had made me feel more times than I wanted to count.

"Uh, okay, I guess?" Chance replied, looking at me curiously. "You sure you wanna do that? I mean we can just go out at different times."

Shaking my head I insisted, "Oh no, they'll still figure it out. You know you're a nice guy and all, but I can't just be seen with just anybody now, so I'll just hop out of here." I bent over the open window in his room and pushed the wooden window frame up so the opening was a little larger. It was still cool, but not cold in the evenings. The grass and dirt outside of his room smelled damp and earthy. I slipped one of my legs out the opening and sat on the windowsill. I smiled up at a shocked Chance I grabbed his shirt and pulled him to my face. I planted a huge kiss on his mouth, and before he was done I pulled away and smiled at him. I was so sick of always being the one on the receiving end of being crapped on by guys, so I cut him off, and finished climbing out of the window.

Once I was completely outside, I saw Chance's round face as he bent over to look out at me. The moon light cast a silver blue light on his face. I looked up into the smiling eyes that were beginning to get some of their good humor back after being completely thrown for a loop by me. I told him I'd see him later. "You gonna be alright, DeLaine?" Chance asked me, looking a little concerned.

I smiled up at him, "Yeah, I am, Chance. *I really am.* See ya!" I walked quietly around the house to where all the cars were parked and I slid into mine. I started it up and drove away. I chuckled all the way home, and thankfully had sobered up a little. I didn't feel too dangerous driving myself. I couldn't believe I'd just done that with Chance, but I also knew that I was done being hidden or treated like shit. I had had a really sweet boyfriend, but he was extremely old fashioned and wanted to control me. He wanted me to marry him and be his little woman. Chance was always using me in one way or another, even when he didn't mean to, but he didn't know how *not* to do that. Shannon had hurt me so much. I still didn't want to think about it all. When I did, it quickly darkened my mood. I just knew that from now on I wanted a guy who would be like Kevin. I wanted someone who would cherish me and love me, and who wouldn't be afraid to show it to the world. *I wanted to matter*. I was never going to matter to Chance, except maybe as a friend. It did feel good getting him back in some ways by acting like he'd always done with me.

I knew that I didn't want to be with Rick again. He'd completely dropped out of sight for the most part. I still heard about him every now and again, but he seemed to avoid anywhere he thought he might see me. I figured he was also over four years older. Maybe he realized that he needed to be hanging out with people his own age, instead of teenagers.

When I got home I was happy that I had realized I had to move forward. Shannon would always have control over me if I didn't move forward. He had made me do *unspeakable* things and he'd hurt me so badly, physically, that even weeks later I still had some last remnants of fading bruises from that night. I'd been so lucky to keep them all hidden. I didn't know how I was going to change things, but I knew that there wasn't much more time left for the school year. I was going to get to go to Wichita Falls! I couldn't wait.

Chapter 12

The rest of the school semester was full of the usual end of year stuff. I had to write my first term paper and was freaked out by it and ended up staying up until 4 a.m. the night before it was due, retyping it over and over. I helped design the program for the UIL banquet that my mom and I went to. I received awards for the One Act Play and even got a special award from some of the teachers for all the artwork I was always doing for the various organizations. I was excited to be at something where I was actually receiving awards and my mom was there and sober. We both got dressed up and I had such a good time.

I went to the Woodway graduation and afterwards I went to a field party for Scotty Cahill, who graduated. I only nursed a beer all night and was thinking about driving up to the Sonic and getting a coke. When I was about to leave, Scotty grabbed my arm and drew me in for a big hug. He was drunk, but he wasn't a belligerent drunk. "DeLaine! I'm so happy you came to my party! Can you believe we graduated?" Scotty exclaimed loudly into my ear.

Laughing, I pulled away and looked into his face that was illuminated by the car lights that were on in the field. "Scotty, I didn't graduate, remember?"

"Oh yeah! Boy, I'm a little drunk! Could you tell?" Scotty grinned sheepishly.

"Yes, dear Scotty. I can tell! I hope you aren't driving," I worried like a mama hen. Scotty shook his head as he pulled me in for another hug.

I was afraid he was going to pass out on my shoulder, but he roused himself and stood up straight as he held me out with his hands clasped around my waist. "DeLaine, I just want you to know I love you. You've been the best friend to me that I've ever had." I smiled at him. He was such a sweet guy. I'd always wished I could've cared for him like I had his stupid brother. "Don't ever lose touch with me, okay?"

"Scotty, you'll always know where to find me," I reassured him.

He leaned down and kissed my cheek. "You know you are still the most bad ass girl I know. Don't think I didn't hear what you did after Sara Barker screwed me over that night. You've always had my back. You're even more bad ass than Rizzo!" Scotty exclaimed as he pulled me in for one more tight hug. "You'll always be my best friend, DeLaine!"

I smiled up at Scotty and kissed his cheek in return. "I love you too, Scott. I always will. Congrats on graduation. Next year it is my turn!" After I finished, he gave me one more lopsided grin and walked away to begin drinking more beer and I'm sure he would sleep in his truck in the field. I was glad it was not going to be me. I'd be safe and snug in my own bed long before he passed out.

I left after my encounter with Scotty Cahill to go to Sonic like I'd already been thinking. After getting my coke, I was bored and decided to drive around a little before going home. As I was driving down Leonard I saw some kids I knew from Calvin hanging out at the carwash. I turned around and pulled in. I saw a boy who called me "Delicious." It was a silly nickname that Kelly had come up with way back in our freshman year. Someone started calling her *Kinky Kelly.* I had almost beaten the crap out of several people for calling me that, but I had given Randy a pass on calling me that the year before, because he'd grown on me. He was one of the crazy boys who was always out partying with us. He was graduating from Calvin the next night and was friends with Rick. He had never called me that around Rick though, which I always thought was funny.

"*Hey DELICIOUS!*" Randy hollered when he saw me pull up into the car wash.

I smiled at him. Randy was sweet, but not anyone I would ever be interested in. He just wasn't my type. I saw a bunch of

Calvin kids hanging out. Mostly it was a bunch of the kicker boys who were about to graduate. "Hey Randy! What's up?" I asked amiably.

"Just kickin' back and drinkin' some beer! Sonic's closed and we're saving up our crazy partyin' for tomorrow night!" Randy crowed, grinning.

I nodded and looked around to see who all was out with him. I saw a boy named Mike Bohannon who was also graduating from Calvin. He had actually knocked me down one day when he had been running through the halls with his buddy, Robby Hart. He probably didn't remember it because he'd only given me a cursory glance to make sure I didn't have a broken neck or something, then was up and running again. Robby Hart of course was there too. I turned back to Randy and we started chatting. He offered me a beer, but I held up my coke. He probably thought I was drinking hard liquor. I didn't care as long as I didn't have to nurse another beer.

Mike Bohannon eventually came over, "So, Randy, why don't you introduce me?"

"Don't you know Delicious?" Randy asked, chuckling.

"Dammit, Randy! *Stop*! You're gonna lose the right to call me that if you don't knock it off!" I growled.

Randy started laughing and patted me on the shoulder, "Nah, man, this is DeLaine Reynolds. She goes to Calvin dude, don't you know her?"

Mike Bohannon shook his head. "I think I'd remember someone named *Delicious*!"

I glared at the blonde, blue eyed cowboy standing in front of me. "It's *DeLaine*! That stupid *'Delicious'* thing is something from my freshman year. I don't like people calling me that anymore. I didn't like 'em calling me that back then. That's why Randy's the *only one* I let get away with it!"

Mike smiled at me. "*DeLaine* it is then. It's nice to meet you."

"Yeah, you too," I was smiling. I looked at Mike Bohannon's eyes and thought of Kevin immediately. They weren't the exact shade of blue, but they were close to summer sky blue. I felt myself begin to blush without any warning.

Mike smiled at me, "So, what are you thinking about, DeLaine? You are awfully pink."

"Oh, I'm, um, it's nothing. You remind me of someone I know from my old home town that's all." I replied.

Again those blue eyes sparkled in the lights from the car wash, "Well, I sure hope it's someone you *like*."

"Oh yeah, *a lot*," I responded before I really thought. Again I felt the blush as it began to deepen. "I mean, yes, it's someone I grew up with. One of my closest, um, friends I guess." I looked down feeling silly and a little embarrassed as I tried to explain to this Calvin kicker why I was blushing. I looked up a little bashfully at Mike Bohannon. I realized he was still looking intently at me and smiling.

"Well, maybe someday I can be *that good* of a friend that you'd blush when you think of me," he stated teasingly.

I looked up at him meeting his gaze directly and asked boldly, "Why Mike Bohannon are you *flirting* with me?"

Mike chuckled softly and tilted his head as he looked down at me. "Maybe I am, DeLaine Reynolds. Would you be upset if I was?"

Looking at him steadily I shook my head, "I don't expect I'd be *too* upset."

"Well, that's good to know. So how come I don't know you?" Mike asked me as he scooted onto the hood of my car.

Smiling at him I told him, "Well you did knock me on my ass in the hall at the first of the year, but you were too busy chasing Robby to pay too much attention to me."

Mike looked over at Robby Hart who was extremely drunk. "What the fuck Rob, you let me run over this girl and didn't stop me so I could see how pretty she is?" Robby glanced over at us bleary eyed and shrugged his shoulders. Mike looked back to me, "I *really* knocked you down? You mean like all the way to the ground? You sure it was *me*? I mean, I would think I'd have stopped and tried to meet you."

I shook my head. "Nope, you did not and yes, I'm *extremely* sure it was you. I pay attention to blonde headed cowboys." I felt the blush creeping back.

"Oh you do, huh?" Mike asked me smirking.

I scooted onto the hood of my Thunderbird and nodded my head. "Yeah, you know, 'cause I like cowboys and especially if they are blondes! You know that whole dumb blonde theory and all."

Mike cocked his head to the side as he looked over at me. "What blonde theory is that?"

I started giggling because I really didn't know what the hell I was trying to say, but he didn't know that. "Oh, you know…"

"No, tell me." He persisted.

I shook my head, "Nah, if you don't know the *blonde theory* then it will probably be wasted on you."

"You're funny, DeLaine Reynolds!" Mike spoke amiably. He leaned over and whispered where only I would hear him, "And even if I can't call you *Delicious*, I must say, that's a *great* name for you too!" I blushed furiously then.

Even though I had stopped because I saw Randy McAlister, I spent the rest of the night sitting on my car talking to Mike Bohannon. I kept looking at his eyes and thinking about Kevin. I wished they *were* Kevin's eyes, but Mike wasn't too bad to pass some time with on a late spring night. I had worked hard to put behind me the whole thing with Shannon Hanks. I just wanted to move forward and forget him. I wanted to enjoy my life. I wanted to find my old sarcastic self. I wanted to get through the next few weeks and get to *Wichita Falls*. I knew I wasn't going to fall in love with Mike Bohannon, but he was fun to flirt with.

When I got ready to leave, Mike asked me if he could have my phone number. I smiled at him and told him that I didn't know if he kept a little black book to collect girls' phone numbers, so he should just give me his. I'd call him. He smiled, "How do I know *you* don't have a little black book too?"

I laughed and hopped off my car and bent through the driver's side window. I grabbed my purse and extracted a tiny address book that was in fact black. I only had a couple of addresses and phone numbers in it and most of them were my girlfriends' numbers and addresses. I had Kevin and Jax in there as well as Levi, but no other boys from Annaville. I came back over to Mike with the tiny three inch tall book and showed it to him. He began to laugh heartily. He plucked it from my fingers and began to look through it. "So, when you go out with a guy do you put stars by their names? Like a grading system on how well they kiss or whatever else?" he wiggled his eyebrows at me.

I rolled my eyes at him, "You know it buddy! I mean, I only have about 35 different guys listed in there…go ahead and look!"

Mike looked through each page in the tiny book, "Unless you have them written in invisible ink I only saw two guys in there and a few girls' names."

I laughed at him and shook my head. "Well you missed one guy completely then 'cause there are *three*. The rest are my friends here and in Wichita Falls where I grew up."

"Really?" Mike began thumbing through the tiny pages again, "So, I see some guy named *Levi Parker* and another named *Kevin Strong*. Where's the other guy?" I pointed out Jax's name under the "G's" and he looked at me curiously. "*Jax*? What kind of name is *Jax*?"

"It's just a nickname. His name is Andrew Jackson. He's my old boyfriend from junior high," I replied matter of factly.

"Uh-oh, poor Jax doesn't even rate *one* star?" Mike asked me with a twinkle in his eyes.

Reaching for the book I squeaked, "I don't rate guys. I haven't had enough boyfriends to have a star system down in place. Unlike you probably, who has gone with at least *5 girls* that I know of!"

Mike Bohannon began to cackle. "Oh so you know who *my* old girlfriends are, huh?"

I felt the damned blush begin creeping through my face. "Yeah, well, only because the girls you've dated aren't exactly the type to keep their mouths shut!" I felt a little bad for sounding so mean but it was true. The girls I knew he had gone with were all pretty big sluts at Calvin. They dated all the kicker boys. They were pretty exclusive to dating only Calvin boys too from the kicker crowd.

Mike whistled and then said, "OUCH! That hurt *Delicious*…oops, I mean *DeLaine*!" He was grinning at me wickedly.

I felt my face unable to keep a straight look and replied, "Well, as long as you forget that damned *Delicious* shit, then I won't be mean about your old girlfriends. By the way now that I think about it, who is your girlfriend *this* week?"

"Damn, girl, you are *ornery*, you know that?" Mike still seemed to keep his good humor about him. "Well, Miss Reynolds, for your information, I'm not going with anyone! I haven't for a few months!" I smiled at him flirtingly. I couldn't help it. He was fun to flirt with. I was having fun and he'd made me forget about how bad I'd been feeling for the last couple of months.

Mike looked at the small black book in his hands again and said, "Well, give me a pen and I'll give you my number! Maybe you'll call me over the summer!" I shook my head and reached back through my car window for my purse and a pen. I didn't think I'd *ever* call Mike, but it was fun just flirting with him.

"I'm leaving for Wichita Falls in a few weeks so I may not call until I'm home from my summer visit up there." I stated.

"Oh, you gonna go meet up with ol' *Jax* from up there?" Mike teased me.

Shaking my head I murmured, "No, I mean, I might see him, but we are just friends now." I was more excited and intent on seeing Kevin than Jax. I wanted to see Jax just so I knew he was alright after the whole bull accident.

"Well, maybe I'll see you some time. Do you go to the dance hall?" Mike asked me. I could tell he was trying to keep me from leaving. I knew I had to get on my way home soon or else I would be late. I nodded and Mike suggested, "Well, next time you go, look for me! Maybe I might ask you to dance."

"Well, thank you so much! I might never get to dance unless you do that!" I began batting my eyes in a sarcastic way.

"Gladly, little lady!" Mike drawled, as he slipped off my car. I was surprised that we'd been sitting on my car talking for over two hours. Randy had left earlier and taken Robby Hart home. The others that were there I really didn't know, except by name only. "Call me some time *Delicious DeLaine*," Mike whispered the last part as he closed my car door behind me. He leaned down to look into my car window that was still rolled down. "Be safe," the sweet blonde, blue eyed kicker whispered as I started my car.

"G'bye," I called softly, as I pulled away. I looked into my rearview mirror and saw he was watching me as I pulled back out onto Leonard Street. I smiled as I thought about the flirty blonde cowboy, who almost had the same color eyes as Kevin did. I realized I kinda liked him, but since I didn't really know him, it was just as well that he gave me his phone number. This way I wouldn't have some bozo calling me and driving me crazy. I figured he would not remember me the next day any way.

Chapter 13

I left for Wichita Falls on Kelly Stubbs' 17th birthday on June 11th. I was anxious the entire way to see Bailey and Kevin. I had gone the whole school year and hadn't contacted Kevin at all. Bailey mentioned him only once in a while. I tried hard not to even ask about him. Since he'd quit school, I knew she didn't see him often. I thought that maybe with the new boyfriend she had, she probably didn't see much of anyone. I wasn't sure if I liked her new boyfriend any better than I had Donny, even though Bailey hadn't said anything bad about him. I just got a weird vibe about him from some of the things she mentioned.

When I got to the bus station late that night, I was happy to see Bailey waiting for me, by herself this time. I missed seeing Jason sometimes and his old, crappy car but he was a dad now and married, which seemed crazy too. We were all growing up, and it seemed a little strange when I thought too hard about it. Bailey grabbed me in probably the tightest hug she'd ever given me before. She seemed a little different even though I wasn't sure exactly why. She actually had tears in her eyes when we parted from the hug.

"Bay, why the tears?" I asked, softly.

"I'm so happy to see you is all," she replied, absently wiping at her eyes.

I smiled at my best friend with the aqua, blue-green eyes. She was even prettier if that could be possible. She already had her golden tan started for the summer, and her hair had blonde streaks through it. She still was the most beautiful girl I knew, I thought. "I'm so happy to see you, Bay! You have no clue what a crazy year this has been!" She laughed and told me that if my letters were any indication that she indeed had an idea. We grabbed my big suitcase that had gone up and down the highway, to and from Wichita Falls and Corpus Christi just as much as I had.

When we were going to sleep later, she told me she had to take medicine at bedtime now and it made her sleepy, so she might go to sleep quickly. I told her it was fine. Since Jason wasn't in his old room any more we just put my stuff in there so there was more room. We lay in her bed and chatted like old times, but I noticed that Bailey did in fact fall asleep much quicker than normal. I looked at the dark ceiling after I heard her breath coming in even time. I wished we were still 13 or 14. I missed our time being that age. I just *thought* that life had sucked back then. I was realizing that getting older didn't mean my life was going to get easier, like I thought it would. Instead, I just had much *different* problems. My mind flashed on Shannon Hanks for the first time in a long time, and I shivered. I hoped that would be the *worst* thing to ever happen to me, because I never wanted to feel that vulnerable or frightened again.

Finally, I felt myself getting tired and my eyelids found their way to closing. I was in the field of yellow flowers. I was happy and peaceful like I always was when I was in that field. I wished I could go out to the lake to that spot where Kevin had taken me to so long ago. I knew that Donna lived near a field like it now, because she still visited my dreams. I wished I could talk to her. I fell asleep missing one tiny girl who loved bigger than anyone else I ever knew.

The next morning when Bailey's mom woke us up with chocolate waffles, I immediately was transported to the first time she had ever done that! It was a happy memory. For some reason I felt like this was a weird summer of memories coming back one last time. I didn't understand that. I felt a sadness that seemed to grip my heart as soon as Bailey fell asleep the night before.

Bailey was off that day, so we made plans to go to the pool. I couldn't wait to see all the people from Milam. I wondered how many still went to the pool. While we were getting our stuff together to go, Bailey began to act a little strange. When I asked her what was wrong she looked at me sadly. "Um, Lala, do you think you'd mind sleeping in Jason's room while you're here? It's just…I take this medicine at night and if you sleep with me, I'll try to stay up. Then I'm really tired all day the next day. I mean, we can sleep together some of the time, but maybe on work nights you can sleep in Jason's room?"

I looked at Bailey curiously. "Uh, sure, Bay. I'm sorry! I really didn't mean to keep you up."

"No! It's cool! You didn't! I wanted you to sleep with me last night, but I know that since I have to work every day, except Tuesdays, I have to get as much sleep as possible. That's the only reason! We'll camp out in the den too, on the pull out bed! That'll be fun too!" Bailey was trying to make it not seem as hurtful even though it still felt that way a bit. I tried not to let my feelings be hurt by her request, but I was wondering why things were suddenly changing so much for us.

We went to the swimming pool, and was happy to see a few of the others that hung out with us, in 8th grade. Everybody was once again coming around us. I wondered if Bailey had to work to gain friends back after she broke up with Donny. I didn't really want to start anything by asking, so I let it be. I was thrilled to see Levi come walking in later. He hugged me hard. I looked at his body and wondered if I'd ever seen a guy with as many muscles as Levi seemed to have. If it was possible, he was more built than he'd ever been. His belly was rippled with muscles which made me blush when I realized I was looking at Levi's body and appreciating it as a *guy's* body. He was one of my best friends, but he was gorgeous as a guy too.

We went out later that night for a quick spin on Kemplar. I kept my eyes peeled for Kevin's car. I still hadn't even mentioned him. Since Bailey hadn't said his name once since I'd gotten there, I wasn't sure what to think. We didn't stay out late because Bailey had to go to work the next morning. When we got back to her house, she went to bed and I went into Jason's old room. I started getting my stuff out, and set it up, so I'd be comfortable in there. I had an old spiral notebook that I wrote in. I didn't really write my thoughts any more like a journal, but I liked playing with book ideas and had since 8th grade. I wanted to write a book about my life, but didn't think anyone would really believe so much stuff could happen to one person. I also didn't want my mom and dad to know *everything* that I'd gone through. Instead, I just played around with story ideas.

When I was propped up in Jason's old bed, I noticed there was a phone still on his nightstand. I thought about calling Kevin and letting him know I was in town. I didn't know if I should or not. I couldn't help that he was the other person on my mind as soon as I got to Wichita Falls. Finally, I picked up the phone after I turned the lights out. I thought in some weird way that maybe with the lights out I wouldn't hurt too much if he hung up on me. The phone rang three times, then I heard Kevin's sleepy voice on the other end. I immediately froze, unsure if I should say anything. I had a mad impulse to hang up the phone, but finally I found my voice, "Kev?" I whispered, softly.

I sat there hearing my heart as it pounded in my head and chest. I hated feeling frightened of the rejection I was sure would come from the boy I still loved. I'd tried so hard to have a real boyfriend and had gotten involved in school just like he wanted. Finally, after what felt like forever, I heard Kevin murmur, "Lainey?"

Relief flooded my pounding heartbeat and I replied quietly, "Yeah, it's me. I'm *here*."

"In *Wichita*?" Kevin asked me, still in a hushed voice.

"Yes," I responded, hoping that he was just asleep and hadn't gotten brain damage from smoking too much pot. "When I said *I'm here*, I assumed you'd know I meant *Wichita*," I spouted, wryly.

Kevin's soft chuckle brought a smile to my face, in the dark of Jason Rains' old bedroom. "Oh, my dear, little, Lainey, you still have that sharp ass tongue on you, don't you?"

I started giggling a little in the dark, "Yeah, you know, I tried to see if I could file it down, but it didn't work. Instead I think I made it a little sharper."

"Dammit, how could it be *sharper*?! What happened to that sweet little girl I met 5 years ago?" Kevin asked with a hint of laughter still in his voice.

"It won't be five years 'til this fall. Oh, and that sweet little girl you met *almost* five years ago…yeah, that was all *an act*. I really fooled you though, you know?" I snickered softly.

Kevin laughed out loud, "Oh hell, Lainey, you've *never* been a sweet *little girl*! You knew how to put my ass in its place! That's what I liked so much about you! You sound good, by the way."

I sat there twisting the curly cord in my index finger. "You too," I finally whispered.

"You gonna come see me?" Kevin asked softly.

"When?" I asked.

"*Now*?" he replied.

I sat there surprised by his answer. I hadn't expected to sneak out. I knew how to do it without getting caught, but I had always done it when Bailey was aware of it. I'd never snuck out without her knowing. I couldn't stand it though. It was a risk I was willing to take. It was Kevin, and he wanted to see me *now*! "Let me get dressed and I'll be there in a few minutes!" I answered, in a breathy voice.

"Be careful, Lainey!" Kevin instructed me.

I hung up the phone quietly, and jumped up. I began running through the room, putting on clothes. I was trying to do it without turning on a lot of light, but I finally managed to find a pair of lavender shorts, with a purple and white striped t-shirt, that was v-necked. I hurried to the old front door and managed to open it just like all the other times I'd done it through the years to sneak out. I was literally running down the sidewalk, in the dark, as fast as my feet would carry me to *my* Kevin. I couldn't believe that in mere minutes I would be looking into the summer, sky blue eyes that I loved the most. I briefly thought about the cowboy from Calvin named Mike Bohannon, and how similar his eyes were but it was such a fleeting thought, it barely registered in my brain.

Just as I got to the end of Granville, standing under the streetlight on the corner stood a tall, blonde headed boy, with broad shoulders. I felt silly running but when I saw him I couldn't make myself slow down and walk like a normal person. Instead I ran, straight up to him and he caught me in his strong arms and twirled me in the air, as our bodies met with a hard thud. I was a little embarrassed for being so eager, but I just couldn't help myself.

"Oh Kevin!" I whispered next to his ear.

He leaned in and smelled my neck. He pulled back after a minute, "You smell *delicious*! What kind of perfume are you wearing? I don't remember you ever wearing that one before!"

I started laughing. He'd never once in all the years I'd known him asked me what perfume I was wearing. "It's something like Night-blooming Jasmine or something. It smells good. I love it!"

Kevin leaned down and his mouth claimed my own, hungrily. I surrendered to his forceful kisses because I had dreamed of this moment for so many months. I ran my hands up into his curls at the back of his neck. I was finally home. I was where I was meant to be, I was sure of it. When we pulled apart he looked at me and wiped the damp curls off of my sweaty brow. "I've missed you so much, Lainey! I want you to know that I wanted to call you so many times, but I made myself back off. I honestly missed you so much though!" he sighed into my ear.

I smiled up at his shadowed face. The face I knew every plane of, whether it was dark or light. I'd looked at this face in so many different types of light over the years, that I could probably draw it from memory if I could draw a face. I stroked his cheek, then put my finger over his mouth. "No more talking! I'm here now! That's what is important!"

"Yes, it is. Let's get to my house! I want to hear all about your year away!" Kevin stated sweetly. I nodded and we crossed out of the side yard of the house on Fairfax Blvd. to go to the opposite side, where Portland Ave. ran into Fairfax. Kevin's large hand engulfed my small one. He kept looking down at me, grinning, as if he thought he might actually be dreaming. I knew the feeling though, so I met each smile with my own.

When we walked into his room I looked around and realized *nothing* had changed much in the four and a half years I'd been walking in there. I looked at the bed and remembered the nights I'd had sex with Kevin in it. I began to feel my face heat up when I thought about what happened the last time I was with Kevin, when I finally figured out why everybody thought sex was so wonderful! He noticed of course, "Why are you blushing?"

I shook my head. "Just thinking about the last time I was in this room with you."

Kevin turned and stood in front of me. I craned my neck to look up into his face. The bathroom light was the only light on. I knew Kevin had been asleep when I had called earlier. He was wide awake now though. I wanted to stay here forever. I wanted him to ask me to marry him like Rick had done. Would I quit going to school for him, I wondered briefly. I realized I'd do anything he wanted if it sounded good. I didn't have a lot of time to think of many other things because Kevin leaned over and kissed me almost achingly. I had never felt so much longing in a kiss from him before, even after Donna had died. I wasn't sure if it was from him or if it was my own longing. I had missed him more than I had even realized.

I didn't think as I stood there, getting lost inside the boy with hair like spun gold and eyes that reminded me of a summer sky. Instead, I began to tug on his T-shirt. Without a moment of hesitation, he lifted it over his head. He returned the favor when he pulled the striped T-shirt over my head. I knew my hair would be crazy curls all over the place, but I didn't care. I knew he didn't either. I shivered as I felt his rough hands glide across my back. I could tell his calloused hands were becoming rougher. I assumed it was because he was working at the gas station still. I hadn't really given him much chance to tell me anything.

By the time we were wrapped around one another, I had forgotten everything that had happened through the year. I no longer remembered Rick, the plays, or even the terror of Shannon. I especially didn't want to remember Shannon. The only thing I was even aware of was Kevin and his young, strong body as it slid over my own. I had gained about 10 pounds back, but I knew I still looked good. I had curves. Even if boys still somehow seemed a little stand offish with me, I noticed the appreciative glances.

Kevin whispered my name over and over, and just as he climaxed, I thought I was going to die when I heard him whisper my name with more love than he'd ever used before. When he buried his nose into my neck, I held on tightly as my own climax racked my body. I didn't think I'd ever love someone as much as I loved Kevin Michael Strong. He was my *everything.* I would measure every boy to him if I couldn't have him. I knew there was no other man in the world I could love the way I'd love him.

Later, as we lay in each other's arms, talking softly, I told him all about the stuff that had happened in school. He was impressed that I'd been in the plays and he laughed when I told him about the kissing scenes with Mattie Maldonado. Eventually I told him about Rick too. He was quiet while I told him. I knew that is what he wanted me to do, but I still felt weird telling him. Kevin knew *everything* about me. I couldn't remember ever hiding anything truly important from him about my life in Corpus. I'd kept some things about Jax private because he didn't need to know them, but for the most part he knew all the most important parts of my life since 7th grade. I realized he was my best friend as well as my lover.

He asked me questions about Rick and why we broke up. When I told him that Rick wanted me to quit school and get married he started laughing. "I'm sure that went over like a turd in a punchbowl, huh?? What a *dumbass*! Asking someone as smart as you to quit school! I'm glad you didn't do that, DeLaine! That would have been the *second* stupidest thing you could ever do!"

I craned my head back and looked into his face. "*The second*? What's the *first*?"

"Lovin' me silly girl! That's the stupidest thing you could ever do!" Kevin replied seriously.

I looked into his hooded eyes. I didn't understand why he was saying that. "Why would you say that?"

"Lainey, baby, I'm *nothin'! I'm nobody*! The real world is not like school! I'm just some dumbass who quit school. I'm not ever gonna be anyone! You though are gonna be somethin'! I just know it! You keep doing all that shit in school! You just wait! You're gonna have a bitchin' senior year!"
he whispered softly.

I shook my head and before I could protest Kevin placed his index finger over my lips to shush me. He replaced the finger with his mouth quietly and I let him. I hated that he thought so badly about himself, but I couldn't stop getting lost in his kisses that night. I had purposely *not* told him about Shannon. I knew that if I told him, he would only feel bad that he'd sent me out looking for a real boyfriend. He didn't need to know that Shannon had hurt me.

I probably never would have told him, except Kevin held my arms by the wrist over my head at one point, and I started crying. I can't explain why I cried, except it reminded me of Shannon holding me down to take advantage of me. I was feeling so amazing one moment, and the next I was a blubbering mess. "Hey, hey, Lainey! *What's wrong?* Did I hurt you?" Kevin asked.

Shaking my head I sniffed the tears back and tried to not be too gross about it. There was no way to sniff like that around a boy without it sounding disgusting I thought. Kevin had only held my hands briefly and had let them go when I began to cry, but I couldn't make myself stop. I hadn't really cried about Shannon hurting me. I hadn't wanted to really admit it after Kelly and Robin had made fun of me when I tried to tell them. I just pretended it didn't happen and I avoided anywhere that I saw Shannon or thought he might be. Finally, I looked up into Kevin's beautiful face. I hadn't wanted to tell him. I wanted to spare him any pain. I wanted to only tell him the good parts of this last year. Even though Rick hadn't ended well, I wanted him to know that I'd done *exactly* what he wanted of me. Telling him about Shannon might make him think less of me, I thought.

Finally, I took a deep breath and admitted, "Rick wasn't the *only* guy I dated. After we broke up I began seeing this other guy named Shannon," I began quietly. I knew if I didn't just tell him at once I'd chicken out and not tell him everything. "We weren't serious or anything, but I wasn't seeing anyone else except him," I explained, as I nestled in Kevin's warm embrace. Our passion was now forgotten for the moment as I let him comfort me. "We, well, I had sex with him, Kevin. I told you the truth about Rick. We *never* had sex, but I got drunk when Rick and I first broke up and Shannon was there. I liked him. He was funny and one thing led to another and we had sex."

I looked up at Kevin's face and saw as he tried to hide the hurt. He kept it stone still, but his eyes told me volumes. I knew I had to continue even though I would rather have poked my own eyes out. "We went out one night. We didn't see each other very long. We took my car because his was in the shop. He was from 'in town' Corpus, so we went over to his old neighborhood and went to a couple of parties. He got really drunk. I wasn't drinking though," I was quick to add, thinking it made a difference. "When we left I was relying on him to help me navigate my way back to our side of town, because I don't really know my way around Corpus Christi." I drew in another deep breath because I knew I was getting to the bad part. “He ended up taking me to a place that is a devil worshipping place.”

“WHAT?” Kevin snarled, sitting up and pushing me back to look into my face.

Suddenly my tears began again because I knew that after this, I would forever be *tainted* to him. “He said he was one, but I don’t know if he is or not. He got really weird though, and well, he wanted to…you know. I didn’t want to, but he scared me and even though I asked him not to hurt me…he did, Kevin. He hurt me and I can’t tell anybody because we’d already seen each other. I knew it would also get messy and my mom would find out and she’d know I had sex.”

Kevin wiped his hand down his face and said, “*Jesus Christ, DeLaine*! I think having *sex* and getting *raped* are two different things! What the fuck? That’s what you’re sayin’ right? This son of a bitch *raped* you?” he growled deep in his throat. I knew he was angry, but I wasn’t sure if he was angry at me, Shannon or the situation. I hung my head down and clutched the sheet from his bed to my chest.

“*I’m so sorry, Kevin*,” I whispered miserably.

“What?” Kevin asked surprised. “Wait a minute! Lainey, do you think I’m angry with *you*?” I nodded my head. He pulled me to him and cried in a choked voice, “No baby, I’m *not* mad at you! Oh fuck! No way darlin’! I told you to go out there! You were doing what I told you to do! You didn’t *ask* for that! *I’m not angry at you*!” Kevin said soothingly as he stroked my back.

“Are you sure, I mean, I guess I was willing to do it as long as he didn’t hurt me,” I lamented miserably.

“No, honey! You were SURVIVING! You did the right thing! You weren’t *willing* to have some asshole terrify you and abuse you. *Baby, I’m not mad at you*! I’m sorry if I scared you!” Kevin reassured me vehemently.

“You didn’t scare me. I just had some weird flashback or something when you held my hands over my head,”

I remarked, quietly. "I just haven't really been able to talk about it with anyone and now I'm talking to you about it. That's messed up, Kevin. It's like one of those weird things that you *don't* tell the guy you love!"

Kevin held me close to him. "You *do* tell him! If you can't tell him, then who do you tell?"

"It's just weird to tell you about having sex with someone else and then…well, you know," I shrugged.

Kevin chuckled then, "DeLaine, we have never had what most would call a *conventional* relationship. We weren't meant to have one of those for some reason. I want you to be able to tell me anything. I know I've been an asshole in the past. I know *I* hurt you the first time," he began.

I jerked back and said, "Shut up Kevin! I don't even want to think about *that!* It *wasn't* the same. I was *never* terrified you were going to kill me. I wasn't afraid you were going to use me as some sort of human sacrifice. You might have taken advantage of something because you were pissed, and I let you because I was pissed, but it was NOT the same! Besides, I don't even count that as anything except an argument. You were drunk and an asshole! I don't count that as anything else!" I insisted.

"Lainey*, I hurt you too,* whether you want to admit it or not. I didn't do it with the intent of hurting you. I can't explain why I felt the need to know I was the *first* one and that I took your virginity that way, but it happened." Kevin responded woefully.

"We're done talking about this now!" I declared with finality. Kevin looked at me curiously. "Now you know about Shannon. I'm sorry I started crying. I guess I just got scared for a minute. I'm okay. I'm sorry I screwed up our time together. I don't ever want to compare what happened with me and you, in that crappy trailer behind Welks' house, and what happened with Shannon. You hurt me, but it wasn't the same. I don't care what you think I don't think you raped me. I think that Shannon *did*, whether my best friends do or not."

Kevin looked at me curiously, "Does Bailey know?"

I sat there and then shook my head. Kevin asked why I hadn't told her and I shrugged my shoulders. "I guess I'm such a screw up anyway compared to her. I don't want her to think I'm *pathetic* now too."

Kevin shook his head, "That's bullshit, DeLaine! Bailey wouldn't think that. She's your best friend. You should tell her!"

"I can't Kev. *I* didn't want to tell *you*. Every time I talk about it I feel dirty, and I let him back into my head one more time. I just want to forget it ever happened and quit thinking about it. Don't tell her!" I cried, pleading with him.

"Honey, I think I might have seen her twice since last summer. I won't tell her anything. But you need to tell her. She's your best friend. I know you think 'cause those other girls didn't believe you that Bailey will think bad, but you know she's different. I know you're close to those girls, but Bailey is Bailey! She loves you. I know she does. She would have killed Geoffrey that one day that she called me…when she and Levi ran to the house on Belfast…if I'd let her. She is a mean little girl! I wouldn't want to fuck with her if I was a chick!" Kevin was grinning.

"I know. I'll think about it. I just want to quit talking about all of it now, okay?" I asked him.

"You got it, Lainey! Just know that if I could come to Corpus, I'd probably go to prison, because I would kill that son-of-a-bitch! I'm not even playing on that one*!*" Kevin stated honestly. I knew he meant every word he said, because his eyes had a hardness to them but they also had a *certainty* behind them as well. I was grateful for once that Kevin couldn't come to Corpus.

We lay in his bed for another hour before I finally had to begin getting dressed. I had to make it back to Bailey's house before the sun came up. I knew her folks got up around 6 in the morning and by the time I was walking back it was 5 a.m. During that hour we made love one more time and this time Kevin didn't hold my hands above my head. He took his time and was more tender than he'd ever been with me before. He'd never been rough, but it was almost as if he wanted me to know that I'd *never* have to worry about him hurting me again.

When we got to Bailey's house, Kevin kissed me tenderly as I stood on the bottom step which brought us face to face with each other. He held me tightly and told me that he'd try to see me again soon. I wondered what he meant by that, but I was happy to have had the whole night with him. I could hardly wait to see him again. I knew that it wouldn't be nearly long enough because my two weeks never were. I hoped we'd get to see each other at least every other day. I couldn't imagine ever loving another man as much as I loved Kevin Strong. I couldn't imagine being with anyone else ever again. I'd been with other boys now, but I wanted to tell Kevin the next time I saw him that I wanted to be faithful to just him until I graduated in 11 months. I couldn't believe he'd been in my life almost 5 years. I'd never had someone in my life that long that wasn't related to me. Now I had him and Bailey.

Chapter 14

The rest of that week was a blur of going to the pool when Bailey was at work and sleeping. Her mom had gotten a job in a retail store, and her dad was gone too. I wandered through their home alone and wondered why I'd even come up. I was bored which was a first for me in Wichita Falls. Everybody else that I cared to spend time with had jobs too.

Bailey seemed different this year as well. I wasn't sure what it was about her, but she seemed *off* in some way. She didn't seem to be her naturally happy self. She was moodier which I found a little weird. She took that medicine every night and was usually asleep by 10:30. I finally asked her what she was taking medicine for and she told me that they had found out she had a chemical imbalance in her brain and the medicine helped to replace whatever chemical was messed up in there. I didn't understand it, but it sure didn't sound good. I hoped my friend was going to be alright. I just knew that things felt too different this summer, which worried me. It didn't help my mood or thinking that this trip might really be for me to say goodbye.

I asked her if I was going to finally get to meet Casey any time soon, but every time she talked to him on the phone, he found some excuse or other to not come over. She would talk to him sometimes for long periods while I was there waiting to spend time with her. He wouldn't want her to get off of the phone. I didn't understand it and I wondered why he was so worried about meeting me. I couldn't think of any other reason why he kept finding excuses while I was there. I wondered what about me worried him. I hoped that surely by the weekend he would come over.

That first Friday night we went riding around on Kemplar all evening. I kept my eyes peeled for Kevin. I finally told Bailey about sneaking out to see Kevin on Thursday. She still didn't say anything to me about him though. I found it odd that she didn't even mention him when she knew how extremely important he was to me.

The next night, Saturday, we ran into a big bunch of the kicker kids and standing in the middle of them was Jax. I was shocked at how tall he'd gotten! He was as tall as Kevin now. He was sitting on the tailgate of his truck in his Wrangler's and a tank top. I thought he looked kinda silly, but he was a guy. They were known to be kinda dumb sometimes I'd realized more and more the older I got. He was wearing a straw cowboy hat as well and holding a beer between his legs.

When Bailey and I parked, he saw Bailey and smiled really big. When he saw me he acted like he didn't even know who I was. I knew that I hadn't seen him in a long time, but surely he remembered me. We walked up to where he was sitting and I realized he was a little drunk. He grabbed Bailey in a big hug and started chatting happily with her. I felt a little hurt that he was ignoring me until Bailey chided him, "Jax, you *do know* that is DeLaine, right?"

Jax snapped his gaze in my direction and yelled, "HOLY SHIT! NO WAY! I'm sorry, DeLaine! I didn't recognize you! DAMN GIRL! You grew up to be hot as hell!" I felt myself blush. I realized that he was used to seeing me with glasses on. I'd dropped some weight and my body proportions had changed. I didn't think that made me unrecognizable to him though, but it seemed as if I was wrong. Jax jumped off the tailgate of the truck and came up to me and wrapped his arms around me in a bear hug. "Damn girl! *You look fine as shit*!" Jax crowed when he stood back.

I felt a little uncomfortable around him for some reason. He was really loud and boisterous when he was drinking. I wished I could have seen him in a quieter setting so I could find out how he *really* was after the whole bull goring fiasco. I knew trying to talk to him with all the cars and loud music and the other kids around made it next to impossible.

"Hey Jax," I was feeling a little shy around this tall cowboy who still had laughing green eyes, even though they were very glassy from drinking. "I heard about your accident. I'm sorry you got hurt!"

"Aww, it's all part of rodeo! It's cool! I can start riding bulls again in another month the doctor says so it's all good!" Jax responded cheerfully.

I stood there dumbstruck. "*What*?!"

"*Riding bulls*, DeLaine! You know, what *I do* in the rodeo! I'm climbing back on next month! Too bad you didn't come in July you could have come see my return!" Jax said smiling.

"Why on Earth are you planning on riding again, Jax?" I asked him, horrified.

Jax set his beer down on the tailgate and began to pull his tank top up. I was impressed with the man's body he was getting, but when he turned I saw the scar from the surgery that had been done to save his life afterward. It was *huge*. It started just under his arm towards his stomach and went all the way around to the middle of his back. "This is why, DeLaine! I'm not letting a fucking bull rule what I do! If I don't get back on I'll be a pussy the rest of my life around them! I'm gonna get back on and ride a whole eight seconds! This can't be what I leave the rodeo over!"

I stood there with my eyes large as I surveyed the damage done to his body. Finally, I nodded my head mutely. I didn't understand his need to get back on a bull when he almost died doing it in the first place. I remembered the first time he'd ridden a bull and hadn't told me he was going to do it. I had been upset with him back then. I'd been so afraid he'd be hurt. It took a few years but my fears were realized. Now I stood looking at the boy I'd known since 2nd grade and wondered what made him want to put his life on the line to ride a huge animal that he *knew* could hurt him or even *kill* him.

Jax had put his shirt down and was climbing back onto the tailgate with his beer. He grinned at me with the impish little grin he used to use to make me feel all breathless in junior high. I was taken back to 6th grade, just for a moment, as I looked at him, remembering a boy who stole a little stuffed puppy out of my locker, one day after school. I remembered how I'd felt a thrumming in my neck from my heart beating so wildly, when he'd stepped in closely to put the puppy back, only to palm it. He'd kept it and ran down the hall. I relived all the moments I'd seen Jax in junior high and talked with him and how we'd been boyfriend and girlfriend. All these memories hummed through me in only a couple of seconds, but I felt like I was seeing a whole different life time.

Within those few seconds, Jax was talking to some of the people who were there hanging out with him. Bailey knew a couple of them, but they obviously weren't that close because she was already done talking and standing beside me. Jax seemed too involved with those around him to pay too much attention to me. I felt a little sad. I had hoped if I saw him, he'd want to find out how my life was going in Corpus. He seemed content to say hi and then move on to his other friends. I stood watching him for a few seconds. I realized this was the last time I'd probably see him, unless we ran into him again like this while I was in town.

"Well, Jax, I think we're gonna go. It was good seeing you," I called, a little uncertainly. I wondered why I wanted him to tell me not to go, that he wanted to talk with me.

Instead, he turned to me and yelled over the din of music and people talking, "Oh yeah, hey it was really good seeing you, DeLaine! Don't party too hard down there in Corpus this year! Can you believe we're gonna be *seniors*? That's some crazy shit, huh?"

I smiled at him and nodded my head. "Yeah, it seems only yesterday you stole J.J. out of my locker."

Jax looked at me uncertainly, as if he didn't know what I was talking about, and then his eyes lit up, "Yeah, that's right! I stole that little stuffed dog right before the tornado! Ha! That's funny, huh? I had completely forgotten about Jax Jr. 'til you said that! Yeah, it's crazy how many years have passed! But we're almost 18! Time to live it up, huh?"

"Yeah, I guess so. I'd love to talk more while I'm here. I have another week if you wanna holler at me at Bay's house," I replied hopefully.

Jax's attention was once again turned away. I realized what I'd said had fallen on deaf ears for the most part. Finally, he looked at me and nodded his head, "Uh, yeah, I'll do that! See you later, DeLaine!" With those words I realized that Jax was dismissing me, and wanted to party with his friends.

I turned to look at Bailey and she shrugged her shoulders and then rolled her eyes. I gave her a weak smile and turned one more time to look at the boy with the meadow green eyes that had been my first, *real* boyfriend. I felt another door closing. I was so sad about it and thought I was stupid for feeling sad. I turned to walk to Bailey's Sunbird. I glanced back one more time to see the smiling cowboy who had kept me in a constant state of confusion for so long and that a part of me loved. I knew that a part of me always would. I smiled one more time as I began to slip silently into Bay's car. I wished him well in my head and realized that the days of sitting at the lake with Jax or in Bailey's room were gone now forever. When Bailey turned her head to begin pulling out of the parking lot we'd parked in, I turned my head so she didn't see the tears that were hovering in my eyes. I knew it was silly, but Jax was a huge part of my past that I was letting go. I hoped he didn't get hurt anymore. I knew I'd probably never see him again.

As we were driving back down Kemplar, Bailey confided, "Yeah, Jax is a lot different now. Since he got hurt he's been drinking a lot. He even came to school drunk one time and almost got caught. Levi covered for him, but he's been partying and hanging out with the kicker crowd that drinks *heavily*." I nodded my head because I didn't trust that I wouldn't begin crying if I tried to talk about him. Bailey seemed to sense that I was upset and so she kept up the flow of talking for a while. She told me that he had gone to a different horse farm this summer to break horses, even though he wasn't supposed to do anything like that until the next month. I wondered why he would be so reckless and as usual Bailey knew my thoughts. "I think since he almost died he's gone a little crazy, thinking he needs to take all these risks. It's almost like he thinks that since he didn't die he's not gonna get hurt again or something. I don't know. I know he and Levi have started hanging out less though.

Looking at Bailey I asked her how she knew that. She hardly acknowledged Levi when he talked to me at the pool. Sheepishly she admitted, "I kinda keep up with Levi. We don't talk or anything in school, but I'm friends with a couple of girls who are friends with his girlfriend and they tell me shit. I don't ever ask anything outright 'cause I don't want his girlfriend thinkin' I'm interested or anything. I don't want Casey getting all jealous because he *hates* Levi…" Bailey trailed off.

I was even more intrigued with her new boyfriend that never seemed to have time to come over while I'd been there. "So, is this Casey guy *ever* gonna come over and meet me?"

"I'm not sure…maybe. I don't know, Lala," Bailey responded quietly. I noticed she wasn't calling me her nickname for me very much this last week either.

"Bay, is everything *okay* with you? I mean, I'm just worried about you is all. What's with this guy, Casey?" I asked her.

Bailey seemed to be concentrating on the traffic in front of us. I let her think about how she wanted to answer for a couple of minutes and just as I was about to push her she admitted quietly, "Lala, Casey and I are having some problems. He's so jealous of everything I do. He tells me all the time he thinks that I'm screwin' around on him, but I'm not! *I swear*! I'm not but sometimes he just acts so crazy. Donny was crazy jealous, but Casey…" my best friend trailed off again. I realized by what she *wasn't* telling me that

Casey wasn't a good guy. I instinctively knew that he was hurting her somehow.

"Bailey, is he *hurting* you?" I asked sternly. I felt the hair on the back of my neck begin to stand up. Bailey looked over at me with a haunted expression and she quickly pulled into a dim parking lot that no teenagers were hanging out in. She pulled into a parking space and put the car into park. Finally, she turned and looked at me and now she was the one with tears shining in her teal colored eyes.

I felt a chill go through me and had goose bumps on my arms. Finally, Bailey looked away from me out the driver's side window and began telling me in a quiet voice. "It only happened once. He swears it will never happen again. He scares me though."

Looking at my best friend I wanted to hold her and I wanted to *kill* Casey at the same time. She had gone steady with Donny and I saw the change in her the summer before, but this year the change was even worse. Finally, I asked, "Bailey, how is he hurting you? Is he *hitting* you?" I prayed that he hadn't hurt her the way Shannon had hurt me. I couldn't stand the thought of my beautiful and cool best friend ever being hurt in that way. I didn't want to think of her being hurt in any manner though. Finally, my best friend began to nod her head, covered her face and cried. I reached over and held her as best as I could since the gear shift was in between the seats. After a few minutes I stated firmly, "Bailey, you have to break up with this bastard! He doesn't want to come meet me because he's afraid I'll know isn't that the reason?"

Bailey pulled away from me, "No, he told me not to tell *anybody*. I haven't told anybody. I don't know how to get away from him. I'm afraid of him. I want him to change and keep hoping he will but he always makes me feel so bad. I've tried to break up with him and that's when he bought me a promise ring. He got me that right after it happened. I just don't know what to do. He's a good guy most of the time, but he gets mad so easily."

I looked at Bailey's tear-streaked face. I couldn't believe the girl who I thought was invincible and able to handle anything was keeping such a huge secret. "Bailey, he is NOT a good guy, even *sometimes*. He just wants you to think that. If he's hit you once, he's going to do it again! Next time it might be worse! You have to break up with him. And he's probably smart not to come around me. I will fuckin' kill him if I see him! I'm not ever going to let someone hurt you while I'm around. Bay, you know what I'm saying is the truth! You know he's gonna hurt you again. He's not going to kill you if you break up with him. Do it over the phone so he isn't even around you. If he comes to your house, tell your mom and dad you don't want him there. Call the cops if you have to, but do not stay with this asshole!" I insisted, vehemently.

My best friend who had found some reason to think I was worthy of being my friend looked like a scared and wounded animal. I'd never known her to act this way. I was mystified what this guy had done to her to frighten her so terribly that she would put up with his crap even for a little while. Bailey was always so cool and aloof. She was friends with everyone and could have *any* boy she wanted. I bet she could have Levi again if she wanted.

Finally, Bailey sniffled, "I don't want Mom and Dad to know."

I felt my heart break listening to her. I understood better than she could ever know about not wanting parents to know that someone had hurt you badly. I'd kept everything about Shannon from my mom. I was afraid she'd get drunk and kill him. I acquiesced, "I understand, but please Bailey, if you don't break up, something bad is going to happen. Maybe when you break up with him you need to tell your mom and dad why. You don't have to tell them when it happened or even tell me either. Just get rid of this creep!"

"I'll try," Bailey assured me. I wasn't so sure she'd do it, but I hoped she would. She wiped her face with the back of her hand and we pulled out of the dark parking lot. We went back to her house after stopping at Sonic for a coke. Neither of us seemed to be in the mood to really cruise with a bunch of dumb teenagers.

While we were sitting in her room eating chocolate donut holes, and drinking cokes, I told her a little more about my last year in school. I had written her most of it, but when I got to Shannon I left out any mention of him. Bailey had known I was seeing him because I'd told her in the beginning about him in a letter. When I quit seeing him I'd only skimmed over it by saying it didn't work out.

"So why didn't things work out with that Shannon guy?" Bailey asked me innocently.

I knew that she would pick up on me skimming past him. She knew me so well. It was scary how much we got into each other's heads sometimes, even 400 miles apart. I looked up at her and whispered, "I don't want to talk about it, Bay. He was an asshole. Let's just leave it at that, okay?" I expected her to prod me more, but she nodded her head while looking at me seriously. I could tell just by the way she looked at me that she was trying to figure out what had happened and was reading my face for any tell-tale signs. I must have managed to keep my face free, for the most part, of expression, because we began talking about other stuff.

I looked at her and asked why she hadn't mentioned Kevin at all since I'd been there. With the exception of me finally telling her I'd snuck out, she still hadn't said one word about him. I noticed he hadn't called at all through the week. I was beginning to get a little worried because he knew how little time I had in town. It was unusual for him to ignore me unless we'd gotten into an argument, but we'd left each other happy and feeling closer than ever I had thought.

Bailey looked at me funny, "Well, I haven't really seen him that much this year. Besides, I thought you were supposed to forget about him and move on. Wasn't that the whole deal this last school year? What was the whole thing with getting a real boyfriend and all that shit, if all you were going to do was come back and go running back to jump in his bed?"

I sat there dumbfounded. Bailey was being hurtful and it wasn't an accident. She actually had a sneer across her face which surprised me! "Bay, you know that I love Kevin. I'm always going to love Kevin. No matter what happens, I'm still planning to come back here after graduation. I'm hoping he and I can finally be together for real."

"Don't get your hopes up, DeLaine! He's dating that slutty Jackie girl. They've been together since you were here last time." Bailey was still using a snotty tone of voice.

I felt like my whole world was collapsing in on itself. Why hadn't Kevin told me? Why had he been with me if he was serious with Jackie? "Are you *sure*?" I asked quietly. I watched as my best friend nodded her head. I remembered what Kevin had told me a long time ago about me always coming before anybody else if he ever started dating someone seriously. I had foolishly believed him. I didn't understand why I'd believed him. That was the most stupid thing in the world to believe I thought. I had been pretty stupid when it came to guys, I knew. Feeling sick to my stomach I only stayed up with Bailey a few more minutes and then I went to Jason's old room. I was sad. I was sad for so many things as I curled up under the covers. I lay there in the dark and thought about how much had changed. Bailey seemed off emotionally. Levi really didn't take the time to come visit me and Jax acted like I was someone he barely knew. Then there was Kevin. He was working and had quit school. He would have graduated last month if he'd stayed in school, I thought. I remembered how he said his grades had gone down so bad that he was in danger of not graduating until my class graduated next year. I sighed as I rolled over and tried to go to sleep. I felt like I didn't belong in Wichita Falls anymore. I didn't understand why everything had to change so much. I was so glad when sleep finally stole me and I didn't dream.

Chapter 15

The next afternoon while we were just hanging out, there was a knock on the door. Bailey jumped up to go answer it. I heard her talking and then she came back into her room. "Um, you have someone here."

"Who?" I asked her curiously.

"Go look," Bailey replied.

I stood up and walked to the front door that she had pushed closed. I was curious that whoever it was she hadn't asked them into the house. I thought it might be Kevin and she left him on the front porch, which would really burn me up. I pulled the heavy door open and there standing on her cement porch was Geoffrey Toole! My step-brother from hell was on her front steps like we were long lost friends. I felt my heart speed up and was totally stunned to find him standing there. Numbly I pushed the glass storm door open and stepped out.

"Hey D.! Oh my God! You got GORGEOUS! Damn, *who knew* you'd grow up so gorgeous!" Geoffrey was laughing. I glared at him, remembering all the times he'd terrorized me and told me what a fat pig and cow I was. I remembered every bruise and every horrible thing he'd ever said or done to hurt me physically or mentally. Now he stood in front of me after not seeing each other in 2 ½ years complimenting me, acting like we were long lost best friends. Then I remembered our brief respite from being at such odds the last time I'd seen him at Christmas, in 1981. Then I remembered all the bad things his mother had done, not just to me through the years, but how much she'd cost my daddy. I thought about the stories Daddy told me about Clarice and Geoff causing him grief when he'd first split with her. I was actually in awe that Geoffrey had the balls to show up like this.

"Hello Geoff," I replied crisply.

"Wow Sister! Why such a cool greeting? You pissed at me or what?" Geoff asked me, still grinning his jackal grin.

"No reason in particular, just wasn't expecting to see you is all," I finally responded again in a crisp tone.

Geoffrey eyed me suspiciously, "I heard you were in town. I live here again. So does Mom! I'd like to go to lunch or dinner with you. I know Mom wants to see you too," he continued smiling.

"I *don't* want to see your mom, Geoff," I snarled, angrily.

"Okay, geez, D.! You don't have to be a bitch!"
Geoff was still grinning at me.

I looked at him and wondered what made him tick. He surely had to have something messed up in his head, I thought. "Not trying to be a bitch," I explained, quietly. "I just *don't* want to see her."

"Will you at least go to lunch with *me* then?" Geoff asked me, now taking down his false cheer.

I thought about it and was curious what his game was. I finally agreed and he told me he'd pick me up the next day, because he was off from the hair salon he worked at. I looked at him curiously and he started laughing and told me that he'd gotten his license to do hair. I wasn't really surprised. Thankfully he didn't hang out too long. I walked back up the stairs wishing I hadn't agreed to go to lunch with him.

When I got inside and told Bailey, she was shocked I had agreed as well. "Why'd you agree Lala?" she asked me. I shrugged my shoulders and told her that I wanted to listen to his reasons behind the shit he'd pulled on my daddy after all the stuff my dad had helped him with. Bailey shook her head, "I hope he doesn't trick you and bring Clarice."

I hadn't really thought about that and then told Bailey that I'd call him and meet him if she'd let me take her to work. She agreed and so I called the number Geoffrey had given me earlier to tell him that I'd just meet him, because I was going to run around in

Bailey's car the next day. He told me where to meet and I warned him again about his mom. "Geoffrey, I mean it! If you bring your mom I will turn around and walk out of the restaurant. I won't want you to ever contact me again, do you understand?" Geoffrey agreed and I felt better about going. I knew I could turn around and leave if I saw Clarice. I also knew I'd have no qualms about doing it either.

The next day when I met Geoff for lunch, I was surprised at how effeminate he had begun to act. I knew he'd been gay for a couple of years, but he was even more girly than he'd been when we were younger. He sat there and chatted away like I was his best girlfriend. He told me about the guys he'd been seeing. I felt myself blanch a time or two when he talked about the men in his life because I'd never known an openly gay person before. I wasn't sure how I felt about all of this. I felt wrong in so many ways because I'd grown up believing if someone was gay that was gross.

While we talked, I found myself glancing away from him a lot, looking at all the other customers in the restaurant. For some reason I didn't want to even see Geoffrey. I couldn't stand him. I knew it was not because he was gay either. I couldn't stand the *falseness* he represented. He wanted to act like we'd been close, and that I was his little sister and he was my big brother, but in fact he'd been my tormenter while growing up with him.

I was so glad when our lunch was over. I had filled him in with just basic information because I didn't trust that he wasn't on a scouting expedition for his mother. For all I knew she wanted to put another *hit* on me. He could be gathering information about what I was doing now so she could hire a hit man to come kill me. Geoffrey grabbed me in a huge hug when we walked outside into the baking, hot parking lot. I was glad I had ended up parking across the lot from where he was parked. There would be no long goodbye. I wanted to get away from him and do it quickly and cleanly. I hoped that this was the last time I saw him.

After I was done, I drove by Kevin's house to say hi to his mom. I'd gone by there a couple of times the week before but she was never home. I wanted to see her while I was in town so I decided to take a chance that she might be there finally. I was excited when I saw her sedan parked in the driveway. I thought about Bailey telling me about Kev and the Jackie chick being serious. I wondered what his mom thought about that. She had also wanted me to go get a life in Corpus too. I wondered if she would even want to see me. I almost turned around and didn't go, but in the long run, I wanted to see her one last time too if possible. Even though I didn't want to admit it, I knew that in some way this might possibly be my last time to see some of the people who meant so much to me. This was my last summer as a kid. The next year I'd be a high school graduate, and I hoped going to college the following year. It was a real possibility that I wouldn't get to come back here like I hoped to do. I would do everything I could, but I was learning more and more that life's plans for me sometimes didn't always meet up with what I wanted.

I rang the doorbell and as if she were expecting me Mrs. Strong opened the door and gave me her warm and inviting smile. I wondered how she could have a smile just like her son's that made me feel as if I was finally *home* when they weren't even biologically related. I just knew that looking at Jean Strong made me happy, just as much as looking at Kevin did. She opened the door and wrapped me close to her in her warm and loving embrace. I felt an overwhelming urge to begin crying as soon as I was safely held in her arms. I managed to keep myself together because I didn't want her to think I'd flipped out. When she pulled away from me she exclaimed, "Oh my dearest, DeLaine! I am so glad you were able to come up this summer! I wondered if you would get that chance or not. You're about to be a senior next year! Where in the world has all the time gone?" She remarked almost absently. She caught herself talking to no one in particular and then shook her head and laughed her rich, warm laughter. "Listen to me just prattling on! Kevin told me you were in town the other day. He's so busy these days…" she began to talk about Kevin, but then I realized that she seemed to be actually breaking off her thoughts in a way to block off telling me anything I might not know already. I smiled at her wanting to tell her I knew about Jackie. I decided not to though. It still caused my heart to hurt when I thought about it too often.

We went into the quiet house and sat in the back family room. She asked me all about my school year. I told her the surface stuff. I let her know about the plays and theater arts. I told her only a tiny bit about Rick and she clucked her tongue and told me she was sorry it didn't work out. I told her that he was a good guy, but he wanted me to quit school. Jean Strong looked directly at me and stated, "DeLaine, I've tried to never really tell you what to do. I know that you and Kevin have a…how should I put this? You each love one another, and I've known that since he brought you here for your 13th birthday dinner. He'd never asked to do anything like that for any other girl. I knew you were both just babies, but you are getting older now. So, I'm going to tell you something and I want you to listen to me. Do not *ever* give up your education for any boy. *Life is too fleeting.* You don't understand what I mean by that, but just trust me. Your life is going to go a lot faster than you could ever realize. You are young right now. You think that a couple of years is forever. Forever goes really fast in the long run. So, please promise me, you *will* finish high school! If you have the opportunity to go to college, *do it*! Kevin has told me how smart you are, and I've known it from our conversations. I'm disappointed that Kevin quit, but I understand why he did it." She stopped suddenly and looked down. I was a little glad because she had leaned forward and seemed so intense.

Finally, Mrs. Strong picked up her train of thought and continued, "Just know that no matter what the future holds for you, you are *always* welcome in my home. You will always be a part of Kevin and my dear Donna. You have brought out the best in my son, even if he doesn't know it. So, no matter what happens in your future, whether you move back here or not, just know that you will always be welcome here. You will always be someone *I love*."

I felt the stupid tears prick my eyes without warning. I knew that this might be the last time I ever got to sit and talk to Mrs. Strong. She'd always loved me without question and had always made me feel welcome. I hated this sad feeling that was following me throughout my trip this summer. I never expected that this is what my favorite time of the year was going to be about. I knew I needed to say something because she'd been so good to me. I licked my lips and finally croaked, "Mrs. Strong, I'm grateful you've always been there for me." I felt the tears escape and was angry and embarrassed.

Jean Strong stood up and motioned for me to stand as well. I did without question and she immediately pulled me to her. She always had a way of making me feel protected, special and loved just like her son had. "DeLaine, honey, it has been my privilege to be there for you. Don't think that this is a goodbye, because I fully expect you to come back to see me again! I just wanted to have a little heart to heart with you while we had the chance since we're alone right now."

I nodded my head as she held me out and looked deep into my brown eyes. She smoothed the curls on the side of my head and tucked them behind my ears. She cleared her throat, "Honey, I don't know what the future holds for you. I love you so much and only want you to have a happy life. I'm a mama and that's what we want for our children. You feel as much a part of me as Kevin and Donna! You needed someone to love you and I was only too happy that God brought you to my kitchen on a chilly, fall night in 1979. I've watched you blossom into this beautiful and capable young woman who is strong! You are so much stronger than you realize. You continue to grow and try new things. Keep reaching out and keep learning! Your intellect will be what you have for the rest of your life. If you are unable to go to college don't despair. There are a lot of people who never got to go to college, but you keep learning new things. No matter how you do it! And don't you ever let a boy or man tell you that you *can't* do something! You can do anything you set your mind to! That even goes for my son!" She laughed nervously and I smiled at her.

Our visit felt like it was ending even though I hadn't been there that long. I knew instinctively though that it was time for me to leave for some reason. It seemed as if Jean Strong was feeling the same way. Before I left she told me she wanted me to have something so I followed her. I was surprised when she walked into Donna's room. I couldn't imagine what she wanted me to go in there for. She had given me the angel bear I'd given Donna and there was so little left that I thought she would want to part with.

As I walked through the doorway, I was struck that the room was still stuck in a time warp. Jean Strong could not let go of the little girl that had lived in this room. It still had little girl pink walls and the pretty white furniture. I felt a deep sense of loss when I walked in because going inside of there always made me miss Donna so much. I watched as Kevin and Donna's mom walked to the white bookcase that still held the books that Donna loved so much. I felt like the room was a hallowed ground and so I stood patiently as I watched his mom dig through the shelves a little.

Turning around, Jean Strong held a book and a Barbie doll in her hands. "I can't bear to part with her *Velveteen Rabbit* book. I know that she gave you that book one Christmas but you always read to her so willingly and she loved that. Her second favorite book was this *Adventures of Winnie the Pooh.* I wanted you to have it. Maybe one day you will read it to your children and you will remember my sweet, little Donna." I saw a tear slip down her face. Then she held out the Barbie doll. It was a brunette doll and was dressed in a pretty pink dress. "Donna told me one time that your step-mother Clarice had sold all of your Barbies, when you moved to Belfast. It really bothered her. She wanted to always get a Barbie for you. I told her that you were too old for them, but she refused to believe that since she was a little older than you. I finally gave in to her the October before she…well, before she got sick and had to leave us. She wanted to get one that reminded her of you in honor of your birthday. She told me that it was going to be her *DeLaine Barbie* and that when you came to see her you could play with that one. I've been meaning to give it to you as well, but I just couldn't bear to give much of her stuff away. I know that eventually I'm going to have to let go of this room. It isn't healthy for me to keep it this way. Until then though, I want to know her things are here. I still come in and dust them and make sure the room gets aired out but…." Kevin's mom trailed off. She looked away and wiped at the tears that were freely flowing from her eyes.

"Thank you so much," I whispered as a way to have her attention turn back to me.

Smiling, she said, "You are more than welcome. I know that she would be happy that you have these."

"I'm honored to have them and will…well, I'm happy to have them. I will keep them *always*," I responded softly as I held the book and the doll in my hands.

Laughing a little Mrs. Strong exclaimed, "Oh my goodness! I know you have other things to get to honey! You don't want to hang out with a bawling, old woman all day! You probably have a date at the pool for a little while or something like that. I don't want to keep you!" She began to steer me back out of the room and down the hallway to the foyer. She told me how happy she was that I made time to come see her and that she'd tell Kevin I came by. I hoped that it would remind him that I didn't have much more time left.

Embracing me at the door for what felt like the last time, Jean Strong held on to me just a little longer than normal. When she pulled away she told me, "I love you, Miss DeLaine Reynolds! I couldn't love you any more if you were my own daughter! You are such a special young woman! Don't *ever* forget that! You will have an amazing life! And when you come here, I want you to come see me, okay?"

I nodded and as I was walking out of the storm door I turned and looked at Kevin's mom one last time. "I don't know if I ever thanked you, but thank you for loving me. I love you, Mrs. Strong."

Laughing, she admitted, "I know you do Darlin' and no thanks needed for anything! I love you, DeLaine!" I looked at her with a small, sad smile and turned out into the glaring, hot afternoon and climbed into Bailey's Sunbird. I couldn't stop the torrent of tears as I backed out of the short driveway and began the less than 90 second drive to Bailey's empty house.

Levi came by that afternoon to see me and we went for a ride in his old green pickup that he'd restored. It was a 1960's model, but I didn't know what year. I just knew it was old and he'd put a lot of work into it. I was happy to see him and he came in when we got back to Bailey's. We were all three sitting on Bailey's bedroom floor, like old times. I was happy to see them actually talking to each other. I knew they'd come together for Jax's accident, but the way they acted I was never sure if they were friendly or not.

While he was there, Bailey's phone rang and I tensed up wondering if it was Casey. When Bailey handed the phone to me I was hoping desperately that it was Kevin. When I heard Geoff's voice on the other end I was horribly disappointed.

"*Hey Sister!* Are you busy?" he asked in a bright voice.

I tried not to groan and instead rolled my eyes at Bailey and Levi, "Um, well, I've got company, *why*?"

Geoffrey asked who was visiting me. He guessed it was Jax and when I said no he picked Kevin. I told him that it was Levi and he let the information drop in the dust of his next statement. "Well, um, I was gonna come by and say hi if you're going to be there."

I sat for a minute and felt trapped. Finally, I explained, "Well, I can't visit very long. I'm going to do something in a little while." Geoffrey assured me that he wasn't going to stay long, he just wanted to see me one more time before I left that following weekend. He was only going to be free this evening. "Okay, come over I guess," I conceded, hoping I didn't sound eager to see him. I didn't want him to think that we were some kind of best friends or anything stupid like that! He told me he'd be there in an hour and I told him that would be fine. When I got off the phone I told my best friend and her former boyfriend.

Bailey rolled her eyes and asked me what he wanted to do. I shrugged my shoulders. I didn't have a clue, but I wanted him to do it and leave as soon as possible. Levi suggested we run to the store before he got there. He needed to get some dip and I really wanted to smoke. Bailey politely declined riding with him. I knew it was because she was afraid someone would see her and tell Casey. I wished she'd just tell him to get lost.

I climbed into the old, light green truck. Since there was no air conditioner in it, we rolled the windows down. I felt the hot air blow around my head as it helped to dry the sweat that was rolling down my neck and cheeks. Levi and I talked briefly about our senior year. He never mentioned his girlfriend which I found a little strange, but I didn't want to push him on it. I enjoyed riding with him the short distance just acting silly and like the kids we were. I was grateful to be able to smoke a cigarette since I wasn't able to smoke much when I was at Baileys. Levi grimaced when I lit the cigarette, but he didn't say anything. I knew he wanted me to quit, but I wasn't there.

It seemed I was smoking more now that my mom knew. I hated it too because cigarettes had gone up to over a $1.00 per pack. They were $1.25 most places, but sometimes I paid $1.50 and that always burned me up. Of course now that my mom knew, she would buy me a carton at a time which was only $10 and it would last me almost two weeks. Ray didn't like me smoking either so Mom had suggested that I just smoke in my room when he was home.

When Levi got me back to Bailey's we all stood outside as the sun began to set behind the houses. I was happy to see Bailey acting more like her old self around Levi. I told them I wanted to get a couple of pictures of them before I left. I ran inside and got my little 110 camera I'd brought up. When I came out I got a couple of goofy pictures of Levi and then one of them together. Levi took the camera then and took pictures of me and Bailey together, and then she took one of me and Levi. Glenda came outside and saw us taking pictures and offered to take one of all three of us. I was happy she'd offered to do that because I didn't have a photograph of all three of us. I couldn't wait to get the film developed because I knew that I'd love all the pictures. Thankfully I had makeup on and my hair wasn't too windblown from the trip in Levi's truck. I even snapped a photo of Glenda being playful. We all stood outside laughing and enjoying the evening as it began to finally cool off some. I saw a car slow down and when I realized who was in it I could feel my flaming winged Goddess that lived deep within me unfurl her wings.

Bailey, Levi and Glenda all saw the car too. Levi said he had to leave and gave me a big hug. He was gone within a few seconds and Bailey and her mom decided to go into the house too. I knew Glenda was curious about why the sudden change in our playful mood, but I could hear Bailey talking to her as they climbed the stairs to the porch. I stood in the driveway as the car pulled in, glaring at the passenger inside. Once the car came to a stop Geoffrey jumped out and yelled, "Hey Sister! Mom came by when I was leaving and she really wanted to see you!"

I looked from Geoffrey to the woman I probably hated with every fiber of my being. I couldn't remember ever hating anyone in my life, but I understood that the feeling I felt for Clarice was always going to be *hatred.* I walked stiffly to the driver's side because I didn't want her to think about getting out of the car. She hit the electric button on her window and I was staring into the face of the woman who had abused me mentally, not to mention emotionally for years. This was the woman who had made my life a living hell and standing on the opposite side of the car was the spawn she had created who had done so much to me as well. I had dreamed of this day and in my mind I always told Clarice off. I realized my chance was sitting right in front of me. Instead of spouting off, I waited to see what she had to say.

"Hey Kid! Geoff told me you looked great! He wasn't lying! How are you? How's school in Corpus?" Clarice asked as if we were long lost friends who happened to run into one another.

Looking down at her face that was covered by large sunglasses I felt myself tighten up. I wanted to yell and scream at her. I wanted to tell her what a bitch I thought she was, but none of those words came out. Instead I replied steadily, "I'm fine, Clarice. School is good."

She looked up at me expecting me to expound on everything and when I didn't she explained, "I just wanted to come by and see you since you were in town. I'm glad Geoff told me you were here."

I faintly shook my head, "Well, you've seen me. Not much to tell you."

Clarice looked at me with a strange expression on her face. I hoped by my tone and my body language that she was getting the hint that she was not welcome in my life in any way. "Well, I won't keep you. I know you said you had plans when Geoff called. I'm glad I got to see you. I really miss you kiddo!"

Finally I couldn't help myself. "Why, because you don't have anyone who can wash your clothes the way you want? Or wait, maybe it's that you have to vacuum your own floors and cook your own meals now. Of course if you're really screwing some rich guy, who obviously got you a boob job, then you probably have a maid to order around. You have to pay her unlike me, huh?"

Sitting there I noticed Clarice features begin to change under the humongous sunglasses. "I don't know why you have to act like that, DeLaine. I was always good to you. I hope you are doing okay. Maybe it is just being around your mom that has given you that mouth. Anyway, I'm leaving so you can go do whatever it is you have planned."

I cocked my head to the side, "No, my mom didn't give me this mouth. I *always* had it. I just knew if I ever told you what I really wanted to you'd beat me with that fucking belt. You've seen me, Clarice. I don't want to *ever* see you again, do you understand me. I don't want you to ever call my house or threaten me or my family again. I'm not scared of you any longer. You are a *piece of shit* to me. So don't sit there and pretend that we had a loving bond. You *used me* and then you stole from my daddy and YOU are the one who *destroyed* his dream. You told me not to let him know about Geoffrey beating me because I would destroy his happiness with his dream. Well, I kept that fucking secret you *sick bitch*… it was YOU who did the destroying and for that…I will NEVER forgive you."

After saying that to her, I felt a little light headed. I couldn't believe that I'd actually said it to her. I was in shock. I never raised my voice, but I was certain that the tone and my ever expressive face got my point across plainly. Finally, she declared in a sharp tone, "As you wish, DeLaine. You might want to watch how you talk to adults though. You might think you are grown, but you are just a wet behind the ears ungrateful brat! I hope that life treats you better than you just treated me."

"Don't worry, Clarice! It will…you know why?" I asked her. She cocked her head sideways this time and I continued, "Because I refuse to let trash like you ever be in my life again. I will never have another bitch like you in my life to contaminate it. I hope you get everything you deserve!" With that last statement I turned and began walking around the car towards the porch.

Geoffrey jumped out of the car and ran up behind me. I was braced for him to hit me. I was going to turn around and knock the hell out of him if he did. I clenched my fist and when he tapped my shoulder I turned around ready to strike. Instead I found him standing there with a troubled expression on his face. "D. why the hell did you say all of that? I was hoping seeing her would make you feel better about her. She really *did* just want to come say hi! She doesn't want to do anything bad to you or to Russ!"

"Geoffrey, just take your bitch mother and leave please. I don't want to ever see her again. I told you that and I meant it. You brought her anyway. I don't appreciate you doing that. Just leave," I insisted.

"Fuck, D.! When did you become such a mean bitch?" Geoffrey asked me as if he was truly puzzled by my behavior.

"Geoffrey, I *had* to become a mean bitch because of your mother and YOU! Don't pretend we were the fucking *Brady Bunch* because we weren't. Go away. You've seen me and she's seen me. I have plans!" I turned my back on him and began to walk off.

"Have a nice life you *stupid cow*! You know you and Kevin will *never* be together right? You're gonna go back to Corpus and probably get pregnant with some Mexican baby and live on welfare because you are such a fucking loser! So you have a nice life!" Geoffrey yelled after me. He knew the barb about Kevin would hurt me, but I didn't care. I continued walking up to the porch. When I got to the door I turned and saw the car pulling out of the drive way. I also saw them both look at me one more time and couldn't help myself. I had to flip them off for good measure. I was grateful I'd had the guts to at least tell them both how I truly felt. It wasn't the big show down I'd always imagined, but it was better than never having my say.

Bailey and I went to the pool on her day off. I knew I wouldn't come back again while she was at work. I was honestly ready to go back to Corpus. I couldn't believe it. Kevin still had been missing and I had decided I was going to call him that evening. I wanted to see him. I was puzzled why he wouldn't call or come over. Honestly, I was more hurt than anything. We'd reconnected my second night here and I thought things were great only to hear *nothing* else from him.

That evening I called his number and it only rang and rang. I hung up the phone and decided to call late. That way he'd be home. After I went to bed in Jason's old room and I picked up the phone and dialed his number again. After five rings Kevin's sleepy voice answered. I felt my heart leap into my chest.

"Hey, Kev! Did you forget I was here?" I asked him jokingly.

He sat there for a long time, and I wondered if he'd fallen back to sleep after answering. Finally, he answered in a voice that was no longer sleepy sounding, "No, Lainey, I know you're still here. I've been really busy with work. By the time I get home I just eat and go to bed. I want to see you before you leave, just not tonight. I've got to get some sleep. Maybe this weekend?"

I sat there feeling disappointed. I finally replied, "Um, yeah, that's cool I guess. Just call me." Kevin assured me he would and we got off the phone. He didn't even act like he wanted to talk. I felt crushed and wondered even more if I would lose him forever. I wanted to tell him that I didn't want to date anyone and wanted him to wait for me the next 11 months until I could come back to be with him. I rolled over in the bed and fell asleep thinking of summer, sky blue eyes. I was surprised though because they somehow seemed to wash out just a shade which I thought was odd. Sleep didn't let me dwell on it too long because it came and took me away as I spiraled down into the darkness of it.

Chapter 16

The rest of the week flew by, even though I didn't really do anything except hang out at Bailey's house all day reading and even doing a little writing. I couldn't understand why things seemed so different, but thought it was probably because we were all getting older. Friday evening came along, but Bailey didn't feel like going out. She wanted to stay home and we slept in the den watching movies. We had moved her phone in there because the cord was so long it could be moved to almost everywhere in the house. Around 10:30 the little princess phone began to trill, but Bailey was on it before it completely rang to the second ring. "Here, it's for you," She stated a little grumpy.

I took the phone and prayed it wasn't Geoffrey again. I was relieved to be met by the warm, velvet purr of Kevin's voice inside the receiver of the phone. "Hey, Kev!" I answered happily.

Without preamble Kevin asked, "You wanna sneak out and come over for a little while?" He didn't have to ask me twice. I told him I did! He told me to come to his house around midnight. I was thrilled. I only had tonight and Saturday night left! I told Bailey and she told me to sneak out through the back. If I walked through the kitchen, the old floorboards in there would creak. They were next to her mom and dad's room. She said it sometimes woke her dad up and she didn't want him to know I'd snuck out. I figured it would be fine. I felt my body begin to hum with anticipation at being around Kevin again and hoped he would spend all the next day and evening with me!

At 11:30, after everyone else was asleep for the night, I slipped out of the bed from the hideaway couch where we were camped out. I listened as I slipped on my tennis shoes. I didn't bother to put anything else on. I was already in shorts and a big t-shirt. Kevin had seen me in a lot worse and this way I could get there and not waste time with changing or getting caught. I slipped out the back door into the Bailey's backyard.

Bailey's dad was a mason so their backyard was really a work yard. It wasn't full of grass or pretty patio furniture. Instead their boat was parked over by the ten foot tall, cinder block fence. The rest of the yard contained all his equipment and a work truck. I'd only been in Bailey's backyard a couple of times, but I knew where the back gate was, so I walked over to it. I was shocked when I found it was padlocked. I looked around me in the moonlight and wondered how I was going to get over a ten foot tall fence. I had never been outdoorsy or remotely athletic. I had never climbed a tree or even wanted to. I didn't climb fences either, especially ones that were made from cement blocks!

Frantically, I tried to figure out how I would get out of the backyard. Bailey had forgotten to tell me about the back gate being locked. I scanned the yard, and finally my gaze fell on their boat that I'd ridden on plenty of times at the lake. I looked at the trailer it was on and thought that if I climbed on top of the trailer, then the boat, I could probably get to the top of the fence. I went over to the trailer and did exactly what I'd seen in my mind to do. Once I was safely straddling the cement blocks, having the soft skin of my thighs scratched up, I realized that I hadn't thought about the drop off the other side. I was also terrified of heights. Being ten feet up in the air made me realize just how bad that fear was. I looked over my shoulder at the neighbor's fence and saw they'd installed a wooden privacy fence like everybody else in the neighborhood. Bailey's dad was a mason, so it only made sense he'd erect a huge cinder block fence instead of the traditional wood one.

I wasn't sure how I could possibly drop down without breaking my ankle or a leg even. Finally, I took a deep breath. I rolled onto my stomach, along the top of the fence, until I was dangling over the side. I felt the rough cement as it bit into the tender flesh on my abdomen where my night shirt had gotten pulled up in all of my maneuvering. I took a big breath and decided I'd come too far to chicken out now. If I didn't do it, I might not get to see Kevin. I lowered myself as far as I could over the side and dropped into the carpet grass on the side yard. I saw Bailey's bedroom window that Kevin always tapped on when he snuck me out. I wished now that we hadn't already made the bed out in the den before Kevin called. It would have been so much easier to sneak out of the house the old way.

Once I emerged from the shadows, between the two houses, I wondered how long it had taken me to get over that stupid fence. I turned and looked at it and realized that I didn't know how I would ever get back over it. On the other side I'd had the boat and its trailer to climb, but on this side there wasn't anything like that. I felt my heart suddenly begin slamming away in my chest. I turned and looked down the darkened street that would lead me to Kevin's and once again back at the fence.

I was over the fence. There wasn't anything I could do at the moment about getting back across it so the only thing I knew to do was go ahead and go to Kevin's. I hoped I could figure out something between now and when I got back. I took another deep breath as I made my way down the slope of the yard onto the sidewalk that ran along Granville. I'd walked this sidewalk so many times in my life I knew where each crack was it seemed. I knew the places to look out for in the dark and the ones to completely avoid altogether. I even knew if I ran down that sidewalk that there were some of the bad places I could literally jump over. I was running by then when that thought raced through my mind. I wanted to get to Kevin just as badly as I had the second night I was in Wichita Falls. It had already been 10 days ago. I couldn't believe that Kevin had blown me off all that time until tonight. Part of me felt hurt, but another part of me didn't care as long as I got to be with him for a while.

Once again I saw his long, lean form standing under the streetlight at the corner of Granville and Fairfax Blvd. waiting on me. I ran straight into his arms again. I felt the overwhelming urge to cry and hang on him as soon as I felt his arms go around me. I felt like I was losing him and everything else that was dear to me in Wichita and I was afraid. This time my summer vacation had felt so odd and different. I was terrified that all the things I'd dreamed about were about to fall away from me.

Kevin pulled back after a minute or so and asked, "Hey Little Lainey Reynolds! Why you holding on so hard?"

I pulled away finally and cried, "Kevin I was so afraid you weren't going to call me, and I was going to leave and *never* see you again."

The golden haired boy that I'd loved since I was 13 smiled his slow *King Kevin* smile, "Not a chance darlin'! I haven't forgotten you were in town! Just a lot of shit on my plate right now! C'mon, let's go to my house. I don't want a cop seeing us out here in the middle of the night." I nodded and we walked over to Portland where the brick house Kevin had lived in since he was 5 years old stood.

When we got inside of his room, I felt on familiar ground. He lay across his bed and pulled me with him. We kissed a couple of times, but this night felt much different than the first night I'd been here. This time Kevin talked softly to me as he held me. None of the conversation was of any real importance. He didn't tell me he wanted me to have a life or find a boyfriend. He never brought up Shannon again or anything else that I'd told him about. We talked about inane subjects like movies and his car. He was still working at the gas station, but he'd been made a mechanic because he'd been learning so much and had gotten a little bit of a raise.

After an hour of just lying side by side, talking about nothing in particular I finally declared, "Kevin, I want to come back here at the end of this school year. I want to be with you. I don't want to date anybody else. I want to go to school and graduate and move back to Wichita."

Kevin lay there silently, never pulling away from me. He continued to stroke my back softly, up and down, in an absent manner. I wondered if I'd freaked him out or if he didn't really want me at all any longer. After what felt like forever, Kevin sighed, "Lainey, go to school. Do good and when the spring gets here we can talk. You might find the love of your life this year. You don't know. You don't want *me* though. You want *'King Kevin'* from 8th grade. I'm just a dumbass who quit school and smokes too much pot and still lives with his mom and dad. Shit, I'm 19 and I'm still living with my folks!"

I didn't pull my face off of his chest to look at him. I was angry. I wanted to hit him. I also thought that this was his way of telling me he didn't want me. I tried hard not to cry. After a while I rose up on my elbow and looked into the eyes that I'd thought about for countless hours. "Kevin, please don't say that about yourself. You *aren't* a dumbass! I don't care about anything you just said. I don't want *King Kevin* from 8th grade. HE was an *arrogant asshole*! I figured out who *King Kevin* was really! That's who I want and that is who you've always been to me. Please, say you'll wait for me. Please tell me not to go to Corpus and find another *real* boyfriend! Please!!!"

Kevin's gaze felt like it was burning a hole into me. Sighing again, he whispered, "Lainey, I'm not going to tell you to do anything. I'm just telling you that you *don't* want me. I'm serious about that. You are going to do what you want to do. Just don't plan your life around *me*. Plan it for you!"

Tearing up I cried, "But the plans I have for *me* include YOU!"

"Honey, don't ever live for a guy! *Live for you*! I mean that! Guys are all assholes, including me! Trust me on this one! Just be happy, Lainey. Do what you think will make you happy, but please baby be careful. There are so many guys out there who will hurt you. You've already found that out. Just be careful, okay?" Kevin insisted as he stroked the side of my face softly. I nodded my head and then I leaned over to kiss him. I want him to make love to me again. I wanted to feel our bodies join together in the delicious way he'd shown me before. I wanted to feel that oneness with him again. It seemed the more I was with him that way the more I wanted to be with him that way.

As if he could read my mind Kevin pulled away, "You need to get back to Bay's. You didn't get here until almost 12:20 and we've been laying here for two hours."

"Seriously?" I exclaimed in shock. Kevin smiled at me sweetly and nodded his head. "Will I see you again before I have to leave, Kev?"

Looking at me oddly he nodded his head. "Yeah, I have to work tomorrow, but I'll come see you tomorrow night, since I know you're leaving early Sunday." I smiled at him and sat up to put my shoes on. I couldn't believe it was almost 3 a.m. I realized I still had to figure out how I was going to get back over the cinderblock fence. I hated leaving Kevin's warm bed. I wished I could just stay the night with him like I'd done before so we could make love, but I was hopeful that we would the next night before I left.

Once we walked out into the warm night air, I thought of different ways to get over the fence. I told Kevin about what all I'd gone through climbing over it. He'd had a good laugh from it. I had to show him my war wounds I'd gotten trying to climb over just to come see him. I laughed about it too because with Kevin I was free to be as klutzy as I was, because I didn't have anything to prove to him. I asked him before we got to the end of Portland if he was walking me all the way to Bay's house. He didn't answer right away. I wondered if he'd even heard me. Just as I was about to repeat myself Kevin asked, "Lainey, do you mind walking by yourself. I'm really tired and I've got to be at work in like less than 4 hours. Just call and let my phone ring once so I know you got there safe okay?" I was surprised because Kevin *always* walked me back usually. I'd hoped if he did he could at least help boost me over the fence. I didn't want to seem like a nag or a baby since he did have to get up early. I nodded my head and tried to give him a bright smile.

When we got to Fairfax Blvd. it was a little creepy, because there were no cars at all anywhere up or down the road. Kevin started walking across the street to Granville. I was surprised because he'd just told me he wasn't going to go all the way. Just as we got to the middle of the four lane road, Kevin grabbed my hand and turned me to him. He didn't say one word but he pulled me to him in the most intense embrace I'd ever felt from him. He kissed me with every ounce of passion I'd ever felt up to that point in my life. I literally began to feel dizzy from the kiss he gave me. I literally lost all sense of time and space as our mouths were melted together in the middle of Fairfax at 3 in the morning. I could still feel the heat in the asphalt of the road as it radiated up. It only matched the heat I felt in my face as I kissed him.

Kevin was holding me by my upper arms in a death grip. When he finally pulled away from me he looked deep into my eyes. I felt breathless after kissing him. He'd kissed me with passion and aching need before, but this kiss felt like something you might see in a romantic movie. It was fraught with raw emotion. I didn't understand it. I looked up into the eyes that were shadowed. I knew the exact shade of blue they were. There was only one other person in the entire world I'd ever seen with that color of eyes before, and she was now a beautiful angel in Heaven.

"*Lainey…I love you.* Don't ever forget that no matter what happens in life! *I honestly do love you.*" Kevin repeated as he looked at me intensely.

I looked at him surprised. He never said it out loud. He'd only told me for real a couple of times. He told me he didn't say it out loud. I'd told him more times than I could count how I felt about him. I'd always known after a certain point that he loved me and cared for me, but I had contented myself with the fact that he wouldn't say it out loud. My heart began to hammer hard in my chest.

"Is everything *okay,* Kevin?" I asked worriedly.

The smile that could make my entire insides do a flip flop flashed in my face as we stood in the middle of Fairfax. "Yeah, Lainey! Everything is fine. *Just remember...*I love you!" With that he leaned down and kissed me a little more gently and told me to remember to call and let the phone ring once. He wouldn't raise any alarm for an hour, but to hurry if I could! I smiled and nodded my head.

I turned around to walk away from him and just as I got to the last lane closest to Granville I heard footsteps running up behind me. Kevin grabbed my arm and turned me back around, kissing me soundly one last time under the street light. When we pulled apart I looked up at the silver lighted boy in front of me and felt a chill pass through me. I suddenly felt like crying. Instead, I was able to keep the tears from pricking in my eyes for a change. He never said anything else; he just cupped my face in his hands and looked into my eyes. Looking at him questioningly he simply shook his head and then turned to walk back to the Portland side of the street. I walked on to the other side of Fairfax Blvd. I turned one last time and smiled at the beautiful boy, who was really a man now, who stood on the other side of the street from me. I couldn't wait until the next night. Kevin raised his arm and spread his long, graceful fingers apart in a wave. I copied his movements and then turned to begin my jog back up Granville. Since Kevin wasn't walking me home I wanted to get back to Bailey's as soon as I possibly could.

I had puzzled over the whole fence thing and realized that the neighbor's backyard gate was right next to the cinderblock fence. If I could get myself up on the wooden side, then hopefully I could pull myself up over the cement blocks. Once I reached the side yard of Bay's house I checked the neighbor's gate and quietly opened it. I was glad to know they didn't have a giant, snarling dog to come running up to me. I looked at the corner of the wooden fence. I saw the brace boards and realized if I could get a toe hold up it, I could get on over the cinderblocks which rose above the top of the wood. Thankfully it went much easier than I thought. By the time I was over and sitting on the side of the boat trailer, trying to catch my breath, and quiet my hammering heart, I'd only managed to rip off three of my long fingernails and scraped up my knee bad enough for it to sting. I was so happy I'd gotten to see Kevin though and couldn't wait for the next night. I thought that the goodbye kiss he'd given me in the middle of Fairfax was probably the most romantic kiss he'd *ever* given me though. I lay on top of the covers, next to Bailey, as she slept peacefully. I thought about that kiss over and over. I had already called Kevin's number and just rang it once and hung up. I relived the kiss until I finally dozed off just as the sun was beginning to brighten the sky to gunmetal gray.

My last day at Bailey's was spent mainly just hanging out. She told me that she was seriously going to break up with Casey after I left. I was happy to hear it. She promised she'd tell her parents if he tried to hurt her. I wanted her to be rid of this creep. I told her to leave creepy guys alone. She smiled at me and told me she would. Things felt a little better between us. I was happy that even if it took until my last day we at least were leaving like we always did. Full of anticipation until we could get together again!

I told her all about everything I'd talked about with Kevin the night before. She nodded her head, not saying much. I wondered a little about her response, but I didn't want to shake the pleasant day we were spending. Later that evening we went down Kemplar one last time. I said goodbye to some of our friends who we'd hung out with in 8th grade together. I once again hated the fact that I was leaving. I wondered why I'd wasted so many days wondering why I'd bothered coming. It seemed every time it was the last night I always felt a sense of bittersweet melancholy just having to say goodbye to everything I'd grown up with all over again.

I waited until 10:30 to call Kevin's house, because I was hoping I'd see him while we were out on Kemplar. When he didn't answer I hoped that it just meant he was still out and he'd show up at *walked you home and stopped in the middle of Fairfax. I hope you know what he's talking about.*

Just so you know, I told him what a sorry bastard he was for breaking your heart like this after everything you'd done to be with him. He didn't argue with me. He just said that you deserved someone much better than him anyway. I don't think he really loves her. I think he's just doing what he thinks is the right thing. I think he really loves <u>*you,*</u> *Lala, but now he's gonna be a dad. It sucks. I can't imagine Kevin Strong being anybody's dad, but look at Jason! He's a dad now too.*

I'm so sorry Lala!

I love you!

Bay-Bay

I sat on my bed and reread the letter at least three times before the words actually sank in. When they finally did, I realized that *every* dream I had about Kevin was now *over*. He was getting *married*. He was going to be a *daddy*. He would *never* be *my* husband. *We* would *never* have children together. I couldn't believe it. I felt myself choking as I cried. Soon I could barely get my breath. I couldn't believe that my entire world was now over for good. I just thought making me move from Wichita Falls had ended my life. I realized it was nothing compared to this. It wasn't like we were 14 and 15 and he had a girlfriend who he was kissing on the skating rink floor to make me jealous. This was *real* life. This was serious. This was about being someone's husband and dad. He would *never* be mine. I couldn't believe that everything I'd lived for since I was 13 was now completely and resolutely *over*.

Chapter 17

On Friday morning my mom came into my room. I was laying in my bed still. I'd been lying there since the day I'd gotten Bailey's letter. I hadn't taken a shower since Tuesday. I didn't see much sense in getting up. I wondered if a person could just die from a broken heart. My heart wasn't just broken it was ripped in two! I wanted to quit breathing. I'd cried all through the night and hadn't even come out for anything to eat.

"DeLaine, honey, I'm worried about you," my mom said as she sat on the edge of my bed. I wouldn't even look up at her. "What is going on? You've been depressed since you got home and now you aren't eating or even coming out of your room. You need to talk to me so I can help."

Looking at the closet door just past where my mom was sitting I held onto my Velveteen bunny. I didn't know if I could tell her without crying. Finally, I rolled over and picked up the letter from Bailey that I read every half hour at least. I handed it to my mom and then lay there waiting to listen to her rant and rave about Kevin being an asshole.

Mama read the letter. I knew that she was reading it a second time because it was so short it didn't take even a minute to read. I wondered why she hadn't started cussing yet, but was waiting on it. Finally, she set the pretty floral stationary down on her leg and looked at me. I could feel my tears seeping again out of my eyes. "I'm *so sorry,* honey. I know how much Kevin's always meant to you. I'm so *so* sorry that you are hurt. I hate to say this, but you are going to be hurt more in life than I want you to, but it is going to happen. I think you've begun to see that the last few years. You just have to pick yourself back up and go back out there and try again."

I rolled my eyes and rolled over where my back was now to my mom. She patted me on the shoulder and told me that she knew that I was not only hurt but angry, pissed off, and ready to beat the hell out of somebody because that is how she would feel if she were me. I let the tears just drip out of my eyes on the pillow case. I sniffed the snot back a few times until I couldn't stand it any longer because I couldn't breathe. I rolled back over towards my mom and my nightstand. I grabbed some more tissues out of the almost empty box. I sat up and blew my nose noisily. I looked at my mom and whispered, "But he's *Kevin,* Mom! He wasn't supposed to *ever* hurt me. He saved me so many times. *Why* would he save me only to hurt me so much I want to *die*?"

Mama pulled me to her and whispered into my dank curls, "I don't know, Bug. I don't understand why things have to happen the way they do. I wish I knew what to tell you. I can only let you know that I love you. That's not ever going to change. I'm always your mom! I know it isn't worth much when you are so hurt, but one day you will understand how much I love you. I would do anything in the world to fix anything that makes you cry!"

I pulled away from her and grabbed for more tissues. I ended up grabbing the last ones out of the box and Mom smiled at me. She told me she'd get me more and I smiled a watery smile. After more noisy nose blowing, I tried to tell Mom about Kevin kissing me goodbye. I didn't tell her I'd snuck out. I left out the second night I was there too. I told her that the whole time I was in Wichita this time I felt like I was telling everybody goodbye *again* and it was so weird. Thankfully, my mom was sober and listened to me without interrupting. "I wanted to move back after graduation," I finally admitted freely to my mom.

"I suspected as much," Mama surprised me by saying.

"You did? *How*?" I asked her stunned.

Mama smiled knowingly, "DeLaine, you're *my* daughter. I know you so much better than you think. I know how unhappy you were to leave there. It would have been so much better if I'd still been there and you never would have had to leave. Life didn't work out that way though. I've tried to make sure you got to go back as much as possible because I knew how much you missed your friends there. I've been terrified of you leaving, but I know that you will one day and I can't stop you."

I sniffled a little more, "Well, I don't think I'll be moving up there after senior year now. I wanted to move up there to have an apartment with Bailey and so I could be with Kevin finally *for real*. Now I can't *ever* go back."

My mom smiled at me, "Well, first of all, Kevin isn't the last boy in the world. If you choose to move up there to get an apartment with Bailey, we'll cross that bridge when we come to it. For now, sweetheart, enjoy being *young*. You are going to be broken hearted more. I can't protect you from it. Enjoy this year. It's your last year of high school. I wish I'd had the opportunity to even have a senior year. I want you to enjoy everything as much as you can because you get to be a grown-up a lot longer than you get to be a kid. Trust me on this one, okay?" I looked solemnly at her and nodded my head. "Okay, it is Friday. I'll give you one more day to lie in bed and feel bad, but tomorrow you are getting up and getting dressed. Maybe we can go to the mall or something. Then you call Kelly and Robin and go out with them! There's a dance tomorrow night, right?" I nodded my head again. "Okay. It's settled then. I'm bringing something in here for you to eat and drink. Watch some TV. Kevin's *always* going to be in your heart, DeLaine. Nobody can take that from you. He just wasn't the one!" I watched as she walked out of my door and realized that I'd always thought that he *was* the one. I couldn't imagine anyone else being that one for me.

Once my mom was out of my room I lay back on my pillows and turned up the radio. Cyndi Lauper's ballad "Time After Time" came on. I couldn't help crying again as I listened to the melancholy words that sang to my broken heart…suitcase of memories…*time after time*.

www.ingramcontent.com/pod-product-compliance
Lightning Source LLC
Chambersburg PA
CBHW020934310726
48980CB00007B/768/J

* 9 7 8 0 5 7 8 7 0 2 9 3 3 *